Laurence Sterne, Percy Hetherington Fitzgerald

The story of my Uncle Toby

Laurence Sterne, Percy Hetherington Fitzgerald

The story of my Uncle Toby

ISBN/EAN: 9783743372863

Manufactured in Europe, USA, Canada, Australia, Japa

Cover: Foto ©Andreas Hilbeck / pixelio.de

Manufactured and distributed by brebook publishing software (www.brebook.com)

Laurence Sterne, Percy Hetherington Fitzgerald

The story of my Uncle Toby

MY . . . , *&c.*,

P. . . . A.,
AUTHOR O. . . . A DONNA,"

PHILADELPHIA:

PORTER & COATES.

1889.

LIFE OF LAURENCE STERNE.

HE life of one who was a clergyman and prebendary in a cathedral town, a writer of sermons and odd romances, and a student of old books, would not seem to promise much that was exciting or adventurous. Yet, the life of Laurence Sterne has an unexpected flavour of romance and incident; which, from his cradle literally to his grave, dashes his life with an oddity and eccentricity, that only too faithfully reflects the extravagance of his Tristram. When a child he fell into a mill race, and was carried under the wheel, his life being saved by almost a miracle; and when he died his remains were snatched from the grave by resurrection men and sold for dissection.

An Archbishop of York, after being sorely persecuted in the days of Cromwell, left behind him a large family; the eldest of whom, Simon Sterne, was established at Elvington, in Yorkshire. Roger Sterne, youngest son of this squire, and father of the famous Laurence, was put into the army, and, like my uncle Toby, had nothing in the world but his commission to start him in life.

His regiment, the thirty-fourth, took its share in Marlborough's wars; and in 1711, during the campaign, the young officer married a Mrs. Agnes Herbert,

A

widow of a captain of good family, and daughter
besides of a notorious army contractor and money
lender, in whose debt the officer was. This poor lady was
destined to have an unhappy time of it, following her
husband from quarter to quarter, encumbered with her
young children. On coming home to her father's father,
at Clonmell, his famous son Laurence was born, on
November 24th, 1713. And as if to mark the occasion
in the most dismal fashion, the regiment was "broke"
on that very day, and the officers cast adrift upon
the world. Later it was re-established under Colonel
Chudleigh ; and then commenced for the family,
steadily increasing up to seven, a series of disastrous
wanderings all over England and Ireland, with peril,
shipwreck, and many hardships on the long journeys ;
the young family was much thinned by death.
About the year 1724, Laurence was taken by his
father to the Free School, at Halifax, where, under
the care of an able master, Mr. Lister, he remained
till he was nineteen ; being all but adopted by the
officer's elder brother, Squire Richard Sterne, of
Elvington. Three years later, his father and the
regiment embarked for the siege of Gibraltar. When
quarrelling with a Captain Philips, (more probably
Philpotts, as an officer of that name was in his corps),
he was run through the body, and died in consequence
at Jamaica, in the year 1731. A goose was the cause
of this fatal difference. Though he survived the
immediate effects of the wound, it wore away his
health ; "and when he was sent to Jamaica," says his
son in an affectionate passage, which shows that he
had heart, and tenderly recalled the father from whom,
with boyish delight, he had heard the story of the
Flanders wars—"he soon fell by the country fever,
which took away his senses first and made a child of
him ; and then, in a month or two, walking about
continually without complaining, till the moment he
sat down in an arm-chair, and breathed his last."—

At that time Laurence Sterne was still at school, and, on being soundly flogged for perpetrating the favourite boy's prank, of writing his name on the ceiling, was comforted by his master with the prophecy that he was a lad of genius who would come to preferment. No doubt, he was a clever, eccentric boy ; and Colonel Ord, of Longridge, near Berwick-on-Tweed, who came to the school shortly after Sterne left, saw the name still upon the ceiling, and found the tradition of his humour still preserved, and instances of his wit quoted. When he grew famous, a morning paper recorded, that it was his way to learn when he pleased, and not oftener than once a fortnight.

After leaving school, his cousin, of Elvington, who treated him like a son, sent him to Jesus College, Cambridge, where, in July, 1733, he obtained a sizarship. There he read a good deal, and established an unfortunate friendship with the loose and witty John Hall Stevenson, author of "Crazy Tales," whose companionship must be accountable for much of Sterne's outrages against decency. Mr. Cole, the antiquary, remembered Hall as "an ingenious young gentleman, and very handsome." In March, 1735, Laurence matriculated, and, in January, 1736, took his Bachelor degree. In the March of the same year, he was ordained deacon, and in August, 1738, priest. No man was ever more unsuited to wearing the gown.

He now came to York, where his uncle, Dr. Jaques Sterne, precentor of the cathedral, a noisy ecclesiastical politician, had obtained for him the vicarage of Sutton ; and in the meanwhile courted his first love, Miss Lumley, of Staffordshire. This was to be the weak part in Mr. Sterne's life—an unrestrained and incurable tendre for the fair sex. This he excused by the indulgent names of flirtation, innocent passion, and the like. But such fickleness is evidence of a certain untrueness of heart—a want of manliness and honour. The whole course of his life was to be

dotted with these "affairs of the heart," which at last
grew indispensable to his spirits and comfort ; as he
rather absurdly proclaimed that, in one of these fits,
he never could be guilty of a dirty action, and that
it kept his moral sense healthy.   It might be objected
that the desertion of one of the objects of his evanes-
cent passions, was something like a dirty action ; but it
must be allowed that the Rev. Mr. Sterne was as it were
privileged, and "wrote so beautifully" on love, and
was so devoted to the sex, that his ways and manners
were well known.   His courting of Miss Lumley was
romantic enough.   He wrote her passionate die-away
letters ; but some fantastic misconception as to money
matters prevented them coming to an understanding.
At last, she fell into a consumption, and then showed
her lover her will, in which he had been left everything.   " This generosity overpowered me," says Mr.
Sterne ; and on the 30th March, 1741, they were
married at the cathedral.

    They were quite unsuited to each other, though few
ladies would have suited the agreeable and mercurial
clergyman ; but she had a homely, matter-of-fact mind.
There can be no question but that she sat for Mrs.
Shandy, and there are various traits of her in her husband's letters, which almost prove this likeness.   She
must have been plain also, if we can trust a curious pen-
and-ink etching of her, which M. Stapfer has published
in his monograph.   The late Mr. Hawthorne saw a pair of
crayon portraits of both husband and wife, and was struck
by her unpleasant expression.   With books, painting,
fiddling, and shooting, Sterne spent his time at Sutton—
so he tells his daughter—leaving out some love-making,
which he pursued at York, and much merry-making,
at Skelton Castle with Hall Stevenson, where he paid
frequent visits, met some of the abandoned " Monks
of Medmenham," and pored over the curious old books
in the library.   Here it was that he was captivated by
the piquant oddities of such writers as Bishop Hall,

Sir Thomas Browne, Bruscambille, and the author of the "Moyen de Parvenir," who helped him so much in his Tristram. "Crazy Castle," (Skelton) was a most congenial, quaint old place, and its old halls and towers saw many a wild prank. In the meantime his first child Lydia was born, in the year 1745, who only lived one day. The following year he obtained a prebend in the Cathedral, worth about £50 a-year, through the interest of his wife's family. He now figured as a "wit" in the cathedral society, and preached a series of strangely dramatic sermons, wholly unsuited to a country congregation, but which were modelled on the fantastic efforts of some eccentric mediæval preachers. Under his uncle's patronage, he plunged into the virulent politics of the day, but soon quarrelled with him, because he could not bring himself to write party paragraphs in the newspapers, though it was suspected he did so a good deal on his own account. In 1747, his second daughter was born, and christened Lydia. In the same year he preached a charity sermon in York, and in 1752, another, before the Judges of Assize, in the cathedral. This was an honour. But he was to have other, more congenial, matters on his hands, and in 1759 was to fall in love with a Miss Catherine de Fourmantelle, a young Huguenot girl, who had come to York from France. This lady he pursued after his favourite fashion, half-paternal, half-pious, or wholly sentimental, and it must be said that his letters are very charming love-letters. . After some cathedral wranglings, in which he took part with his pen, and wrote a strange squib, called "The History of a Warm Watch Coat," he began to set to work on his great book, "Tristram Shandy." This was originally quite a local satire, but owing to the publisher's advice, he struck out many of the allusions and made it more general. It was offered to the London publishers for £50, which was thought too great a risk, so he resolved to print it at his own expense.

There was great excitement in York attendant on its coming out, for it was known to contain much personality. It was published in December, 1759, and in two days, Hinxham, the York bookseller, had sold more than 200 copies at five shillings each. It contained many local portraits and sketches,—among others, that of Dr. Burton, an accoucheur of repute, as Dr. Slop, Dr. Mead as Dr. Kunastrokius, himself as Yorick, his father as Uncle Toby, Mrs. Sterne, and Miss Fourmantelle, with all sorts of stray allusions.

The shire was in a storm. He was abused, remonstrated with, and exhorted to excise largely for his second edition. Prudent friends warned him that he was sacrificing his chances of preferment. He was told from London that his book could not be put into the hands of any woman of character. He replied that he only wrote to be famous, and that he scorned to kneel in the dust to any patron. In this independence he certainly was genuine. The following year he went up to London for the season, where, as Mr. Forster says, no one was so talked of and admired as "the tall, thin, hectic-looking Yorkshire parson."

He put up in Pall Mall, and his rooms were besieged with fine company. Within twenty-four hours he was engaged to ten noblemen and men of fashion. Lord Chesterfield, Lord Rockingham, Fox, Garrick, Lords Lyttleton, Spencer, and Edgcumbe were all eager for his company. But what was strange, all the bishops came to call on him. Warburton, the Bishop of Gloucester, was enchanted with him, and gave him a purse of gold. Such episcopal patronage to the author of a clever but indecent book was surely encouragement to go on. Lord Falconberg gave him the perpetual curacy of Stillington, worth about £70 a-year. Then he was taken to Court, supped with Prince Edward, and, in short, received attention enough to overset the head and sense of any poor country parson. He had quite forgotten the Huguenot lady, who wished him to advance her interest among his great friends, and who at last followed him to town. He could not spare her a day, or even an hour, though he had solemnly assured her she was to succeed his wife, and that he would cling to her in death. A strange finale to the adventure is endorsed on the packet which contains her letters, by a Mrs. Weston. That lady) states that Sterne courted the girl five years, had then deserted her, and married Mrs. Sterne : that the young lady in consequence had lost her wits, and that she was the original of Maria of Moulins. Dates dispose of Mrs. Sterne's part in the matter ; but there is no doubt of his promise to marry the young Frenchwoman, as well as of his desertion, and the rest is not unlikely. Flattery and self-indulgence, and above all, the indulgence in false sentiment, in which the world encouraged him, blinded him to the sufferings of others.

Warburton's odd present had now got noised abroad, and Dr. Hill put a very natural construction on it. Tristram, when he grew up, was to have a travelling tutor, and Warburton, he insinuated, was to have been pitched on as a model.

It seems probable that the proud and unscrupulous man would try to buy off so dangerous a satirist. When we think how he denounced Wilkes's indecency, it was not likely that he would favour one who followed at a humble distance, so he tried to make the object of his episcopal patronage more decent and respectable, by friendly warnings. When these were not attended to he complacently began to fear that "the man was an irrevocable scoundrel."

Meanwhile Sterne was pelted from "cellar to garret," in the newspapers and reviews, pursued with rhymes and squibs of the most ribald kind. I have seen a unique little caricature, representing him as standing in his robes in front of the Venus de Medici, with this inscription—

"Behold the learned prebend, wise and grave,
To tawdry wit become a selfish slave."

But these attacks only added to his popularity. He dressed up his old Sutton sermons— from the specimen in Tristram the public were eager to have more—and for them, and a second edition of Tristram (exhausted in three weeks), he received £480.

At last he returned to Yorkshire, after a three months' brilliant campaign in Town, where he had made his name both in letters and socially. He moved to Coxwould, his new living, leaving his curate to look after Sutton and Stillington, and established himself at a quaint old house still standing, and which he christened "Shandy Hall." It is known by that name to this day. But he could not rest long there. Before the winter he had his two fresh Shandys ready, and by Christmas was in town again. This time he was more than six months away, "cantering it along on his haunches," and enjoying himself. By Christmas he had again two of his little volumes ready, and, as usual, came up with them himself. But this winter he had a second chest attack—he had broken a vessel in his lungs at Cambridge — and was disordered. Tristram was beginning to flag ; an account of his travels, done in a Shandean fashion, would stimulate a languid public, and in 1762 he started for Paris.— There he made nearly as great "a success" as in London. D'Holbach's and other noted *salons* were thrown open to him. Choiseul was curious as to this odd "Chevalier Shandy," about whose eccentricity he heard so much, and the Duke of Orleans paid him the questionable compliment of adding his portrait to a gallery of eccentric men that he had formed. Two of his Shandyisms were retailed about Paris ; one his compact with the licentious Crebilon, that they should write books against each other's proceedings, and divide the profits ; the other, his pretending to know and taking off a certain diplomatist, at a dinner party, without being aware that the diplomatist was sitting next to him. He now sent for his wife and daughter, with whom he set off for Toulouse, where they were to pass the winter. A number of English families were settled there, the Hodges', Hewetts', and others ; and Mr. Sterne set on foot theatricals and all kinds of amusement.

After the winter was over, the family migrated to Bagniéres, and thence to Montpellier, where the French were vastly amused with Mrs. Sterne's pertinacious pursuit of her lord, who bore it "with the patience of an angel," until he caught a fever, and was almost at the point of death, under the barbarous treatment of the Montpellier doctors, who gave him "cocks flayed alive," and other strange nostrums. He fled from them to Paris, where he got well at once, and preached in the Ambassador's chapel, before a strange collection of individuals—libertines and *beaux esprits* of all kinds. There is something very profane and disagreeable in this notion ; but the scene would make a dramatic subject for a painter. He was then smitten with the tenderest pains that human wight ever underwent. "I wish thou couldst conceive how deliciously I cantered away with it the first month—two up, two down—always upon my haunches along the street, from my hotel to here ; at first once, then twice, then three times a day ; until I was within an ace of setting up my hobby-horse within her stable for good and all ; I might as well, considering how the enemies of the Lord have blasphemed thereon." In this light and profane fashion did the Rev. Laurence regard his attachments.

In August, 1764, he was back again at York, on the whole, scarcely improved by his travels. His wife, tired of his vagaries, had determined to stay in France, and fixed herself at Montauban with her daughter, where, as far as money went, they could not complain of his neglecting them. The gay Laurence

was utterly unfitted for the hum-drum duties of husband or father ; society was grown to be indispensable.
He found time to "knock off" a couple of very lean
Shandys, which appeared in January, 1765. But he
was now merely trying to fill out his yearly contribution, and swelled his chapters with bits of fooling
that seemed almost an affront to his readers. He
proposed taxing the public regularly for many years
to come, and making his Tristram a sort of annual.
He spent some time in London ;—went to Bath,—
fell in love with Lady Percy, and then, finding his
health growing worse, and his "plaguy cough" fastening on him, determined to fly to the continent. About
the middle of October he set off on his famous Sentimental Journey,— met those adventures at Calais
which have made Dessein's Hotel famous,—had a
fresh success at Paris, and set off for Italy. He passed
by Rome, Milan, Turin ; was everywhere received into
the best society, and lived a dissipated rackety life.
Coming home, he went out of his way to hunt up his
wife and daughter, and then returned home, prophesy-
ing that he should live these ten years. With the
Christmas of 1766, he had flown to town with his
wares, a single volume of Tristram—the last, as it
proved to be,—two new volumes of Sermons, and his
"Sentimental Journey," nearly complete, which he
intended should run to four volumes.

His lodgings were at 41, Old Bond Street, at a bag-
wig maker's, and the house is still to be seen. The
subscription list for his Sermons sparkled with
famous names, English and foreign ; but, by this time
he had grown so infatuated with the pleasures of town-
life, and so reckless as to appearance, that the public
were every day growing more and more scandalized.
A memorial was sent in to his Archbishop, calling
attention to the discredit brought on the Church by
such a minister going uncensured, and, it might be
fairly added, to his long desertion of his cure. But

there were only too many of his cloth to keep him in
countenance, and the excuse of his miserable health
was a genuine one. His Archbishop, too, was easy.
The worst feature was his "Tristram," which was growing less witty only to become more indecent. And
soon he was to raise fresh scandal among his friends
by the notorious " Draper " episode. This was with an
Indian lady who had come over an invalid, leaving
her husband and family at Bombay. He met her at
his friends the James'—people whose affectionate sym-
pathy and interest ought to disprove much that has
been said about Sterne's falsity of heart and sham
sentiment. They were kind sensible friends, who
knew his faults and warned him about his follies.
Mrs. Draper was more interesting than handsome, and
was quite flattered by the extravagant admiration of
so fashionable and celebrated a professor of the Ars
Amoris. But this adoration began to be talked of, and
was only interrupted by the recall of the lady to
India ; not, however, before some officious friend had
reported it to his wife and daughter in France.

The father had to defend himself, after a lame
fashion, to his child Lydia ; and must have at that
moment felt how degrading and childish, even in one
of his age, were such passions—for he was now not
very far from sixty. When Eliza had gone down to
Deal, where the Indiaman was lying, he began to write
her those celebrated letters, " Yorick to Eliza," which
must be placed on the shelf with the Sorrows of
Werther, and other records of blighted love. He
also sent her portions of a most curious journal of his
daily life, which he kept for her benefit. Half of this
history is now in possession of Mr. Gibbs, of Bath, the
rest has been lost. A very minute and curious narrative,
and which seemed to me, from the glimpses and
extracts with which I have been favoured, to be of
singular value, as a picture of town life and manner
a century ago, and certainly a most genuine and un-

affected specimen of Sterne's writing. This journal
was submitted to the late Mr. Thackeray, when he
was preparing his well known Lecture on Sterne, but
was returned as being of no assistance. This seems
incomprehensible, unless it be explained by the well
known story of the Abbé Vertot, who, when offered some
valuable documents for his History of the Knights of
Malta, declined them, on the plea that "his siege was
over" and he could not alter it. Scattered through it
are many good stories, accounts of dinners and suppers
with men of fashion, and some rather coarse anecdotes.
The letters of Yorick to Eliza are a strange jumble of
love, piety, and artful argument, and full of vehement
protestations of eternal fidelity. As it was through
the vanity of the lady they came to be published, it
seems highly probable that there were interpolations
as well as omissions, and there are several passages
which support such a view.

On the 3rd of April, the East Indiaman, Earl of Chat-
ham, sailed away. "Eliza" must have been a woman
of extraordinary powers of fascination ; and Raynal
has left in his History of the Indies, an almost frantic
panegyric on her charms.—She came back to England
about four years after Sterne's death. But in one of these
prodigious "ship letters,"—which are indeed treatises,
and which she sent from India—she gives us a real
prosaic conclusion to the Yorick and Eliza romance.
She there says that Mr. Sterne had treated her badly,
that she had discovered him to be heartless and selfish.
She herself died, in 1778, was buried at Bombay, but
has a monument in Bristol Cathedral, which proclaims
that—" in her genius and benevolence were united."
She adds another to the list of ordinary women, like
Burns' Clarinda, whom the admiration of men of
genius has made immortal.

After her departure, a sort of depression seemed to
come over the lover—a kind of rueful dissatisfaction
with himself, and hate of the life he was leading, which

might be set down to the kindly admonitions of Mrs.
James. His health was growing worse every hour, and
he had to change the air and get to the country. This
restored him; but he wrote to his old friend, Stevenson,
"that his heart ought to be merry, as he never felt so
well since he left college, and should be a marvellous
happy man, but for some reflections which bow down
my spirits. But if I live but even three or four years,
I will acquit myself with honour and—no matter . . ."
These are remarkable words, considering the man to
whom they are addressed. His wife and daughter at
last returned to him, in obedience to his pressing
entreaties. At this time there may be noticed a more
subdued and gentle tone in him; he was having
compunction and forebodings—and perhaps, with a
more judicious partner than Mrs. Sterne was, helping
a daughter whom he loved extravagantly, some radical
change might have been effected. Here was the re-
deeming point :—on this daughter he doted ; and for her
sake, with all his extravagance and pleasures, he kept
his Lydia and her mother well supplied with means.

He now left them in York in the season, and a few
days after Christmas in 1767, started on his last ex-
pedition to town.—" Now, I take Heaven," he wrote
solemnly to a friend, " my heart is innocent, and the
sport of my pen is just equal to what I did in my
boyish days when I sat astride of a stick and galloped
away." This may be the apology for his speech and
manners : not for his Sentimental Journey, which was
now ready to be published ; his only excuse for which
deliberate defiance to decency, is the encouragement
of friends and the tacit approval of really good
people, like the James'. *Double entendre*, if it was
but ingenious and elegant, became a polite accomplish-
ment. It did seem strange that just about the week
in which came out this book, from which so much was
expected, he himself should be seized with the short
last illness which swept him from the world. That

extraordinary book, so picturesque, so full of colour—
but so corrupt in its tone, was actually to begin to
make a new reputation for him, and make him a classic
in France. But he was not to know of this success.
At the beginning of March his old enemy came to
attack him again ; though it was nightly balls and his
rackety life that invited the attack. He was worn
out by the illness, and his treatment wasted him yet
more. There was no one but his friend Mr. James
to look after him. "I wish I had thee to nurse me,"
he piteously wrote to his daughter, "but I am denied
that." This denial may have been occasioned by his
own faults, or by his wife's peculiar temper ; in either
case it is hard not to pity the dying humourist, for
such he was. He was little more than a week ill.
His last letters from his deathbed show a warmth
and tenderness that went deeper than that sham
sentiment with which he was charged. To Mrs.
James, when he was first seized, he wrote a little
note, which, as it has never been published, may be
given here—

"Mr. Sterne's kindest and most friendly compli-
ments to Mrs. James, with his most *sentimental* thanks
for her obliging enquiry after his health. He fell ill
the moment he got to his lodgings, and has been
attended by a physician ever since—he says 'tis owing
to Mr. Sterne's taking James's powder, and venturing
out on so cold a day ; but Mr. Sterne could give a
truer account. He is almost dead, yet still hopes to
glide like a shadow to Gerard Street in a few days, to
thank his good friend for her good will. All compli-
ments to Mr. James—and all comfort to his good
lady."

One later from his death-bed, commending his
daughter to that lady's charge, is piteous and almost
despairing beyond description. He seems to have
been completely deserted, and it stands to the discredit of Mrs. Sterne, whatever her causes of com-

plaint, that neither she nor his daughter were by his bedside. On the Friday following, which was March 13th, 1768, towards four o'clock in the afternoon, the end came on. He complained of cold in his feet and limbs, and the woman who attended him, began to rub. But he felt the cold mounting higher. A footman sent to enquire after him from a merry party, where Garrick, Hume, and Lord March were dining, came up stairs just as he was expiring, saw the wasted arm lifted suddenly, as if to ward off a blow, caught the words, "now it is come!" and saw him then fall back in death. This was the report he brought to the gentlemen who were dining, and who "were very sorry." In a burst of affectation in his Tristram, he wished to die thus deserted : and must have felt how cruelly his wish had been gratified. We may wonder too, did the thought of the legacy of mischief he had bequeathed to the world in the shape of licentious writing further distract his last moments ; or when the woman was rubbing his knee, did he think of Trim's story of the Beguine, and of the coarse satyr-like colour he there imparted to such an office of charity. There were ghastly circumstances following his death. He was buried in the new burying-ground at Bayswater. His publisher, Becket, and Mr. Salt, of the India House—Elia's Sam Salt—being his only mourners. Only two nights after, the resurrection-men took his body, sent it down to Cambridge, where, as a Mr. Collignon, the Professor, was anatomizing it, it was recognized by a friend. This was all on the grim side of Shandeism, as he would have called it, and certainly from the beginning to the end, his life is evidence of the genuine character of his work.

The design of Tristram Shandy, Sterne's great work, is not original, and is founded, in the main, on Rabelais, and Martinus Scriberus, and in its details is an imitation of the old humour of some two or three centuries before. The inditing a sort of

grotesque biography :—a grave, solemn account of
the birth, education, and bringing up of a child, was
a favourite way of laughing at the follies and hobbies
of the times. The library of his friend, Hall Stevenson, overflowed with strange books of this description, written with a serious earnestness and gravity,
on trifling and odd subjects, and which, indeed, is
the secret of the Shandean humour. This solemnity
is found in the works of Bruscambille, Montaigne,
Bishop Hall, Rabelais, and many more ; in the curious
Latin squibs in which men of letters of the sixteenth
century delighted—in Erasmus' dialogues—in passages of Swift and Fielding. "Jonathan Wild,"
"Gulliver," and Essays like the "Modest Proposal,"
are all in this key. This gravity is utterly absent in
modern attempts at humour, and is perhaps the cause
of the general decay of wit. Sterne has been detected
in abundant instances of plagiarism in this direction,
but the charge has been made too much of. The
truth is, these are the weakest portions of Tristram.
They are affectations and excrescences, drawn in as
it were by head and shoulders to fill up the measure.
For he reckoned on his work as a steady income,
and proposed to tax the public every year. Gradu-
ally he found his resources failing him, and the undertaking a drudgery : and to stimulate public interest, had recourse to these borrowings, which soon
took the shape of familiarities and freedoms that
amounted almost to effrontery. Such were the blank
and marbled pages, wrong headings of chapters, "the
careless squirtings" of his ink, resources to fill up
his stipulated two volumes. Further proof of this
is found in his inartistic and abrupt dragging of his
Uncle Toby and Mr. Shandy abroad, which was no-
more than the insertion of his own travelling diary,
merely to fill in a volume. But his real strength
was in character—the admirable touchings—the
knowledge of human springs of action. Where he was

dealing with my uncle Toby or Yorick or Mr. and Mrs.
Shandy, he was on firm ground. As may, perhaps,
be found in reading the present little volume, his bits
of grotesque, his freedoms and familiarities, may be
dispensed with, and with little loss of effect. For the
first time, these characters of the very first rank, with
all the domestic scenes in which they figure, may
be now laid on the drawing-room table and read with
delight.

To the French nation at large, Tristram has always
been unintelligible, although it has been translated
several times. But the Sentimental Journey enjoys a
high popularity. It is a unique book, amazing for its
perfect flavour, and picturesque tone—but it is dis-
figured by meaningless "grossièretés," indelicacies
that are as inartistic as they are scandalous. The
merited retribution has been an abridgment of at
least one half its popularity. Sterne's sermons are
strangely theatrical, and utterly inappropriate in a
church. And though they have obtained the imma-
ture approbation of Mr. Gladstone, in his "Essay on
Church and State," they have nothing genuine about
them. They are full, too, of indecorous Shandeisms,
modelled on stock jests and stories relating to mediæval
preachers. His letters are admirable, genuine, free,
graphic, and entertaining in the highest degree. A
new essay of his was lately published by M. Stapfer,
an acute French writer, which is admittedly his writing,
and which I have no hesitation in pronouncing
genuine, from internal evidence which seems to have
escaped M. Stapfer, viz., that the description of the
garden and orchard corresponds to Sterne's own.

It might have been expected that a Life of Sterne,
published a few years ago, would have brought out
some worthy English criticism on the works of
such a writer. But it was reserved for the
French to contribute to literature a true appreciation of so great a writer. M. de Montégut, in

one of those admirable and exhaustive articles in the *Revue des deux Mondes*, furnished a specimen of fine yet deep French criticism, which will hold a permanent place ; while M. Stapfer, in his " Monograph," founded on " The Life," has exhibited a *finesse* and delicacy in the appreciation of an English writer, marvellous in a foreigner. Mr. Elwin, in the " Quarterly," had, many years before, given a discriminating view of Sterne's life and writings, while the late Mr. Thackeray's shallow estimate of Sterne's character was merely the sensation of the hour. There was something almost ludicrous in the venomous way in which he assailed the great writer, fastening especially on what he thought the hypocritical side of his character: the sham sentiment, the "leering" Tartuffeism, and mock humanity. It has always seemed that there could be but one solution : a consciousness of the same unreality in the modern writer's own satire against social vices.

Without pursuing this comparison further, it may be pointed out into what gross blunders his rage against Sterne betrayed him. The whole tone of the lecture in which he criticised Sterne is unbecoming; as where he calls him " a mountebank," and jeers at some of his most famous passages, on the ground of their insincerity. This tone seems to amount to an utter insensibility to fine poetic colour; as, for instance, in those charming little series of sketches which have made Dessein's Court-yard at Calais famous—like the désobligeant, which has been painted again and again. He could cavil at this pretty etching—" Four months had elapsed since it had finished its career of Europe in the corner of Monsieur – Dessein's court-yard, and having sallied out thence but a vamped-up business at first, though it had been twice taken to pieces on Mount Sennis. . . . . . Much, indeed, was not to be said for it, but something might, and when a few words will rescue

misery out of her distress, I hate the man who can
be a churl of them." This, said Mr. Thackeray, was
only more of the mountebank—"Does anyone believe
that this is a real sentiment—that this luxury of
generosity—this gallant rescue out of misery of an
old cab is genuine feeling ? " Such lack of fine sense
is inconceivable. Sterne, as anyone can see, never
dreamed of such a view; it is a pleasant bit of
trifling—*persiflage* almost : just as one would say—
" I took pity on the thing." But it is impossible to
argue on such *nuances*—they make their own appeal.
In worse taste was his sneer at the description of the
dead ass—famous all the world over—"Tears and
fine feelings, and a white pocket-handkerchief, and a
funeral sermon, horses and feathers, and a procession
of mutes, and a hearse, with a dead donkey inside.
Pshaw, mountebank !" Here, again, is an utter misconception, as the whole pathos centres in the
mourner for the dead ass.

But his mistakes as to facts are more serious : such
a collection of blunders was rarely collected into a
few pages. He says that Richard Sterne was Archbishop of York in the time of James II.; but that
prelate died in the reign of Charles II. "Roger
Sterne was a lieutenant in Handiside's regiments,"
but Roger never served in that corps. "He married
the daughter of a noted sutler"—she was the sutler's
daughter-in-law. "One relative of his mother's
took her and her family under shelter for ten
months at Mullingar ; another descendant of the
Archbishop's housed them for a year at his castle near
Carrickfergus." This is all confused. The ten months
were spent at Elvington, not at Mullingar ; and it was
a relative of his father, not of his mother, that so
entetrained them. The mother's relative, too, lived
in Wicklow, not in Mullingar, and kept them six
months. Finally, to make the shuffle complete, the
collateral descendant of the Archbishop's had no

castle at Carrickfergus, though the regiment had been
recently quartered there. Laurence remained at
Halifax School, not "till he was eighteen years old,"
but till he was twenty ; and he remained at Cambridge not five years, but four. Some of the English,
too, is very curious : it is strange to hear a man like
Mr. Thackeray talking of anyone getting "a preben-
dary of York," meaning a prebend. This, too, is
odd : "He married the daughter of a noted sutler,
and marched through the world with this companion,
*following the regiment, and bringing many children to
poor Roger Sterne.*" (!) This is converting the father
into the mother. Again, when he says : "The captain was an irascible, but kind and simple little man,
Sterne says, and informs us that his sire was run
through the body at Gibraltar," it is made to appear
that it was the sire who informs us. But there are
more serious perversions still. There is a free and
easy letter in Latin, in which Sterne says he was
"sick of his wife," and which Mr. Thackeray, to make
Sterne's conduct more questionable, says was written
in the year 1767, at the same time that he was so devoted to Mrs. Draper. The letter is actually undated ;
but the context, where Sterne mentions his own age
fixes the date at about 1753 or 1754, near thirteen
years earlier. Again, he says that this Mrs. Draper
had hardly sailed when "the coward" was at a
coffee-house writing to another lady, Lady Percy, and
offering his affections to her. This is a precise charge
of duplicity and disloyalty ; but there is no date to
the letter. Again Sterne was warning Mrs. Draper
against some people he disliked ; but Mr. Thackeray,
who had not read the letters carefully, jumped at the ‑
conclusion that this was a sneer at the lady's husband.
The context proves conclusively that "the gentility"
Sterne was warning her against was that of some
people who were odious to him, and whose influence
with her he had tried to undetermine even by a false-

hood. The class of English writers to which Sterne
belongs is small—the species is almost the genus—and
it is unfortunate that such an attack should have come
from a writer of kindred genius.

No memorial of any kind exists to his memory.
There remains indeed the marvellous portrait by Sir
Joshua, of which the well known engraving gives a
very imperfect idea, the eyes in the picture being
lighter and a little cruel, and the mouth more good-
humoured. But it is hoped that this neglect of the
memory of so remarkable a writer will soon be repaired.
The Dean of York has given permission for a memorial to be placed in the cathedral, and the Archbishop
of York has promised a contribution. Whatever have
been the failings of Bishop Warburton's " irrevocable
scoundrel," the creator of my uncle Toby, the author
of the pathetic story of Le Fever, deserves at least a
tablet and inscription.

I am aware that there are great objections to what
has been called a " Bowlerized edition ;" but I think
it will be found that Sterne suffers less from this process than would be supposed. All the passages by
which his reputation has been made may be read by
" boys and virgins ;" the coarse portions are for the
most part digressions ; the author goes out of his way
to seek those nasty piquancies. But all the while
there remains the interest in Mr. Shandy's household,
and his visitors, the arguments of Yorick and uncle
Toby with their host, the latter's campaigns and court-
ship—in short, a little story. I may lay claim to some
little ingenuity in the arrangement of these scenes,
especially in finding a conclusion for Sterne's incom-
plete work, by shifting some passages from the middle
of the book. I have also made some other transposi-
tions, which become almost legitimate when it is considered that Sterne himself was respectively antici-
pating or shifting the events of his little narrative.

I have also carefully collated the text with the original editions, published in Sterne's life-time, and restored much of the effective though irregulative punctuation which later printers have removed.

PERCY FITZGERALD.

CONTENTS.

CHAPTER VIII.

CHAPTER IX.

CHAPTER X.

CHAPTER XI.

CHAPTER XII.

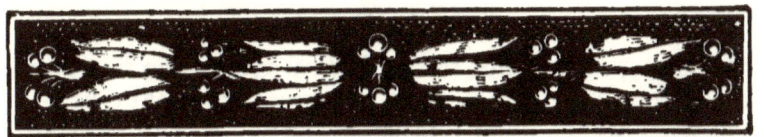

THE STORY OF MY UNCLE TOBY.

CHAPTER I.

PARSON YORICK.

ON the fifth day of November, 1718, was I, Tristram Shandy, Gentleman, brought forth into this scurvy and disastrous world of ours.—I wish I had been born in the moon, or in any of the planets (except Jupiter or Saturn, because I never could bear cold weather,) for it could not well have fared worse with me in any of them (though I will not answer for Venus) than it has in this vile, dirty planet of ours,—which o' my conscience, with reverence be it spoken, I take to be made up of the shreds and clippings of the rest ;—not but the planet is well enough, provided a man could be born in it to a great title or to a great estate ; or could anyhow contrive to be called up to public charges, and employments of dignity or power ;—but that is not my case ;—and therefore every man will speak of the fair as his own market has gone in it ;—for which cause I affirm it over again to be one of the vilest worlds that ever was made ;—for I can truly say, that from the first hour I drew my breath in it, to this, that I can now scarce draw it at all, for an asthma I got in skating against the wind in Flanders,—I have been the continual sport of what the world calls fortune ;

1

and though I will not wrong her by saying she has ever
made me feel the weight of any great or signal evil ;—
yet with all the good temper in the world, I affirm it of
her, that in every stage of my life, and at every turn and
corner where she could get fairly at me, the ungracious
duchess has pelted me with a set of as pitiful misadven-
tures and cross accidents as ever small hero sustained.

In the same village where my father and mother
dwelt, dwelt also a thin, upright, motherly, notable, good
old body of a midwife, who, with the help of a little
plain good sense, and some years' full employment in
her business, in which she had all along trusted little
to her own efforts, and a great deal to those of
Dame Nature,—had acquired, in her way, no small
degree of reputation in the world ;—by which word
world, need I in this place inform your worship that
I would be understood to mean no more of it than a
small circle described upon the circle of the great
world, of four English miles diameter, or thereabouts,
of which the cottage where the good old woman lived
is supposed to be the centre.—She had been left, it
seems, a widow in great distress, with three or four
small children, in her forty-seventh year ; and as she
was at that time a person of decent carriage,—grave
deportment,—a woman moreover of few words, and
withal an object of compassion, whose distress and
silence under it called out the louder for a friendly
lift : the wife of the parson of the parish was touched
with pity ; and having often lamented an inconvenience, to which her husband's flock had for many
years been exposed, inasmuch, as there was no such
thing as a midwife, of any kind or degree, to be got
at, let the case have been never so urgent, within less
than six or seven long miles' riding ; which said seven
long miles in dark nights and dismal roads, the
country thereabouts being nothing but a deep clay,
was almost equal to fourteen : and that in effect was
sometimes next to having no midwife at all ; it came

into her head, that it would be doing as seasonable a
kindness to the whole parish, as to the poor creature
herself, to get her a little instructed in some of the
plain principles of the business, in order to set her up
in it. As no woman thereabouts was better qualified
to execute the plan she had formed than herself, the
gentlewoman very charitably undertook it ; and having
great influence over the female part of the parish, she
found no difficulty in effecting it to the utmost of her
wishes. In truth, the parson joined his interest with
his wife's in the whole affair ; and in order to do
things as they should be, and give the poor soul as
good a title by law to practise, as his wife had given
by institution,—he cheerfully paid the fees for the
ordinary's license himself, amounting in the whole to
the sum of eighteen shillings and fourpence ; so that
betwixt them both the good woman was fully invested
in the real and corporal possession of her office, together with all its rights and appurtenances whatsoever.

Whatever degree of small merit the act of benignity in
favour of the midwife might justly claim,—at first sight
seems not very material to this history ; certain however
it was, that the gentlewoman, the parson's wife, did run
away at that time with the whole of it ; and yet, for
my life, I cannot help thinking but that the parson
himself, though he had not the good fortune to hit
upon the design first,—yet, as he heartily concurred
in it the moment it was laid before him, and as heartily
parted with his money to carry it into execution, had
a claim to some share of it, if not to a full half of
whatever honour was due to it.

The world at that time was pleased to determine
the matter otherwise.

Be it known then, that for about five years before
the date of the midwife's license, the parson had made
himself a country talk by a breach of all decorum ;—
and that was in never appearing better, or otherwise
mounted, than upon a lean sorry jackass of a horse,

1—2

value about one pound fifteen shillings ; who, to shorten the description of him, was full brother to Rosinante.

In the several sallies about his parish, and in the neighbouring visits to the gentry who lived around him you will easily comprehend that the parson, so appointed, would both hear and see enough to keep. his philosophy from rusting. To speak the truth, he never could enter a village, but he caught the attention of both old and young.—Labour stood still as he passed,—the bucket hung suspended in the middle of the well,—the spinning-wheel forgot its round,— even chuck-farthing and shuffle-cap themselves stood gaping till he had got out of sight ; and as his move- ment was not of the quickest, he had generally time enough upon his hands to make his observations,—to hear the groans of the serious, and the laughter of the light-hearted ;—all which he bore with excellent tran- quillity.—His character was,—he loved a jest in his heart—and as he saw himself in the true point of ridicule, he would say, he could not be angry with others for seeing him in a light in which he so strongly saw himself : So that to his friends, who knew his foible was not the love of money, and who therefore made the less scruple in bantering the extravagance of his humour,—instead of giving the true cause,—he chose rather to join in the laugh against himself ; and as he never carried one single ounce of flesh upon his own bones, being altogether as spare a figure as his beast,—he would sometimes insist upon it that the horse was as good as the rider deserved.

At different times he would give fifty humorous and opposite reasons for riding a meek-spirited jade of a broken-winded horse, preferable to one of mettle ;— - for on such a one he could sit mechanically, and meditate as delightfully *de vanitate mundi et fugâ sæculi*, as with the advantage of a death's-head before him ;—that, in all other exercitations, he could spend his time, as he rode slowly along,—to as much account as in his study ;—that he could draw up an argument in his sermon,—or a hole in his breeches, as steadily on the one as in the other ;—that brisk trotting and slow argumentation, like wit and judgment, were two incompatible movements.—But that upon his steed— he could unite and reconcile everything,—he could compose his sermon,—he could compose his cough,— and, in case nature gave a call that way, he could likewise compose himself to sleep.—In short, the parson upon such encounters would assign any cause but the true cause,—and he withheld the true one, only out of a nicety of temper, because he thought it did honour to him.

But the truth of the story was as follows :—In the first years of this gentleman's life, and about the time when a superb saddle and bridle were purchased by him, it had been his manner or vanity, or call it what you will,—to run into the opposite extreme.—In the language of the county where he dwelt, he was said to have loved a good horse, and generally had one of the best in the whole parish standing in his stable always ready for saddling ; and as the nearest mid- wife, as I told you, did not live nearer to the village than seven miles, and in a vile country,—it so fell out that the poor gentleman was scarce a whole week together without some piteous application for his beast ; and as he was not an unkind-hearted man, and every case was more pressing and more distressful than the last,—as much as he loved his beast, he had never a heart to refuse him ; the upshot of which was generally this, that his horse was either clapped, or spavined, or greased ;—or he was twitter-boned, or broken-winded, or something, in short, or other had befallen him, which would let him carry no flesh ;—so that he had every nine or ten months a bad horse to get rid of,—and a good horse to purchase in his stead.

What the loss in such a balance might amount to, *communibus annis*, I would leave to a special jury of sufferers in the same traffic to determine ;—but let it be what it would, the honest gentleman bore it for many years without a murmur, till at length, by repeated ill accidents of the kind, he found it necessary to take the thing under consideration ; and upon weighing the whole, and summing it up in his mind, he found it not only disproportioned to his other expenses, but withal so heavy an article in itself, as to disable him from any other act of generosity in his parish. Besides this he considered, that with half the sum thus galloped away he could do ten times as much good ; and what still weighed more with him than all other considerations put together was this, that it confined all his charity into one particular channel, and where, as he fancied, it was the least wanted, namely, to the child-bearing part of his parish ; reserving nothing for the impotent,—nothing for the aged,—nothing for the many comfortless scenes he was hourly called forth to visit, where poverty, and sickness, and affliction dwelt together.

For these reasons he resolved to discontinue the expense ; and there appeared but two possible ways to extricate him clearly out of it ;—and these were, either to make it an irrevocable law never more to lend his steed upon any application whatever,—or else be content to ride the last poor devil, such as they had made him, with all his aches and infirmities, to the very end of the chapter.

As he dreaded his own constancy in the first,—he very cheerfully betook himself to the second ; and though he could very well have explained it, as I said, to his honour,—yet, for that very reason, he had a spirit above it ; choosing rather to bear the contempt of his enemies, and the laughter of his friends, than undergo the pain of telling a story, which might seem a panegyric upon himself.

I have the highest idea of the spiritual and refined sentiments of this reverend gentleman, from this single stroke in his character, which I think comes up to any of the honest refinements of the peerless knight of *La Mancha*, whom, by the bye, with all his follies, I love more, and would actually have gone further to have paid a visit to, than the greatest hero of antiquity.

But this is not the moral of my story: The thing I had in view was to show the temper of the world in the whole of this affair.—For you must know, that so long as this explanation would have done the parson credit,—the devil a soul could find it out,—I suppose his enemies would not, and that his friends could not. —But no sooner did he bestir himself in behalf of the midwife, and pay the expenses of the ordinary's licence to set her up,—but the whole secret came out ; every horse he had lost, and two horses more than ever he had lost, with all the circumstances of their destruction, were known and distinctly remembered.—The story ran like wildfire—" The parson had a returning " fit of pride which had just seized him ; and he was " going to be well mounted once again in his life ; " and if it was so, 'twas plain as the sun at noon-day, " he would pocket the expense of the licence, ten " times told, the very first year :—So that everybody " was left to judge what were his views in this act of " charity."

What were his views in this, and in every other action of his life,—or rather what were the opinions which floated in the brains of other people concerning it, was a thought which too much floated in his own, and too often broke in upon his rest, when he should have been found asleep.

About ten years ago this gentleman had the good fortune to be made entirely easy upon that score,—it being just so long since he left his parish,—and the whole world at the same time behind him,—and stands accountable to a Judge of whom he will have no cause to complain.

But there is a fatality attends the actions of some men : Order them as they will, they pass through a certain medium which so twists and refracts them from their true directions—that, with all the titles to praise which a rectitude of heart can give, the doers of them are nevertheless forced to live and die without it.

Yorick was this parson's name, who, by what I can remember of him, and by all the accounts I could ever get of him, seemed not to have had one single drop of Danish blood in his whole crasis ; in nine hundred years, it might possibly have all run out :—I will not philosophize one moment with you about it ; for, happen how it would, the fact was this :—that instead of that cold phlegm and exact regularity of sense and humours you would have looked for in one so extracted, —he was, on the contrary, as mercurial and sublimated a composition,—as heteroclite a creature in all his declensions ;—with as much life and whim, and *gaieté de cœur* about him, as the kindliest climate could have engendered and put together. With all this sail, poor Yorick carried not one ounce of ballast ; he was utterly unpractised in the world ; and, at the age of twenty-six, knew just about as well how to steer his course in it, as a romping, unsuspicious girl of thirteen : so that upon his first setting out, the brisk gale of his spirits, as you will imagine, ran him foul ten times in a day of somebody's tackling ; and as the grave and more slow-paced were oftenest in his way,—you may likewise imagine, 'twas with such he had generally the ill luck to get the most intangled. For aught I know there might be some mixture of unlucky wit at the bottom of such *fracas :* for, to speak the truth, Yorick had an invincible dislike and opposition in his nature to gravity ;—not to gravity as such ;—for where gravity was wanted, he would be the most grave or serious of

mortal men for days and weeks together ;—but he was
an enemy to the affectation of it, and declared open
war against it, only as it appeared a cloak for ignorance, or for folly ; and then, whenever it fell in his
way, however sheltered and protected, he seldom gave
it much quarter.

But, in plain truth, he was a man unhackneyed and
unpractised in the world, and was altogether as in-
discreet and foolish on every other subject of discourse
where policy is wont to impress restraint. Yorick had
no impression but one, and that was what arose from
the nature of the deed spoken of ; which impression
he would usually translate into plain English without
any periphrasis,—and too oft without much distinction of either personage, time, or place ;—so that
when mention was made of a pitiful or an ungenerous
proceeding, he never gave himself a moment's time
to reflect who was the hero of the piece,—what his
station,—or how far he had power to hurt him hereafter ;—but if it was a dirty action,—without more
ado,—The man was a dirty fellow,—and so on :—and
as his comments had usually the ill fate to be
terminated either in a *bon mot*, or to be enlivened
throughout with some drollery or humour of expression, it gave wings to Yorick's indiscretion. In a
word, though he never sought, yet at the same time,
as he seldom shunned occasions of saying what came
uppermost, and without much ceremony ; he had but
too many temptations in life, of scattering his wit and
humour,—his gibes and jests about him.—They were
not lost for want of gathering. To speak the truth, he
had wantonly involved himself in a multitude of
small book-debts of this stamp, which, notwithstanding Eugenius's frequent advice, he too much
disregarded ; thinking that as not one of them was
contracted through any malignancy ;—but, on the
contrary, from an honesty of mind, and a mere

jocundity of humour, they would all of them be crossed out in course.

Eugenius would never admit this ; and would often tell him, that one day or other he would certainly be reckoned with ; and he would often add, in an accent of sorrowful apprehension,—to the uttermost mite. To which Yorick, with his usual carelessness of heart, would as often answer with a pshaw !—and if the subject was started in the fields,—with a hop, skip, and a jump, at the end of it ; but if close pent up in the social chimney corner, where the culprit was barricadoed in, with a table and a couple of arm-chairs, and could not so readily fly off in a tangent, Eugenius would then go on with his lecture upon discretion in words to this purpose, though somewhat better put together.

Trust me, dear Yorick, this unwary pleasantry of thine will sooner or later bring thee into scrapes and difficulties, which no after-wit can extricate thee out of.—In these sallies, too oft, I see, it happens, that a person laughed at, considers himself in the light of a person injured, with all the rights of such a situation belonging to him ; and when thou viewest him in that light too, and reckons up his friends, his family, his kindred and allies,—and musters up with them the many recruits which will list under him from a sense of common danger ;—'tis no extravagant arithmetic to say, that for every ten jokes, thou hast got an hundred enemies ; and till thou hast gone on, and raised a swarm of wasps about thine ears, and art half stung to death by them, thou wilt never be convinced it is so.

Revenge from some baneful corner shall level a tale of dishonour at thee, which no innocence of heart or integrity of conduct shall set right.—The fortunes of thy house shall totter,—thy character, which led the way to them, shall bleed on every side of it,—thy faith questioned,—thy works belied, thy wit forgotten,—thy learning trampled on. To wind up the last scene of thy tragedy, Cruelty and Cowardice, twin ruffians, hired and set on by Malice in the dark, shall strike together at all thy infirmities and mistakes :—The best of us, my dear lad, lie open there,—and trust me,— trust me, Yorick, when to gratify a private appetite, it is once resolved upon, that an innocent and an help-less creature shall be sacrificed, 'tis an easy matter to pick up sticks enough from any thicket where it has strayed, to make a fire to offer it up with.

Yorick scarce ever heard this sad vaticination of his destiny read over to him, but with a tear stealing from his eye, and a promissory look attending it, that he was resolved, for the time to come, to ride his tit with more sobriety.—But, alas, too late! a grand con-federacy was formed before the first prediction of it.— The whole plan of the attack, just as Eugenius had foreboded, was put in execution all at once,—with so little mercy on the side of the allies,—and so little suspicion in Yorick, of what was carrying on against him,—that when he thought, good easy man ! full surely preferment was o' ripening, they had smote his root, and then he fell, as many a worthy man had fallen before him.

Yorick, however, fought it out with all imaginable gallantry for some time ; till overpowered by numbers, and worn out at length by the calamities of the war,— but more so by the ungenerous manner in which it was carried on,—he threw down the sword ; and though he kept up his spirits in appearance to the last, he died, nevertheless, as was generally thought, quite broken-hearted.

A few hours before Yorick breathed his last, Euge-nius stept in with an intent to take his last sight and last farewell of him. Upon his drawing Yorick's curtain, and asking how he felt himself, Yorick, look-ing up in his face, took hold of his hand,—and, after thanking him for the many tokens of his friendship to

him, for which, he said, if it was their fate to meet
hereafter,—he would thank him again and again,—he
told him, he was within a few hours of giving his
enemies the slip for ever.—I hope not, answered
Eugenius, with tears trickling down his cheeks, and
with the tenderest tone that ever man spoke,—I hope
not, Yorick, said he.   Yorick replied, with a look up,
and a gentle squeeze of Eugenius's hand, and that was
all,—but it cut Eugenius to his heart.—Come, come,
Yorick, quoth Eugenius, wiping his eyes, and sum-
moning up the man within him,—my dear lad, be
comforted,—let not all thy spirits and fortitude forsake
thee at this crisis when thou most wantest them;—who
knows what resources are in store, and what the power
of God may yet do for thee?—Yorick laid his hand
upon his heart, and gently shook his head;—for my
part, continued Eugenius, crying bitterly as he uttered
the words,—I declare I know not, Yorick, how to part
with thee,—and would gladly flatter my hopes, added
Eugenius, cheering up his voice, that there is still
enough left of thee to make a bishop,—and that I may
live to see it.   I beseech thee, Eugenius, quoth Yorick,
taking off his night-cap as well as he could with his
left hand,—his right being still grasped close in that
of Eugenius,—I beseech thee to take a view of my
head.—I see nothing that ails it, replied Eugenius.
Then, alas! my friend, said Yorick, let me tell you,
that 'tis so bruised and mis-shapened with the blows
which **** and ****, and some others, have so un-
handsomely given me in the dark, that I might say
with Sancho Panca, that should I recover, and
"Mitres thereupon he suffered to rain down from
"heaven as thick as hail, not one of 'em would fit it."
Yorick's last breath was hanging upon his trembling
lips ready to depart as he uttered this;—yet still it
was uttered with something of a Cervantic tone;—
and as he spoke it, Eugenius could perceive a stream
of lambent fire lighted up for a moment in his eyes;—

faint picture of those flashes of his spirit, which (as
Shakspeare said of his ancestor) were wont to set the
table in a roar !

Eugenius was convinced from this, that the heart
of his friend was broke ; he squeezed his hand,—and
then walked softly out of the room, weeping as he
walked. Yorick followed Eugenius with his eyes to
the door,—he then closed them,—and never opened
them more.

He lies buried in a corner of his churchyard, in the
parish of ————, under a plain marble slab, which
his friend Eugenius, by leave of his executors, laid
upon his grave, with no more than these three words
of inscription, serving both for his epitaph and elegy :

Ten times in a day has Yorick's ghost the consolation
to hear his monumental inscription read over with
such a variety of plaintive tones, as denote a general
pity and esteem for him ; a foot-way crossing the
churchyard close by the side of his grave,—not a
passenger goes by without stopping to cast a look
upon it,—and sighing as he walks on,
Alas, poor YORICK !

CHAPTER II.

MY FATHER AND MOTHER.

PON looking into my mother's marriage settlement, in order to satisfy myself and reader in a point necessary to be cleared up, before we could proceed any further in this history;—I had the good-fortune to pop upon the very thing I wanted, which is so much more fully expressed in the deed itself, than ever I can pretend to do it, that it would be barbarity to take it out of the lawyer's hand :—It is as follows :

"𝔄𝔫𝔡 this 𝔈𝔫𝔡𝔢𝔫𝔱𝔲𝔯𝔢 𝔣𝔲𝔯𝔱𝔥𝔢𝔯 𝔴𝔦𝔱𝔫𝔢𝔰𝔰𝔢𝔱𝔥, That the
" said Walter Shandy, merchant, in consideration of
" the said intended marriage to be had, and, by God's
" blessing, to be well and truly solemnized and con-
" summated between the said Walter Shandy and
" Elizabeth Mollineux aforesaid, and divers other good
" and valuable causes and considerations him there-
" unto specially moving,—doth grant, covenant, con-
" descend, consent, conclude, bargain, and fully agree
" to and with John Dixon and James Turner, Esqrs.,
" the above-named trustees, &c., &c.—to wit,—That
" in case it should hereafter so fall out, chance,
" happen, or otherwise come to pass,—That the said
" Walter Shandy, merchant, shall have left off busi-
" ness before the time or times that the said Elizabeth
" Mollineux shall, according to the course of nature,

" or otherwise, have left off bearing and bringing
" forth children ;—and that, in consequence of the
" said Walter Shandy having so left off business, he
" shall, in despite, and against the free-will, consent,
" and good-liking of the said Elizabeth Mollineux,—
" make a departure from the city of London, in order
" to retire to, and dwell upon, his estate at Shandy
" Hall, in the county of —— or at any other country
" seat, castle, hall, mansion-house, messuage, or grange-
" house, now purchased, or hereafter to be purchased,
" or upon any part or parcel thereof :—That then, and
" as often as the said Elizabeth Mollineux shall
" happen to be *enceinte* with child or children severally
" and lawfully begot, he the said Walter Shandy shall,
" at his own proper cost and charges, and out of his
" own proper monies, upon good and reasonable
" notice, which is hereby agreed to be within six
" weeks of her the said Elizabeth Mollineux's full
" reckoning, or time of supposed and computed deli-
" very,—pay, or cause to be paid, the sum of one
" hundred and twenty pounds of good and lawful
" money, to John Dixon and James Turner, Esqrs.
" or assigns,— upon TRUST and confidence, and for and
" unto the use and uses, intent, end, and purpose
" following :—That is to say,—That the said sum of
" one hundred and twenty pounds shall be paid into
" the hands of the said Elizabeth Mollineux, or to be
" otherwise applied by them the said Trustees, for the
" well and truly hiring of one coach, with able and
" sufficient horses, to carry and convey the body of
" the said Elizabeth Mollineux, and the child or
" children which she shall be then and there *enceinte*
" and pregnant with,—unto the city of London ; and
" for the further paying and defraying of all other
" incidental costs, charges, and expenses whatsoever,
" —in and about, and for, and relating to, her said
" intended delivery and lying-in, in the said city or
" suburbs thereof. And that the said Elizabeth

" Mollineux shall and may, from time to time, and
" at all such time and times as are here covenanted
" and agreed upon,—peaceably and quietly hire the
" said coach and horses, and have free ingress, egress,
" and regress throughout her journey, in and from the
" said coach, according to the tenor, true intent, and
" meaning of these presents, without any let, suit,
" trouble, disturbance, molestation, discharge, hin-
" drance, forfeiture, eviction, vexation, interruption,
" or incumbrance whatsoever.—And that it shall
" moreover be lawful to and for the said Elizabeth
" Mollineux, from time to time, and as oft or often
" she shall well and truly be advanced in her said
" pregnancy, to the time heretofore stipulated and
" agreed upon,—to live and reside in such place or
" places, and in such family or families, and with
" such relations, friends, and other persons within the
" said city of London, as she, at her own will and
" pleasure, notwithstanding her present coverture,
" and as if she was a *femme sole* and unmarried,—
" shall think fit.—And this Indenture further witnes-
" seth, That for the more effectually carrying of the
" said covenant into execution, the said Walter
" Shandy, merchant, doth hereby grant, bargain, sell,
" release, and confirm unto the said John Dixon and
" James Turner, Esqrs., their heirs, executors, and
" assigns, in their actual possession, now being, by
" virtue of an indenture of bargain and sale for a
" year to them the said John Dixon and James
" Turner, Esqrs., by him the said Walter Shandy,
" merchant, thereof made; which said bargain and
" sale for a year, bears date the day next before
" the date of these presents, and by force and
" virtue of the statute for transferring of uses into
" possession,—All that the manor and lordships of
" Shandy in the county of —— with all the rights,
" members, and appurtenances thereof; and all and
" every the messuages, houses, buildings, barns,

" stables, orchards, gardens, tofts, crofts, garths,
" cottages, lands, meadows, feedings, pastures,
" marshes, commons, woods, underwoods, drains,
" fisheries, waters and water-courses ;—together with
" all rents, reversions, services, annuities, fee farms,
" knight's fees, views of frank-pledge, eschcats,
" reliefs, mines, quarries, goods and chattels of felons,
" and fugitives, felons of themselves, and put in
" exigent, deodands, free warrens, and all other
" royalties and seignories, rights and jurisdictions,
" privileges and hereditaments whatsoever.—And
" also, the advowson, donation, presentation and free
" disposition of the rectory or parsonage of Shandy
" aforesaid, and all and every the tenths, tithes, glebe-
" lands "—In three words,—" My mother was to lay
" in, (if she chose it) in London."

But in order to put a stop to the practice of any
unfair play on the part of my mother, for which a
marriage article of this nature too manifestly opened a
door, and which indeed had never been thought of at
all, but for my uncle Toby Shandy ;—a clause was
added in security of my father, which was this :—
" That in case my mother hereafter should, at any
" time, put my father to the trouble and expense of a
" London journey upon false cries and tokens ;—that
" for every such instance she should forfeit all the
" rights and title which the covenant gave her to
" the next turn ;—but to no more,—and so on, *toties
" quoties*, in as effectual a manner, as if such a cove-
" nant betwixt them had not been made."—This, by
the way, was no more than what was reasonable ;—
and yet, as reasonable as it was, I have ever thought
it hard that the whole weight of the article should
have fallen entirely, as it did, upon myself.

But I was begot and born to misfortunes ;—for my
poor mother, whether it was simply the mere swell
of imagination and fancy in her ; or how far a strong
wish and desire to have it so, might mislead her judg-

2

ment ;—in short, whether she was deceived or deceiving in this matter, it no way becomes me to decide. The fact was this : That, in the latter end of September, 1717, which was the year before I was born, my mother having carried my father up to town much against the grain,—he peremptorily insisted upon the clause ;—so that I was doomed by marriage articles, to have my nose squeezed as flat to my face as if the destinies had actually spun me without one.

My father, as anybody may naturally imagine, came down with my mother into the country, in but a pettish kind of humour. The first twenty or five-and-twenty miles he did nothing in the world but fret and tease himself, and indeed my mother too, about the cursed expense, which he said might every shilling of it have been saved ;—then what vexed him more than everything else was the provoking time of the year,—which, as l told you, was towards the end of September, when his wall-fruit and greengages especially, in which he was very curious, were just ready for pulling :—"Had he been whistled up to London, "upon a tomfool's errand, in any other month of the "whole year, he should not have said three words "about it."

For the next two whole stages, no subject would go down, but the heavy blow he had sustained from the loss of a son, whom it seems he had fully reckoned upon in his mind, and registered down in his pocket-book, as a second staff for his old age, in case Bobby should fail him. "The disappointment of this, he "said, was ten times more to a wise man than all the "money which the journey, &c. had cost him, put "together,—rot the hundred and twenty pounds,—he "did not mind it a rush."

From Stilton, all the way to Grantham, nothing in the whole affair provoked him so much as the condolences of his friends, and the foolish figure they should both make at church the first Sunday ;—of which in the satirical vehemence of his wit, now sharpened a little by vexation, he would give so many humorous and provoking descriptions,—and place his rib and self in so many tormenting lights and attitudes in the face of the whole congregation;—that my mother declared, these two stages were so truly tragi-comical, that she did nothing but laugh and cry in a breath, from one end to the other of them all the way.

From Grantham, till they had crossed the Trent, my father was out of all kinds of patience at the vile trick and imposition which he fancied my mother had put upon him in this affair—"Certainly," he would say to himself over and over again, "the woman "could not be deceived herself;"—— In short, he had so many little subjects of disquietude springing out of this one affair, all fretting successively in his mind as they rose upon it, that my mother, whatever was her journey up, had but an uneasy journey of it down.—In a word, as she complained to my uncle Toby, he would have tired out the patience of any flesh alive.

Though my father travelled homewards, in none of the best of moods,—pshawing and pishing all the way down,—yet he had the complaisance to keep the worst part of the story still to himself ;—which was the resolution he had taken of doing himself the justice, which my uncle Toby's clause in the marriage settlement empowered him ; nor was it till thirteen months after, that she had the least intimation of his design ; —when my father, happening to be a little chagrined and out of temper,—took occasion as they lay chatting gravely in bed, talking over what was to come,—to let her know that she must accommodate herself as well as she could to the bargain made between them in their marriage deeds ; which was to lie-in of her next child in the country to balance the last year's journey.

My father was a gentleman of many virtues,—but

2—2

he had a strong spice of that in his temper which might, or might not, add to the number.—'Tis known by the name of perseverance in a good cause, and of obstinacy in a bad one : of this my mother had so much knowledge, that she knew 'twas to no purpose to make any remonstrance,—so she e'en resolved to sit down quietly, and make the most of it.

As the point was agreed, or rather determined, that my mother should lie-in of me in the country, she took her measures accordingly; for which purpose she began to cast her eyes upon the midwife, whom you have so often heard me mention; and before the week was well got round, as the famous Dr. Manningham was not to be had, she had come to a final determination in her mind,—notwithstanding there was a scientific operator within so near a call as eight miles of us,—absolutely determined to trust her life, and mine with it, into no soul's hands, but this old woman's only. Now this I like, when we cannot get at the very thing we wish, never to take up with the next best in degree to it,—no; that's pitiful beyond description. Only what lessened the honour of it somewhat, in my mother's case, was, that she could not heroine it into so violent and hazardous an extreme, as one in her situation might have wished, because the old midwife had really some little claim to be depended upon,—as much, at least, as success could give her ; having, in the course of her practice of near twenty years in the parish, brought every mother's son of them into the world without any one slip or accident which could fairly be laid to her account.

These facts, tho' they had their weight, yet did not altogether satisfy some few scruples and uneasinesses which hung on my father's spirits in relation to his choice.—To say nothing of the natural workings of humanity and justice,—or of the yearnings of parental and connubial love, all which prompted him to leave as little to hazard as possible in a case of this kind ;—he felt himself concerned in a particular manner, that all should go right in the present case ;— from the accumulated sorrow he lay open to, should any evil betide his wife and child in lying-in at Shandy Hall.—He knew the world judged by events, and would add to his afflictions in such a misfortune, by loading him with the whole blame of it.—"Alas " o'day! had Mrs. Shandy, poor gentlewoman! had " but her wish in going up to town just to lie-in and " come down again ;—which they say, she begged and " prayed for upon her bare knees,—and which, in my " opinion, considering the fortune which Mr. Shandy " got with her,—was no such mighty matter to have " complied with, the lady and her babe might both of " 'em have been alive at this hour."

This exclamation, my father knew, was unanswerable ;—and yet it was not merely to shelter himself,— nor was it altogether for the care of his offspring and wife that he seemed so extremely anxious about this point ; my father had extensive views of things,—and stood, moreover, as he thought, deeply concerned in it for the public good, from the dread he entertained of the bad uses an ill-fated instance might be put to.

He was very sensible that all political writers upon the subject had unanimously agreed and lamented, from the beginning of Queen Elizabeth's reign down to his own time, that the current of men and money towards the metropolis, upon one frivolous errand or another,—set in so strong,—as to become dangerous to our civil rights ;—though, by the bye,—a current was not the image he took most delight in,—a distemper was here his favourite metaphor, and he would run it down into a perfect allegory, by maintaining it was identically the same in the body national as in the body natural, where blood and spirits were driven up into the head faster than they could find their ways down ;—a stoppage of circulation must ensue, which

was death in both cases. There was little danger, he
would say, of losing our liberties by French politics
and French invasions :—but he verily feared that in
some violent push we should go off all at once in a
state of apoplexy ;—and then he would say, "*The
" Lord have mercy upon us all !*"

   "Why are there so few palaces and gentlemen's
" seats," he would ask, with some emotion, as he
walked across the room, " throughout so many deli-
" cious provinces in France ? Whence is it that the
" few remaining chateaus amongst them are so dis-
" mantled,—so unfurnished, and in so ruinous and
" desolate a condition ?—Because, sir," (he would say)
" in that kingdom no man has any country interest to
" support ;—the little interest of any kind which any
" man has anywhere in it is concentrated in the court,
" and the looks of the Grand Monarch : by the sun-
" shine of whose countenance, or the clouds which
" pass across it, every Frenchman lives or dies."
   For all these reasons, private and public, put
together,—my father was for having the man midwife
by all means,—my mother by no means. My father
begged and entreated she would for once recede from
her prerogative in this matter, and suffer him to
choose for her ;—my mother, on the contrary, insisted
upon her privilege in this matter to choose for herself,
—and have no mortal's help but the old woman's.
What could my father do ? He was almost at his wit's
end ;—talked it over with her in all moods ;—placed
his arguments in all lights ;—argued the matter with
her like a Christian—like a heathen,—like a husband,—like a father,—like a patriot,—like a man ;—
My mother answered everything only like a woman ;
which was a little hard upon her ;—for as she could
not assume and fight it out behind such a variety of
characters,—'twas no fair match ;—'twas seven to
one.—What could my mother do ?—She had the
advantage (otherwise she had been certainly over-

powered) of a small reinforcement of chagrin personal at the bottom, which bore her up, and enabled her to dispute the affair with my father with so equal an advantage,—that both sides sung *Te Deum.* In a word, my mother was to have the old woman,—and the operator was to have licence to drink a bottle of wine with my father and my uncle Toby Shandy in the back parlour,—for which he was to be paid five guineas.

I would sooner undertake to explain the hardest problem in geometry than pretend to account for it, that a gentleman of my father's great good sense could be capable of entertaining a notion in his head so out of the common track ;—and that was in respect to the choice and imposition of Christian names, on which he thought a great deal more depended than what superficial minds were capable of conceiving.

The hero of Cervantes argued not the point with more seriousness,—nor had he more faith,—than my father had on those of Trismegistus or Archimedes, on the one hand,—or of Nyky and Simkin on the other. How many Cæsars and Pompeys, he would say, by mere inspiration of the names, have been rendered worthy of them? And how many, he would add, are there, who might have done exceeding well in the world, had not their characters and spirits been totally depressed and Nicodemus'd into nothing?

I see plainly, sir, by your looks (or as the case happened), my father would say,—that you do not heartily subscribe to this opinion of mine,—Your son !—your dear son,—from whose sweet and open temper you have so much to expect.—Your Billy, sir !—would you, for the world, have called him Judas ?—Would you, my dear sir, he would say, laying his hand upon your breast with the genteelest address,—and in that soft and irresistible *piano* of voice, which the nature of the *argumentum ad hominem* absolutely requires,— Would you, sir, if a Jew of a godfather had proposed the name for your child, and offered you his purse

along with it, would you have consented to such a
desecration of him?—O my God! he would say,
looking up, if I know your temper right, sir,—you are
incapable of it ;—you would have trampled upon the
offer ;—you would have thrown the temptation at the
tempter's head with abhorrence.—In a word, I repeat
it over again ;—he was serious ;—and, in consequence
of it, he would lose all kind of patience whenever he
saw people, especially of condition, who should have
known better,—as careless and as indifferent about
the name they imposed upon their child,—or more so,
than in the choice of Ponto or Cupid for their puppy
dog.

This, he would say, looked ill ;—and had, moreover,
this particular aggravation in it, viz. That when once
a vile name was wrongfully or injudiciously given,
'twas not like the case of a man's character, which,
when wronged, might hereafter be cleared ;—and,
possibly, some time or other, if not in the man's life,
at least after his death,—be, somehow or other, set to
rights with the world : But the injury of this, he
would say, could never be undone ;—nay, he doubted
even whether an act of parliament could reach it.

It was observable, that though my father, in consequence of this opinion, had, as I have told you, the
strongest likings and dislikings towards certain names ;
—that there were still numbers of names which hung
so equally in the balance before him, that they were
absolutely indifferent to him. Jack, Dick, and Tom,
were of this class : These my father called neutral
names :—affirming of them, without a satire, that there
had been as many knaves and fools, at least, as wise
and good men, since the world began, who had indif-
ferently borne them ;—so that, like equal forces acting
against each other in contrary directions, he thought
they mutually destroyed each other's effects ; for which
reason, he would often declare, he would not give a
cherry-stone to choose amongst them. Bob, which was

my brother's name, was another of these neutral kinds
of Christian names, which operated very little either
way ; and as my father happened to be at Epsom,
when it was given him,—he would oft-times thank
heaven it was no worse. Andrew was something
like a negative quantity in algebra with him ;—'twas
worse, he said, than nothing—William stood pretty
high :—Numps again was low with him :—and Nick,
he said, was the devil.

But, of all the names in the universe, he had the
most unconquerable aversion for Tristram ;—he had
the lowest and most contemptible opinion of it of
anything in the world,—thinking it could possibly
produce nothing in *rerum natura*, but what was
extremely mean and pitiful : so that in the midst of
a dispute on the subject, in which, by the bye, he was
frequently involved,—he would sometimes break off
in a sudden and spirited Epiphonema, or rather Ero-
tesis, raised a third, and sometimes a full fifth, above
the key of the discourse,—and demand it categorically
of his antagonist, whether he would take upon him to
say, he had ever remembered,—whether he had ever
read,—or even whether he had ever heard tell of a
man, called Tristram, performing anything great or
worth recording !—No,—he would say,—Tristram !—
The thing is impossible.

CHAPTER III.

CAPTAIN SHANDY AND HIS HOBBY-HORSE.

WONDER what's all that noise, and running backwards and forwards for, above stairs, quoth my father, addressing himself, after an hour and a half's silence, to my uncle Toby,—who, you must know, was sitting on the opposite side of the fire, smoking his social pipe all the time, in mute contemplation of a new pair of black plush-breeches which he had got on :—What can they be doing, brother ?—quoth my father,—we can scarce hear ourselves talk.

I think, replied my uncle Toby, taking his pipe from his mouth, and striking the head of it two or three times upon the nail of his left thumb, as he began his sentence,—" I think," says he :—but to enter rightly into my uncle Toby's sentiments upon this matter, you must be made to enter first a little into his character, the outlines of which I shall just give you, and then the dialogue between him and my father will go on as well again.

His humour was of that particular species, which does honour to our atmosphere ; and I should have made no scruple of ranking him amongst one of the firstrate productions of it, had not there appeared too many strong lines in it of a family likeness, which showed that he derived the singularity of his temper more from blood, than either wind or water, or any

modifications or combinations of them whatever : and
I have, therefore, ofttimes wondered, that my father,
though I believe he had his reasons for it, upon his
observing some tokens of eccentricity in my course
when I was a boy,—should never once endeavour to
account for them in this way ; for all the Shandy
Family were of an original character throughout :—I
mean the males,—the females had no character at all,
—except, indeed, my great aunt, Dinah, who, about
sixty years ago, was married by the coachman ; for
which my father, according to his hypothesis of
Christian names, would often say, she might thank
her godfathers and godmothers. It will seem very
strange that an event of this kind, so many years
after it had happened, should be reserved for the
interruption of the peace and unity, which otherwise
so cordially subsisted, between my father and my
uncle Toby. One would have thought, that the whole
force of the misfortune should have spent and wasted
itself in the family at first,—as is generally the case :—
but nothing ever wrought with our family after the
ordinary way. My uncle Toby Shandy, was a gentleman, who, with the virtues that usually constitute the
character of a man of honour and rectitude,—possessed one in a very eminent degree, which is seldom
or never put into the catalogue ; and that was a most
extreme and unparalleled modesty of nature. Whichever way my uncle Toby came by it, 'twas nevertheless
modesty in the truest sense of it ; and that is, not in
regard to words, for he was so unhappy as to have very
little choice in them,—but to things ;—and this kind
of modesty so possessed him, and it arose to such a
height in him, as almost to equal, if such a thing could
be, even the modesty of a woman ; which happening
to be somewhat subtilized and rarified by the constant
heat of a little family pride,—they both so wrought
together within him, that he could never bear to hear
the affair of my aunt Dinah touched upon, but with

the greatest emotion.—The least hint of it was enough
to make the blood fly into his face ; but when my
father enlarged upon the story in mixed companies,
which the illustration of his hypothesis frequently
obliged him to do,—the unfortunate blight of one of
the fairest branches of the family, would set my uncle
Toby's honour and modesty o' bleeding ; and he would
often take my father aside, in the greatest concern
imaginable, to expostulate and tell him, he would give
him anything in the world, only to let the story rest.

My father, I believe, had the truest love and tenderness for my uncle Toby, that ever one brother bore
towards another, and would have done anything in
nature, which one brother in reason could have desired
of another, to have made my uncle Toby's heart easy in
this, or any other point.   But this lay out of his power.

My father, as I told you, was a philosopher in grain,
—speculative,—systematical ; and my aunt Dinah's
affair was a matter of as much consequence to him, as
the retrogradation of the planets to Copernicus.

This contrariety of humours betwixt my father and
my uncle, was the source of many a fraternal squabble.
The one could not bear to hear the tale of family
disgrace recorded—and the other would scarce ever
let a day pass to an end without some hint at it.

For God's sake, my uncle Toby would cry,—and for
my sake and for all our sakes, my dear brother
Shandy,—do let this story of our aunt's and her ashes
sleep in peace ; how can you,—how can you have so
little feeling and compassion for the character of our
family :—What is the character of a family to an
hypothesis ? my father would reply.—Nay, if you
come to that—what is the life of a family ?—The life
of a family !—my uncle Toby would say, throwing
himself back in his arm-chair, and lifting up his
hands, his eyes, and one leg.—Yes, the life,—my father
would say, maintaining his point, how many thousands
of them are there every year that comes, cast away

(in all civilized countries at least)—and considered as nothing but common air, in competition of an hypothesis. In my plain sense of things, my uncle Toby would answer,—every such instance is downright Murder, let who will commit it.—There lies your mistake, my father would reply ; for in *Foro Scientiæ* there is no such thing as Murder.—'tis only Death, brother.

My uncle Toby would never offer to answer this by any other kind of argument, than that of whistling half a dozen bars of Lillibullero,—You must know it was the usual channel through which his' passions got vent, when anything shocked or surprised him ;—but especially when anything, which he deemed very absurd, was offered.

Now the hobby-horse which my uncle Toby always rode upon, was, in my opinion, a hobby-horse well worth giving a description of, if it was only upon the score of his great singularity ; for you might have travelled from York to Dover, from Dover to Penzance in Cornwall, and from Penzance to York back again, and not have seen such another upon the road ; or if you had seen such a one, whatever haste you had been in, you must infallibly have stopped to have taken a view of him.

In good truth my uncle Toby mounted him with so much pleasure, and he carried my uncle Toby so well, that he troubled his head very little with what the world said or thought about it. But to go on regularly, I only beg you will give me leave to acquaint you first how my uncle Toby came by him.

The wound in my uncle Toby's groin, which he received at the siege of Namur, rendering him unfit for the service, it was thought expedient he should return to England, in order, if possible, to be set to rights. He was four years totally confined—part of it to his bed, and all of it to his room ; and in the course of his cure, which was all that time in hand, suffered unspeakable miseries,—owing to a succession of exfo-

liation from the *os pubis*, and the outward edge of
that part of the *coxendix* called the *os ileum*,—both
which bones were dismally crushed, as much by the
irregularity of the stone, which I told you was broke
off the parapet,—as by its size,—(though it was pretty
large) which inclined the surgeons all along to think,
that the great injury which it had done my uncle
Toby's groin, was more owing to the gravity of the
stone itself, than to the projectile force of it—which he
would often tell him was a great happiness.

My father at that time was just beginning business
in London, and had taken a house ;—and as the truest
friendship and cordiality subsisted between the two
brothers,—and that my father thought my uncle Toby
could nowhere be so well nursed and taken care of as
in his own house,—he assigned him the very best
apartment in it.—And what was a much more sincere
mark of his affection still, he would never suffer a
friend or an acquaintance to step into the house on
any occasion, but he would take him by the hand,
and lead him upstairs to see his brother Toby, and
chat an hour by his bedside.

The history of a soldier's wound beguiles the pain
of it ;—my uncle's visitors at least thought so, and in
their daily calls upon him, from the courtesy arising
out of that belief, they would frequently turn the discourse to that subject,—and from that subject the discourse would generally roll on to the siege itself.

These conversations were infinitely kind ; and my
uncle Toby received great relief from them, and would
have received much more, but that they brought him
into some unforeseen perplexities, which, for three
months together, retarded his cure greatly ; and if he
had not hit upon an expedient to extricate himself out
of them, I verily believe they would have laid him in
his grave.

I must remind the reader, in case he has read the
history of King William's wars,—but if he has not,—

I then inform him, that one of the most memorable attacks in that siege, was that which was made by the English and Dutch upon the point of the advanced counterscarp, between the gate of St. Nicholas, which inclosed the great sluice or water-stop, where the English were terribly exposed to the shot of the counter-guard and demi-bastion of St. Roch; the issue of which hot dispute, in three words, was this; that the Dutch lodged themselves upon the counter-guard,—and that the English made themselves masters of the covered way before St. Nicholas's gate, notwithstanding the gallantry of the French officers, who exposed themselves upon the glacis sword in hand.

As this was the principal attack of which my uncle Toby was an eye-witness at Namur,—the army of the besiegers being cut off, by the confluence of the Maes and Sambre, from seeing much of each other's operations,—my uncle Toby was generally more eloquent and particular in his account of it; and the many perplexities he was in, arose out of the almost insurmountable difficulties he found in telling his story intelligibly, and giving such clear ideas of the differences and distinctions between the scarp and counterscarp,—the glacis and covered-way,—the half-moon and ravelin,—as to make his company fully comprehend where and what he was about.

What rendered the account of this affair the more intricate to my uncle Toby, was this,—that in the attack of the counterscarp before the gate of St. Nicholas, extending itself from the bank of the Maes, quite up to the great water-stop,—the ground was cut and cross cut with such a multitude of dykes, drains, rivulets, and sluices on all sides,—and he would get so sadly bewildered and set fast amongst them, that frequently he could neither get backwards or forwards to save his life; and was ofttimes obliged to give up the attack upon that very account only.

These perplexing rebuffs gave my uncle Toby

Shandy more perturbations than you would imagine ;
and as my father's kindness to him was continually
dragging up fresh friends and fresh inquirers,—he
had but a very uneasy task of it.

No doubt my uncle Toby had great command of
himself,—and could guard appearances, I believe, as
well as most men ;—yet any one may imagine, that
when he could not retreat out of the ravelin without
getting into the half-moon, or get out of the covered
way without falling down the counterscarp, or cross
the dyke without danger of slipping into the ditch,
but that he must have fretted and fumed inwardly ;—
he did so ; he could not philosophise upon it ;—'twas
enough he felt it was so,—and having sustained the
pain and sorrows of it for three months together, he
was resolved some way or other to extricate himself.

He was one morning lying upon his back in his
bed, the anguish and nature of the wound upon his
groin suffering him to lie in no other position, when a
thought came into his head, that if he could purchase
such a thing, and have it pasted down upon a board,
as a large map of the fortification of the town and
citadel of Namur, with its environs, it might be a
means of giving him ease.—I take notice of his desire
to have the environs along with the town and citadel,
for this reason,—because my uncle Toby's wound was
got in one of the traverses, about thirty toises from
the returning angle of the trench, opposite to the
salient angle of the demi-bastion of St. Roch ;—so
that he was pretty confident he could stick a pin upon
the identical spot of ground where he was standing
when the stone struck him.

When my uncle Toby got his map of Namur to his
mind, he began immediately to apply himself, and
with the utmost diligence, to the study of it; for
nothing being of more importance to him than his
recovery, and his recovery depending, as you have
read, upon the passions and affections of his mind, it

behoved him to take the nicest care to make himself so far master of his subject, as to be able to talk upon it without emotion.

In a fortnight's close and painful application, which, by-the-bye, did my uncle Toby's wound, upon his groin, no good,—he was enabled, by the help of some marginal documents at the feet of the elephant, together with Gobesius's military architecture and pyroballogy, translated from the Flemish, to form his discourse with passable perspicuity; and before he was two full months gone,—he was right eloquent upon it, and could make not only the attack of the advanced counterscarp with great order;—but having, by that time, gone much deeper into the art, than what his first motive made necessary, my uncle Toby was able to cross the Maes and Sambre; make diversions as far as Vauban's line, the abbey of Salfines, &c., and give his visitors as distinct a history of each of their attacks, as of that of the gate of St. Nicholas, where he had the honour to receive his wound.

But the desire of knowledge, like the thirst of riches, increases ever with the acquisition of it. The more my uncle Toby pored over his map, the more he took a liking to it.

The more my uncle Toby drank of this sweet fountain of science, the greater was the heat and impatience of his thirst, so that before the first year of his confinement had well gone round, there was scarce a fortified town in Italy or Flanders, for which, by one means or other, he had not procured a plan, reading over as he got them, and carefully collating therewith the history of their sieges, their demolitions, their improvements, and new works, all which he would read with that intense application and delight, that he would forget himself, his wound, his confinement, his dinner.

In the second year my uncle Toby purchased Romelli and Cataneo, translated from the Italian;—

3

likewise Stevinus, Moralis, the Chevalier de Ville,
Lorini, Coehorn, Sheeter, the Count de Pagan, the
Marshal Vauban, Mons. Blondel, with almost as many
more books of military architecture, as Don Quixote
was found to have of chivalry, when the curate and
barber invaded his library.

Towards the beginning of the third year, which was
in August, ninety-nine, my uncle Toby found it necessary to understand a little of projectiles :—and having
judged it best to draw his knowledge from the fountain-
head, he began with N. Tartaglia, who it seems was
the first man who detected the imposition of a cannon-
ball's doing all that mischief under the notion of a
right line—This N. Tartaglia proved to my uncle
Toby to be an impossible thing.

——Endless is the search of truth !   ·

No sooner was my uncle Toby satisfied which road
the cannon-ball did not go, but he was insensibly led
on, and resolved in his mind to enquire and find out
which road the ball did go : for which purpose he was
obliged to set off afresh with old Maltus, and studied
him devoutly.—He proceeded next to Gallileo and
Torricellius, wherein, by certain geometrical rules,
infallibly laid down, he found the precise path to be
a parabola—or else an hyperbola,—and that the parameter of the conic section of the said path, was to the
quantity and amplitude in a direct ratio, as the whole
line to the sine of double the angle of incidence, and
that the semiparameter, —— stop ! my dear uncle
Toby,—stop ! go not one foot farther into this thorny
and bewildered track,—intricate are the steps ! intricate are the mazes of this labyrinth ! Is it fit, good-
natured man ! thou shouldest sit up, with the wound
upon thy groin, whole nights baking thy blood with
hectic watchings ?—Alas ! 'twill exasperate thy symp-
toms,—check thy perspiration,—evaporate thy spirits,
—waste thy animal strength,— dry up thy radical
moisture,—bring thee into a costive habit of body,—

impair thy health, and hasten all the infirmities of thy old age.—O my uncle! my uncle Toby!

In the latter end of the third year, my uncle Toby perceiving that the parameter and semi-parameter of the conic section angered his wound, he left off the study of projectiles in a kind of a huff, and betook himself to the practical part of the fortification only; the pleasure of which, like a spring held back, returned upon him with redoubled force.

It was in this year that my uncle began to break in upon the daily regularity of a clean shirt,—to dismiss his barber unshaven,—and to allow his surgeon scarce time sufficient to dress his wound, concerning himself so little about it, as not to ask him once in seven times dressing how it went on: when lo! all of a sudden, for the change was as quick as lightning, he began to sigh heavily for his recovery,—complained to my father, grew impatient with the surgeon;—and one morning as he heard his foot coming up stairs, he shut up his books, and thrust aside his instruments, in order to expostulate with him upon the protraction of the cure, which, he told him, might surely have been accomplished at least by that time:—he dwelt long upon the miseries he had undergone, and the sorrows of his four years' melancholy imprisonment;—adding, that had it not been for the kind looks, and fraternal cheerings of the best of brothers,—he had long since sunk under his·misfortunes. My father was by: my uncle Toby's eloquence brought tears into his eyes;—'twas unexpected—my uncle Toby, by nature, was not eloquent;—it had the greater effect. The surgeon was confounded;—not that there wanted grounds for such, or greater, marks of impatience, but 'twas unexpected too; in the four years he had attended him, he had never seen anything like it in my uncle Toby's carriage;—he had never once dropped one fretful or discontented word,—he had been all patience,—all submission.

3—2

We lose the right of complaining sometimes by
forbearing it ;—but we often treble the force :—the
surgeon was astonished ;—but much more so, when he
heard my uncle Toby go on, and peremptorily insist
upon his healing up the wound directly,—or sending
for Monsieur Ronjat, the king's serjeant-surgeon, to do
it for him.

When my uncle Toby's wound was near well, and as
soon as the surgeon recovered his surprise, and could
get leave to say as much—he told him, 'twas just
beginning to incarnate ; and that if no fresh exfolia-
tion happened, which there was no sign of,—it would
be dried up in five or six weeks. The sound of as
many Olympiads twelve hours before, would have
conveyed an idea of shorter duration to my uncle
Toby's mind. The succession of his ideas was now
rapid,—he broiled with impatience to put his design
in execution;—and so, without consulting farther with
any soul living,—which, by the bye, I think is right,
when you are predetermined to take no one soul's advice,—he privately ordered Trim, his man, to pack up
a bundle of lint and dressings, and hire a chariot and
four to be at the door exactly by twelve o'clock that
day, when he knew my father would be upon 'Change.
—So leaving a bank-note upon the table for the surgeon's care of him, and a letter of tender thanks for
his brother's—he packed up his maps, his books of
fortification, his instruments, &c., and by the help of
a crutch on one side, and Trim on the other,—my
uncle Toby embarked for Shandy Hall.

The reason, or rather the rise, of this sudden demi-
gration, was as follows :

The table in my uncle Toby's room, and at which,
the night before this change happened, he was sitting
with his maps, &c., about him,—being somewhat of
the smallest, for that infinity of great and small instruments of knowledge which usually lay crowded
upon it—he had the accident, in reaching over for his

tobacco-box, to throw down his compasses, and in stooping to take the compasses up, with his sleeve he threw down his case of instruments and snuffers ;— and as the dice took a run against him, in his endeavouring to catch the snuffers in falling,—he thrust Monsieur Blondel off the table, and Count de Pagan o'top of him.

'Twas to no purpose for a man, lame as my uncle Toby was, to think of redressing all these evils by himself,—he rung his bell for his man Trim ;—" Trim," quoth my uncle Toby, " prithee see what confusion I have here been making—I must have some better contrivance, Trim.—Canst not thou take my rule, and measure the length and breadth of this table, and then go and bespeak me one as big again ?"—" Yes, an' please your honour," replied Trim, making a bow ; " but I hope your honour will be soon well enough to get down to your country seat, where,—as your honour takes so much pleasure in fortification, we could manage this matter to a T."

I must here inform you, that this servant of my uncle Toby's, who went by the name of Trim, had been a corporal in my uncle's own company,—his real name was James Butler,—but having got the nickname of Trim in the regiment, my uncle Toby, unless when he happened to be very angry with him, would never call him by any other name.

The poor fellow had been disabled for the service by a wound on his left knee by a musket bullet, at the battle of Landen, which was two years before the affair of Namur ;—and as the fellow was well beloved in the regiment, and a handy fellow in the bargain, my uncle Toby took him for his servant ; and of excellent use was he, attending my uncle Toby in the camp and in his quarters as valet, groom, barber, cook, sempster, and nurse, and, indeed, from first to last, waited upon him and served him with great fidelity and affection.

My uncle Toby loved the man in return, and what attached him more to him still, was the similitude of their knowledge :—for Corporal Trim (for so, for the future, I shall call him), by four years' occasional attention to his master's discourse upon fortified towns, and the advantage of prying and peeping continually into his master's plans, &c., exclusive and besides what he gained hobby-horsically, as a body-servant, *Non Hobby-horsical per se ;*—had become no mean proficient in the science ; and was thought, by the cook and chambermaid, to know as much of the nature of strongholds as my uncle Toby himself.

I have but one more stroke to give to finish Corporal Trim's character,—and it is the only dark line in it. The fellow loved to advise,—or rather to hear himself talk ; his carriage, however, was so perfectly respectful, 'twas easy to keep him silent when you had him so ; but set his tongue agoing,—you had no hold of him ; he was voluble ;—the eternal interlardings of your Honour, with the respectfulness of Corporal Trim's manner, interceding so strong in behalf of his elocu-tion,—that though you might have been incommoded, —you could not well be angry. My uncle Toby was seldom either the one or the other with him,—or, at least, this fault in Trim broke no squares with 'em. My uncle Toby, as I said, loved the man ;—and be-sides, as he ever looked upon a faithful servant—but as an humble friend,—he could not bear to stop his mouth.—Such was Corporal Trim.

If I durst presume, continued Trim, to give your honour my advice, and speak my opinion in this matter.—Thou art welcome, Trim, quoth my uncle Toby,—speak,—speak what thou thinkest upon the subject, man, without fear. Why then, replied Trim, ˉ (not hanging his ears, and scratching his head like a country lout, but) stroking his hair back from his fore-head, and standing erect as before his division,—I think, quoth Trim, advancing his left, which was his

lame leg, a little forwards,—and pointing with his
right hand open towards a map of Dunkirk, which was
pinned against the hangings,—I think, quoth Corporal
Trim, with humble submission to your honour's better
judgment,—that these ravelins, bastions, curtains, and
horn-works, make but a poor, contemptible, fiddle-
faddle piece of work of it here upon paper, compared
to what your honour and I could make of it, were we
in the country by ourselves, and had but a rood or a
rood and a half of ground to do what we pleased
with : as summer is coming on, continued Trim, your
honour might sit out of doors, and give me the nogra-
phy—(call it ichnography, quoth my uncle)—of the
town or citadel, your honour was pleased to sit down
before,—and I will be shot by your honour upon the
glacis of it, if I did not fortify it to your honour's
mind.—I dare say thou would'st, Trim, quoth my
uncle.—For if your honour, continued the corporal,
could but mark me the polygon, with its exact lines
and angles.—That I could do very well, quoth my
uncle.—I would begin with the fossé, and if your
honour could tell me the proper breadth. — I
can to a hair's breadth, Trim, replied my uncle.—I
would throw out the earth upon this hand towards
the town for the scarp,—and on that hand towards the
campaign for the counterscarp.—Very right, Trim,
quoth my uncle Toby.—And when I had sloped them
to your mind,—an' please your honour, I would face
the glacis, as the finest fortifications are done in
Flanders, with sods,—and as your honour knows they
should be,—and I would make the walls and parapets
with sods too.—The best engineers call them gazons,
Trim, said my uncle Toby.—Whether they are gazons
or sods, is not much matter, replied Trim ; your
honour knows they are ten times beyond a facing
either of brick or stone. —I know they are, Trim, in
some respects,—quoth my uncle Toby, nodding his
head ;—for a cannon ball enters into the gazon right

onwards, without bringing any rubbish down with it, which might fill the fossé (as was the case at St. Nicholas's gate), and facilitate the passage over it.

Your honour understands these matters, replied Corporal Trim, better than any officer in his Majesty's service ;— but would your honour please to let the bespeaking of the table alone, and let us but go into the country, I would work under your honour's directions like a horse, and make fortifications for you something like a tansy, with all their batteries, saps, ditches, and palisadoes, that it should be worth all the world's riding twenty miles to go and see it.

My uncle Toby blushed as red as scarlet as Trim went on ;—but it was not a blush of guilt,—of modesty,—or of anger ;—it was a blush of joy ;—he was fired with Corporal Trim's project and description.—Trim ! said my uncle Toby, thou hast said enough.—We might begin the campaign, continued Trim, on the very day that his Majesty and the allies take the field, and demolish them town by town as fast as——Trim, quoth my uncle Toby, say no more. —Your honour, continued Trim, might sit in your arm-chair (pointing to it) this fine weather, giving me your orders, and I would——Say no more, Trim, quoth my uncle Toby.—Besides, your honour would get not only pleasure and good pastime,—but good air, and good exercise, and good health,—and your honour's wound would be well in a month. Thou hast said enough, Trim,—quoth my uncle Toby (putting his hand into his breeches-pocket)—I like thy project mightily.—And if your honour pleases, I'll this moment go and buy a pioneer's spade to take down with us, and I'll bespeak a shovel and a pickaxe, and a couple of——Say no more, Trim, quoth my uncle Toby, leaping up upon one leg, quite overcome with rapture,—and thrusting a guinea into Trim's hand,—Trim, said my uncle Toby, say no more ;—but go down, Trim, this moment, my lad, and bring up my supper this instant.

Trim ran down and brought up his master's supper,—to no purpose :—Trim's plan of operation ran so in my uncle Toby's head, he could not taste it.—Trim, quoth my uncle Toby, get me to bed.—'Twas all one.—Corporal Trim's description had fired his imagination,—my uncle Toby could not shut his eyes.—The more he considered it, the more bewitching the scene appeared to him ;—so that, two full hours before daylight, he had come to a final determination, and had concerted the whole plan of his and Corporal Trim's decampment.

My uncle Toby had a little neat country-house of his own, in the village where my father's estate lay at Shandy, which had been left him by an old uncle, with a small estate of about one hundred pounds a year. Behind this house, and contiguous to it, was a kitchen-garden of about half an acre ; and at the bottom of the garden, and cut off from it by a tall yew hedge, was a bowling-green, containing just about as much ground as Corporal Trim wished for ;—so that as Trim uttered the words, "A rood and a half of ground to do what they would with,"—this identical bowling-green instantly presented itself, and became curiously painted all at once upon the retina of my uncle Toby's fancy ;—which was the physical cause of making him change colour, or at least of heightening his blush to that immoderate degree I spoke of.

Never did lover post down to a beloved mistress with more heat and expectation than my uncle Toby did, to enjoy this self-same thing in private;—I say in private ;—for it was sheltered from the house, as I told you, by a tall yew hedge, and was covered on the other three sides, from mortal sight, by rough holly and thickset flowering shrubs ;—so that the idea of not being seen did not a little contribute to the idea of pleasure preconceived in my uncle Toby's mind.—

Vain thought ! however thick it was planted out,—or private soever it might seem,—to think, dear uncle Toby, of enjoying a thing which took up a whole rood and a half of ground,—and not have it known !

How my uncle Toby and Corporal Trim managed this matter,—with the history of their campaigns, which were no way barren of events,—may make no uninteresting under-plot in the epitasis and working-up of this drama.—At present the scene must drop,—and change for the parlour fire-side.

CHAPTER IV.

DOCTOR SLOP.

WHAT can they be doing, brother? said my
father.—I think, replied my uncle Toby,—
taking, as I told you, his pipe from his
mouth, and striking the ashes out of it as
he began his sentence; I think, replied he—it would
not be amiss, brother, if we rung the bell.

Pray what's all that racket over our heads, Obadiah!—quoth my father;—my brother and I can
scarce hear ourselves speak.

Sir, answered Obadiah, making a bow towards his
left shoulder,—my mistress is taken very badly.—And
where's Susannah running down the garden there?—
Sir, she is running the shortest cut into the town,
replied Obadiah, to fetch the old midwife.—Then
saddle a horse, quoth my father, and do you go
directly for Dr. Slop, the man-midwife, with all our
services,—and let him know your mistress is fallen
into labour,—and that I desire he will return with
you with all speed.

It is very strange, says my father, addressing
himself to my uncle Toby, as Obadiah shut the
door,—as there is so expert an operator as Dr. Slop so
near,—that my wife should persist to the very last in
the obstinate humour of hers, in trusting the life of
my child, who has had one misfortune already, to the

ignorance of an old woman ;—and not only the life of my child—brother, but her own life, and with it the lives of all the children that might, peradventure, have been born to me hereafter.

Mayhap, brother, replied my uncle Toby, my sister does it to save the expense :—A pudding's end,— replied my father,—the doctor must be paid the same for inaction as action,—if not better,—to keep him in temper.

—Then it can be out of nothing in the whole world,—quoth my uncle Toby, in the simplicity of his heart,—but modesty.—My uncle Toby had not fully arrived at the period's end,—then the world stands indebted to the sudden snapping of my father's tobacco pipe, for one of the neatest examples of that ornamental figure in oratory which rhetoricians style the Aposiopesis.

Though my father was a good natural philosopher, yet he was something of a moral philosopher too; for which reason, when his tobacco pipe snapped short in the middle,—he had nothing to do, as such, but to have taken hold of the two pieces, and thrown them gently upon the back of the fire.—He did no such thing ;—he threw them with all the violence in the world ;—and to give the action still more emphasis,—he started up upon both his legs to do it.

This looked something like heat ; and the manner of his reply to what my uncle Toby was saying proved it was so.

—" By heaven, brother Toby ! you would try the patience of Job ;—and I•think I have the plagues of one already, without it.—Why?—Where?—Wherein? —Wherefore ?—Upon what account ? replied my uncle Toby, in the utmost astonishment.—To think, said my father, of a man living to your age, brother, and knowing so little about women !— I know nothing at all about them,—replied my uncle Toby.—Then, brother Toby, replied my father, I will tell you. If a man was to sit down coolly and consider within himself the whole of that animal called Woman— compare her analogically.—I never understood rightly the meaning of that word—quoth my uncle Toby.— Analogy, replied my father, is the certain relation and agreement which different—Here a devil of a rap at the door snapped my father's definition (like his tobacco-pipe) in two.

Imagine to yourself a little, squat, uncourtly figure of a Doctor Slop, of about four feet and a half perpendicular height, with a breadth of back, and a susquipedality of belly, which might have done honour to a serjeant in the Horse Guards.

Imagine such a one,—for such, I say, were the outlines of Dr. Slop's figure, coming slowly along, foot by foot, waddling through the dirt upon the vertebræ of a little diminutive pony, of a pretty colour,—but of strength,—alack!—scarce able to have made an amble of it, under such a fardel, had the roads been in an ambling condition.—They were not.—Imagine to yourself, Obadiah mounted upon a strong monster of a coach-horse, pricked into a full gallop, and making all practicable speed the adverse way.

Pray, sir, let me interest you a moment in this description.

Had Dr. Slop beheld Obadiah a mile off, posting in a narrow lane directly towards him, at that monstrous rate,—splashing and plunging like a devil through thick and thin, as he approached, would not such a phenomenon, with such a vortex of mud and water moving along with it, round its axis,—have been a subject of juster apprehension to Dr. Slop in his situation, than the worst of Whiston's comets?— To say nothing of the Nucleus; that is, of Obadiah and the coach-horse.—In my idea, the vortex alone of them was enough to have involved and carried, if not the doctor, at least the doctor's pony, quite away with it. What then do you think must the terror and hydrophobia of Dr. Slop have been, when you read (which you are just going to do) that he was advancing thus warily along towards Shandy Hall, and had approached to within sixty yards of it, and within five yards of a sudden turn, made by an acute angle of the garden wall,—and in the dirtiest part of a dirty lane,—when Obadiah and his coach-horse turned the corner, rapid, furious,—pop,—full upon him!—Nothing, I think, in nature, can be supposed more terrible than such a rencounter,—so imprompt! so ill prepared to stand the shock of it as Dr. Slop was!

What could Dr. Slop do!—He crossed himself ✠—Pugh!—but the doctor, sir, was a Papist.—No matter; he had better have kept hold of the pummel.—He had so;—nay, as it happened, he had better have done nothing at all;—for in crossing himself he let go his whip,—and in attempting to save his whip betwixt his knee and his saddle's skirt, as it slipped, he lost his stirrup,—in losing which he lost his seat;—and in the multitude of all these losses the unfortunate doctor lost his presence of mind. So that, without waiting for Obadiah's onset, he left his pony to its destiny, tumbling off it diagonally, something in the style and manner of a pack of wool, and without any other consequence from the fall, save that of being left (as it would have been) with the broadest part of him sunk about twelve inches deep in the mire.

Obadiah pulled off his cap twice to Dr. Slop;—once as he was falling,—and then again when he saw him seated—Ill-timed complaisance;—had not the fellow better have stopped his horse, and got off and helped him?—Sir, he did all that his situation would allow; but the momentum of the coach-horse was so great, that Obadiah could not do it all at once;—he rode in a circle three times round Dr. Slop, before he could fully accomplish it anyhow;—and at the last, when he did stop his beast, 'twas done with such an explo-

sion of mud, that Obadiah had better have been a
league off.

When Dr. Slop entered the back-parlour, where my
father and my uncle Toby were discoursing upon the
nature of women,—it was hard to determine whether
Dr. Slop's figure, or Dr. Slop's presence, occasioned more
surprise to them ; for, as the accident happened so
near the house, as not to make it worth while for
Obadiah to remount him,—Obadiah had led him in as
he was, unwiped, unappointed, unaneled, with all
his stains and blotches on him. He stood like Hamlet's ghost, motionless and speechless, for a full minute
and a half, at the parlour door (Obadiah still holding
his hand) with all the majesty of mud. His hinder
parts, upon which he had received his fall, totally
besmeared,—and in every other part of him, blotched
over in such a manner with Obadiah's explosion, that
you would have sworn (without mental reservation)
that every grain of it had taken effect.

Dr. Slop's presence, at that time, was no less prob-
lematical than the mode of it ; though, it is certain,
one moment's reflection in my father might have solved
it ; for he had apprised Dr. Slop but the week before,
that my mother was at her full reckoning ; and as the
doctor had heard nothing since, 'twas natural and
very political too in him, to have taken a ride to
Shandy Hall, as he did, merely to see how matters
went on.

But my father's mind took unfortunately a wrong
turn in the investigation ; running like the hyper-
critic's altogether upon the ringing of the bell and the
rap upon the door,—measuring their distance,—and
keeping his mind so intent upon the operation, as to
have power to think of nothing else,—commonplace
infirmity of the greatest mathematicians ! working
with might and main at the demonstration, and so
wasting all their strength upon it, that they have
none left in them to draw the corollary, to do good with.

The ringing of the bell, and the rap upon the door, struck likewise strong upon the sensorium of my uncle Toby,—but it excited a very different train of thoughts ;—the two irreconcilable pulsations instantly brought Stevinus, the great engineer, along with them, into my uncle Toby's mind. What business Stevinus had in this affair,—is the greatest problem of all :— It shall be solved.

Let the reader imagine then, that Dr. Slop has told his tale ;—and in what words, and with what aggravations, his fancy chooses : let him suppose that Obadiah has told his tale also, and with such rueful looks of affected concern, as he thinks will best contrast the two figures as they stand by each other. Let him imagine that my father has stepped up stairs to see my mother. And, to conclude this work of imagination—let him imagine the doctor washed,—rubbed down,—and condoled with,—felicitated,—got into a pair of Obadiah's pumps.

Your sudden and unexpected arrival, quoth my uncle Toby, addressing himself to Dr. Slop (all three of them sitting down to the fire together, as my uncle Toby began to speak),—instantly brought the great Stevinus into my head, who, you must know, is a favourite author with me.—Then, added my father, making use of the argument *ad crumenam*,—I will lay twenty guineas to a single crown piece, that this same Stevinus was some engineer or other,—or has wrote something or other, either directly or indirectly, upon the science of fortification.

He has so,—replied my uncle Toby.—I knew it, said my father ;—though, for the soul of me, I cannot see what kind of connexion there can be betwixt Dr. Slop's sudden coming, and a discourse upon fortifications ;—yet I feared it.—Talk of what we will, ~ brother,—or let the occasion be never so foreign or unfit for the subject,—you are sure to bring it in : I would not, brother Toby, continued my father,—I

declare I would not have my head so full of curtains
and horn-works.—That, I daresay, you would not, quoth
Dr. Slop, interrupting him, and laughing most im-
moderately at his pun.

Sir, quoth my uncle Toby, the curtains my brother
Shandy mentions here, have nothing to do with bed-
steads;—though I know Ducange says, "That bed-
curtains, in all probability, have taken their name
from them;—as for the horn-works,—(high! ho! sighed
my father)—which, continued my uncle Toby, my
brother was speaking of, they are called by the French
engineers "*ouvrage à cornes:*" 'tis formed by two epaule-
ments or demi-bastions—they are very pretty, and if you
will take a walk, I'll engage to show you one well worth
your trouble.—I own, continued my uncle Toby, when
we crown them,—they are much stronger, but then
they are very expensive, and take up a great deal of
ground, so that, in my opinion, they are most of use
to cover or defend the head of a camp; otherwise the
double tenaille—By the mother who bore us!—
brother Toby, quoth my father, not able to hold out
any longer,—you would provoke a saint;—here have
you got us, I know not how, not only souse into the
middle of the old subject again:—but so full is your
head of these confounded works, that though my wife is
at this moment in the pains of labour,—and you hear
her cry out, yet nothing will serve you but to carry off
the man-midwife.—Accoucheur,—if you please, quoth
Dr. Slop.—With all my heart, replied my father, I
don't care what they call you,—but I wish the whole
science of fortification, with all its inventors, at the
devil;—it has been the death of thousands,—and
it will be mine in the end.—I would not, I would not,
brother Toby, have my brains so full of saps, mines,
blinds, gabions, palisados, ravelins, half-moons, and
such trumpery, to be proprietor of Namur, and of all
the towns in Flanders with it.

My uncle Toby was a man patient of injuries;—not

4

from want of courage,—I have told you in the fifth
chapter of this second book, "that he was a man of
courage:"—and will add here, that where just occasions presented, or called it forth, I know no man
under whose arm I would sooner have taken shelter ;
nor did this arise from any insensibility or obtuseness
of his intellectual parts ;—for he felt this insult of my
father's as feelingly as a man could do ;—but he was
of a peaceful, placid nature,—no jarring element in it,
—all was mixed up so kindly within him ; my uncle
Toby had scarce a heart to retaliate upon a fly.

—Go—says he, one day at dinner, to an overgrown
one, which had buzzed about his nose, and tormented
him cruelly all dinner time,—and which, after infinite
attempts, he had caught at last, as it flew by him ;—
I'll not hurt thee, says my uncle Toby, rising from his
chair and going across the room, with the fly in his
hand,—I'll not hurt a hair of thy head :—Go, says he,
lifting up the sash, and opening his hand as he spoke,
to let it escape ;—go, poor devil, get thee gone ; why
should I hurt thee ?—This world surely is wide enough
to hold both thee and me.

I was but ten years old when this happened ;—but
whether it was, that the action itself was more in
unison with my nerves at that age of pity, which
instantly set my whole frame into one vibration of
most pleasurable sensation ; or how far the manner
and expression of it might go towards it ;—or in what
degree, or by what secret magic, a tone of voice and
harmony of movement, attuned by mercy, might find
a passage to my heart, I know not ;—this I know,
that the lesson of universal goodwill then taught and
imprinted by my uncle Toby, has never since been
worn out of my mind : and though I would not
depreciate what the study of the *literæ humaniores,*
at the university, has done for me in that respect, or
discredit the other helps of an expensive education
bestowed upon me, both at home and abroad since ;—

yet I often think that I owe one half of my philan-
thropy to that one accidental impression.

My father, in this patient endurance of wrongs,
which I mention, was very different, as the reader
must long ago have noted; he had a much more
acute and quick sensibility of nature, attended with
a little soreness of temper; though this never trans-
ported him to anything which looked like malignity;
—yet, in the little rubs and vexations of life, 'twas
apt to show itself in drollish and witty kind of
peevishness:—he was, however, frank and generous
in his nature;—at all times open to conviction; and
in the little ebullitions of this sub-acid humour
towards others, but particularly towards my uncle
Toby, whom he truly loved;—he would feel more
pain, ten times told (except in the affair of my aunt
Dinah, or where an hypothesis was concerned) than
what he ever gave.

The characters of the two brothers, in this view of
them, reflected light upon each other, and appeared
with great advantage in this affair which arose about
Stevinus.

I need not tell the reader, if he keep a hobby-
horse,—that a man's hobby-horse is as tender a part
as he has about him; and that these unprovoked
strokes at my uncle Toby's could not be unfelt by
him.—No;—as I said above, my uncle Toby did feel
them, and very sensibly too; for as soon as my
father had done insulting his hobby-horse,—he turned
his head, without the least emotion, from Dr. Slop, to
whom he was addressing his discourse, and looked up
into my father's face, with a countenance spread over
with so much good-nature;—so placid;—so fraternal;—so inexpressibly tender towards him;—it pene-
trated my father to his heart; he rose up hastily from
his chair, and seizing hold of both my uncle Toby's
hands as he spoke:—brother Toby, said he,—I beg
thy pardon;—forgive, I pray thee, this rash humour

4—2

which my mother gave me.—My dear, dear brother, answered uncle Toby, rising up with my father's help, say no more about it ;—you are heartily welcome, had it been ten times as much, brother.   But 'tis ungenerous, replied my father, to hurt any man ;—a brother worse ;—but to hurt a brother of such gentle manners, —so unprovoking,—and so unresenting ;—'tis base,— By heaven, 'tis cowardly.—You are heartily welcome, brother, quoth my uncle Toby,—had it been fifty times as much.—Besides, what have I to do, my dear Toby, cried my father, either with your amusements or your pleasures, unless it was in my power (which it is not) to increase their measure?

As my father spoke the last words,—he sat down ;— my uncle Toby exactly followed his example, only that, before he took his chair, he rang the bell, to order Corporal Trim, who was in waiting, to step home for Stevinus ;—my uncle Toby's house being no further off than the opposite side of the way.

Some men would have dropped the subject of Stevinus ;—but my uncle Toby had no resentment in his heart, and he went on with the subject, to show my father that he had none.

Your sudden appearance, Dr. Slop, quoth my uncle, resuming the discourse, instantly brought Stevinus into my head.   [My father, you may be sure, did not offer to lay any more wagers upon Stevinus's head]— Because, continued my uncle Toby, the celebrated sailing chariot, which belonged to Prince Maurice, and was of such wonderful contrivance and velocity as to carry half-a-dozen people thirty German miles, in I don't know how few minutes,—was invented by Stevinus, that great mathematician and engineer.

You might have spared your servant the trouble, quoth Dr. Slop (as the fellow is lame), of going for Stevinus's account of it, because in my return from Leyden, through the Hague, I walked as far as Schevling, which is two long miles, on purpose to take a view of it.

That's nothing, replied my uncle Toby, to what the learned Peireskius did, who walked a matter of five hundred miles, reckoning from Paris to Schevling, and from Schevling to Paris back again, in order to see it—and nothing else.

Some men cannot bear to be out-gone. The more fool Peireskius, replied Dr. Slop. But mark, 'twas out of no contempt of Peireskius at all—but that Peireskius's indefatigable labour, in trudging so far on foot out of love for the sciences, reduced the exploit of Dr. Slop, in that affair, to nothing.—The more fool Peireskius, said he again...Why so?—replied my father, taking his brother's part, not only to make reparation as fast as he could for the insult he had given him, which still sat upon my father's mind;—but partly that my father began really to interest himself in the discourse:—Why so?—said he. Why is Peireskius, or any man else, to be abused for an appetite for that, or any other morsel of sound knowledge; for, notwithstanding I know nothing of the chariot in question, continued he, the inventor of it must have had a very mechanical head; and though I cannot guess upon what principles of philosophy he has achieved it—yet certainly his machine has been constructed upon solid ones, be they what they will, or it could not have answered at the rate my brother mentions.

It answered, replied my uncle Toby, as well, if not better; for, as Peireskius elegantly expresses it, speaking of the velocity of its motion, *Tam citus erat quam erat ventus;* which, unless I have forgot my Latin, is, that it was as swift as the wind itself.

But pray, Dr. Slop, quoth my father, interrupting my uncle (though not without begging pardon for it), upon what principles was this self-same chariot set a-going? Upon very pretty principles, to be sure, replied Dr. Slop;—and I have often wondered, continued he, evading the question, why none of our gentry, who live upon large plains like this of ours— attempt nothing of this kind ; for it would be excellent good husbandry to make use of the winds, which cost nothing, and which eat nothing, rather than horses, which (the devil take 'em) both cost and eat a great deal.

For that very reason, replied my father, "Because they cost nothing, and because they eat nothing,"— the scheme is bad ;—it is the consumption of our products, as well as the manufacture of them, which gives bread to the hungry,—circulates trade, brings in money, and supports the value of our lands :—and though I own if I was a Prince, I would generously recompense the scientific head which brought forth such contrivances ;—yet I would as peremptorily suppress the use of them.

My father here had got into his element,—and was going on as prosperously with his dissertation upon trade as my uncle Toby had before upon his of fortification ;—but, to the loss of much sound knowledge, the destinies in the morning had decreed that no dissertation of any kind should be spun by my father that day ;...for, as he opened his mouth to begin the next sentence,

———

In popped Corporal Trim with Stevinus—but it was too late :—all the discourse had been exhausted without him, and was running into a new channel.

—You may take the book home again, Trim, said my uncle Toby, nodding to him.

But pri'thee, Corporal, quoth my father, drolling,— look first into it, and see if thou can'st spy aught of a - sailing chariot in it.

Corporal Trim, by being in the service, had learned to obey—and not to remonstrate ;—so taking the book to a side-table, and running over the leaves :...

An' please your honour, said Trim, I can see no such thing ;—however, continued the Corporal, drolling a little in his turn, I'll make sure work of it, an' please your honour ;—so taking hold of the two covers of the book, one in each hand, and letting the leaves fall down, as he bent the covers back, he gave the book a good sound shake.

There is something fallen out, however, said Trim, an' please your honour ;—but it is not a chariot, or anything like one...Pri'thee, Corporal, said my father, smiling, what is it then ?—I think, answered Trim, stooping to take it up,—'tis more like a sermon,—for it begins with a text of scripture, and the chapter and verse ;—and then goes on, not as a chariot, but like a sermon directly.

The company smiled.

I cannot conceive how it is possible, quoth my uncle Toby, for such a thing as a sermon to have got into my Stevinus.

I think 'tis a sermon, replied Trim ; but if it please your honours, as it is a fair hand, I will read you a page ;—for Trim, you must know, loved to hear himself read almost as well as talk.

I have ever a strong propensity, said my father, to look into things which cross my way, by such strange fatalities as these ;—and as we have nothing better to do, I should be obliged to you, brother, if Dr. Slop has no objection to it, to order the corporal to give us a page or two of it,—if he is as able to do it as he is willing. An' please your honour, quoth Trim, I officiated two whole campaigns, in Flanders, as clerk to the chaplain of the regiment.—He can read it, quoth my uncle Toby, as well as I can.—Trim, I assure you, was the best scholar in my company, and should have had the next halberd, but for the poor fellow's misfortune. Corporal Trim laid his hand upon his heart, and made an humble bow to his master ;—then laying down his hat upon the floor, and taking up the sermon in his left hand, in order to have his right at liberty,—he advanced, nothing doubting, into the middle of the room, where he could best see, and be best seen by his audience.

—If you have any objection,—said my father, addressing himself to Dr. Slop. Not in the least, replied Dr. Slop ;—for it does not appear on which side of the question it is wrote ;—it may be a composition of a divine of our church, as well as yours, —so that we run equal risks. 'Tis wrote upon neither side, quoth Trim, for 'tis only upon conscience, an' please your honours.

Trim's reason put his audience into good humour,— all but Dr. Slop, who turning his head about towards Trim, looked a little angry.

Begin, Trim,—and read distinctly, quoth my father. I will, an' please your honour, replied the corporal, making a bow, and bespeaking attention with a slight movement of his right hand.

CHAPTER V.

TRIM'S SERMON.

"For we trust we have a good Conscience."—HEBREWS xiii. 18.

TRUST! — Trust we have a good conscience!"

[Certainly, Trim, quoth my father, interrupting him, you give that sentence a very improper accent; for you curl up your nose, man, and read it with such a sneering tone, as if the parson was going to abuse the Apostle.

He is, an' please your honour, replied Trim. Pugh! said my father, smiling.

Sir, quoth Dr. Slop, Trim is certainly in the right; for the writer (who I perceive is a Protestant) by the snappish manner in which he takes up the Apostle, is certainly going to abuse him,—if this treatment of him has not done it already. But from whence, replied my father, have you concluded so soon, Dr. Slop, that the writer is of our church?—for aught I can see yet,—he may be of any church. Because, answered Dr. Slop, if he was of ours,—he durst no more take such a license,—than a bear by his beard. If in our communion, sir, a man was to insult an Apostle,—or a saint,—he would have an old house over his head. Pray is the Inquisition an ancient building, answered my uncle Toby, or is it a modern one?—I know nothing of architecture, replied Dr. Slop.—An' please your honours, quoth Trim, the Inquisition is the vilest —Prithee spare thy description, Trim, I hate the very name of it, said my father.—No matter for that, said Dr. Slop,—it has its uses ; for though I'm no great advocate for it, yet, in such a case as this, he would soon be taught better manners ; and I can tell him, if he went on at that rate, would be flung into the Inquisition for his pains. God help him then, quoth my uncle Toby. Amen, added Trim ; for heaven above knows, I have a poor brother who has been fourteen years a captive in it.—

Come Trim, quoth my father, after he saw the poor fellow's grief had got a little vent,—read on,—and put this melancholy story out of thy head :—I grieve that I interrupted thee ;—but prithee begin the sermon again,—for if the first sentence in it is matter of abuse, as thou sayest, I have a great desire to know what kind of provocation the Apostle has given.

[Corporal Trim wiped his face, and returned his handkerchief into his pocket, and making a bow as he did it,—he began again.]

"Trust !—Trust we have a good conscience ! Surely if there is anything in this life which a man may depend upon, and to the knowledge of which he is capable of arriving upon the most indisputable evidence, it must be this very thing,—whether he has a good conscience or no. In other matters we may be deceived by false appearances ; but here the mind has all the evidence and facts within herself ;—is conscious of the exact share which every passion has had in working upon the several designs which virtue or vice has planned before her."

[The language is good, and I declare Trim reads very well, quoth my father.]

"I own, in one case, whenever a man's conscience does accuse him (as it seldom errs on that side) that he is guilty ; and unless in melancholy and hypochon-

driac cases, we may safely pronounce upon it, that
there is always sufficient grounds for the accusation.

"But the converse of the proposition will not hold
true ;—namely, that whenever there is guilt, the conscience must accuse ; and if it does not, that a man is
therefore innocent.—This is not fact :—So that the
common consolation which some good Christian or
other is hourly administering to himself,—that he
thanks God his mind does not misgive him ; and that,
consequently, he has a good conscience, because he
hath a quiet one,—is fallacious ; and as current as the
inference is, and as infallible as the rule appears at
first sight, yet when you look nearer to it, and try the
truth of this rule upon plain facts,—you see it liable
to so much error from a false application ;—the principle upon which it goes so often perverted ;—the whole
force of it lost, and sometimes so vilely cast away,
that it is painful to produce the common examples
from human life which confirm the account.

"A man shall be vicious and utterly debauched in
his principles ;—exceptionable in his conduct to the
world ; shall live shameless, in the open commission
of a sin which no reason or pretence can justify ;—a
sin by which, contrary to all the workings of humanity,
he shall rule for ever the deluded partner of his guilt ;
—rob her of her best dowry ; and not only cover her
own head with dishonour, — but involve a whole
virtuous family in shame and sorrow for her sake.—
Surely you will think conscience must lead such a
man a-troublesome life ;—he can have no rest night
or day from its reproaches.

"Alas ! conscience had something else to do, all
this time, than break in upon him ; as Elijah re-
proached the God Baal,—this domestic god was either
talking, or pursuing, or was in a journey, or peradventure he slept and could not be awoke.

"Perhaps he was gone out in company with honour
to fight a duel ; to pay off some debt at play ;—or

dirty annuity : perhaps conscience all this time was
engaged at home, talking loud against petty larceny,
and executing vengeance upon some such puny crimes
as his fortune and rank in life secured him against all
temptation of committing ; so that he lives as
merrily "—[If he was of our church though, quoth
Dr. Slop, he could not]—"sleeps as soundly in his
bed ;—and at last meets death as unconcernedly ;
perhaps much more so than a much better man.

" Another is sordid, unmerciful, [here Trim waved
his right hand], a strait-hearted, selfish wretch, incapable either of private friendship or of public spirit.
Take notice how he passes by the widow and orphan
in their distress, and sees all the miseries incident to
human life without a sigh or a prayer. [An' please
your honours, cried Trim, I think this a viler man
than the others.]

" Shall not conscience rise up and sting him on such
occasions ?—No ; thank God, there is no occasion :
*I pay every man his own ;—I have no fornication to
answer to my conscience ; no faithless vows or promises
to make up ; I thank God, I am not as other men,
adulterers, unjust, or even as this libertine, who stands
before me.*

" A third is crafty and designing in his nature. View
his whole life ; 'tis nothing but a cunning contexture
of dark arts and unequitable subterfuges, basely to
defeat the true intent of all laws,—plain dealing, and
the safe enjoyment of our several properties.—You
will see such an one working out a frame of little
designs upon the ignorance and perplexities of the
poor and needy man ;—shall raise a fortune upon the
inexperience of a youth, or the unsuspecting temper
of his friend, who would have trusted him with his life.

" When old age comes on, and repentance calls him
to look back upon his black account, and state it over
again with his conscience,—Conscience looks into the
statutes at large ;—finds no express law broken by

what he has done ;—perceives no penalty or forfeiture
of goods and chattels incurred ; — sees no scourge
waving over his head, or prison opening his gates
upon him :—What is there to affright his conscience?
Conscience has got safely entrenched behind the letter
of the law ; sits there invulnerable, fortified with
𝕮𝖆𝖘𝖊𝖘 and 𝕽𝖊𝖕𝖔𝖗𝖙𝖘 so strongly on all sides ;—that it
is not preaching can dispossess it of its hold."

[Here Corporal Trim and my uncle Toby exchanged
looks with each other.—Ay,—ay, Trim ! quoth my
uncle Toby, shaking his head,—these are but sorry
fortifications, Trim.—Oh ! very poor work, answered
Trim, to what your honour and I make of it.—The
character of this last man, said Dr. Slop, interrupting
Trim, is more detestable than all the rest.—Go on,
Trim, quoth my father.—'Tis a very short sermon,
replied Trim.—I wish it was longer, quoth my uncle
Toby, for I like it hugely.—Trim went on.]

     *   *   *   *   *   *

" Blessed is the man, indeed, as the author of the
book of Ecclesiasticus expresses it, who is not pricked
with the multitude of his sins ; blessed is the man
whose heart hath not condemned him ; whether he
be rich, or whether he be poor, if he have a good heart
(a heart thus guided and informed) he shall at all
times rejoice in a cheerful countenance ; his mind
shall tell him more than seven watchmen that sit
above upon a tower on high."—[A tower has no strength,
quoth my uncle Toby, unless 'tis flanked.]—" In the
darkest doubts it shall conduct him safer than a
thousand casuists, and give the state he lives in a
better security for his behaviour than all the clauses
and restrictions put together, which law-makers are
forced to multiply."

I like the reasoning, said my father, and am sorry
that Dr. Slop has fallen asleep before the time of his
conviction ;—for it is now clear that the parson, as I
thought at first, never insulted St. Paul in the least ;—

nor has there been, brother, the least difference between them.—A great matter, if they had differed,
replied my uncle Toby,—the best friends in the world
may differ sometimes.—True,—brother Toby, quoth
my father, shaking hands with him,—we'll fill our pipes,
brother, and then Trim shall go on.

Well,—what dost thou think of it? said my father,
speaking to Corporal Trim, as he reached his tobacco-
box.

I think, answered the Corporal, that the seven
watchmen upon the tower, who, I suppose, are all
sentinels there,—are more, an' please your honour,
than were necessary;—and, to go on at that rate,
would harass a regiment all to pieces, which a commanding officer, who loves his men, will never do,
if he can help it, because two sentinels, added the
Corporal, are as good as twenty.—I have been a
commanding officer myself in the Corps de Garde a
hundred times, continued Trim, rising an inch higher
in his figure, as he spoke,—and all the time I had the
honour to serve his Majesty King William, in relieving
the most considerable posts, I never left more than
two in my life.—Very right, Trim, quoth my uncle
Toby,—but you do not consider, Trim, that the
towers, in Solomon's days, were not such things as
our bastions, flanked and defended by other works;—
this, Trim, was an invention since Solomon's death;
nor had they horn-works, or ravelins before the
curtain, in his time;—or such a fossé as we make
with a cuvette in the middle of it, and with covered
ways and counterscarps pallisadoed along it, to guard
against a coup de main:—So that the seven men
upon the tower were a party, I dare say, from the
Corps de Garde, set there, not only to look out, but to
defend it.—They could be no more, an' please your
honour, than a corporal's guard.—My father smiled
inwardly,—but not outwardly;—the subject being
rather too serious, considering what had happened, to

make a jest of: So putting his pipe into his mouth, which he had just lighted,—he contented himself with ordering Trim to read on.

"I know the banker I deal with, or the physician I usually call in,"—[There is no need, cried Dr. Slop (waking), to call in any physician in this case]—"to be neither of them men of much religion: I hear them make a jest of it every day, and treat all its sanctions with so much scorn as to put the, matter past doubt. Well;—notwithstanding this, I put my fortune into the hands of the one;—and what is dearer still to me, I trust my life to the honest skill of the other.

"Now, let me examine what is my reason for this great confidence. Why, in the first place, I believe there is no probability that either of them will employ the power I put into their hands to my disadvantage;—I consider that honesty serves the purposes of this life;—I know their success in the world depends upon the fairness of their characters,—in a word,—I'm persuaded that they cannot hurt me without hurting themselves more.

"But put it otherwise, namely, that interest lay, for once, on the other side; that a case should happen wherein the one, without stain to his reputation, could secrete my fortune, and leave me naked in the world;—or that the other could send me out of it, and enjoy an estate, by my death, without dishonour to himself or his art:—In this case, what hold have I of either of them?—Religion, the strongest of all motives, is out of the question;—interest, the next most powerful motive in the world, is strongly against me:—What have I left to cast into the opposite scale, to balance this temptation?—Alas! I have nothing,—nothing but what is lighter than a bubble:—I must lie at the mercy of Honour, or some such capricious principle—Straight security for two of the most valuable blessings—my property and my life!

"In how many kingdoms of the world"—[Here Trim

kept waving his right hand, from the sermon to the extent of his arm, returning it backwards and forwards to the conclusion of the paragraph.]

"In how many kingdoms of the world has the crusading sword of this misguided saint-errant spared neither age, nor merit, nor sex, nor condition?—and, as he fought under the banners of a religion which set him loose from justice and humanity, he showed none; mercilessly trampled upon both,—heard neither the cries of the unfortunate, nor pitied their distresses!"

[I have been in many a battle, an' please your honour, quoth Trim, sighing, but never in so melan-choly an one as this:—I would not have drawn a trigger in it, against these poor souls,—to have been made a general officer.—Why, what do you understand of the affair? said Dr. Slop, looking towards Trim, with something more of contempt than the Corporal's honest heart deserved.—What do you know, friend, about this battle you talk of?—I know, replied Trim, that I never refused quarter in my life to any man who cried out for it:—but, to a woman, or a child, continued Trim, before I would level my musket at them, I would lose my life a thousand times.—Here's a crown for thee, Trim, to drink with Obadiah to-night, quoth my uncle Toby, and I'll give Obadiah another, too.—God bless your Honour, replied Trim; I had rather these poor women and children had it.—Thou art an honest fellow, quoth my uncle Toby.—My father nodded his head,—as much as to say—And so he is.

But pri'thee, Trim, said my father, make an end,—for I see thou hast but a leaf or two left.

Corporal Trim read on.]

"I will add no farther to the length of this sermon, than by two or three short and independent rules deducible from it.

"First, whenever a man talks loudly against religion, always suspect that it is not his reason, but his passions which have got the better of his creed. A bad life and a good belief are disagreeable and troublesome neighbours, and where they separate, depend upon it, 'tis for no other cause than for quietness' sake.

"Secondly, When a man, thus represented, tells you in any particular instance,—that such a thing goes against his conscience,—always believe he means exactly the same thing as when he tells you such a thing goes against his stomach ;—a present want of appetite being generally the true cause of both.

"In a word,—trust that man in nothing who has not a conscience in everything.

"And, in your own case, remember this plain distinction, a mistake in which has ruined thousands,— that your conscience is not a law :—No, God and reason made the law, and have placed conscience within you to determine ;—not, like an Asiatic cadi, according to the ebbs and flows of his own passions, but like a British judge in this land of liberty and good sense, who makes no new law, but faithfully declares that law which he knows already written."

FINIS.

Thou hast read the sermon extremely well, Trim, quoth my father.—If he had spared his comments, replied Dr. Slop, he would have read it much better.— I should have read it ten times better, sir, answered Trim, but that my heart was so full.—That was the very reason, Trim, replied my father, which has made thee read the sermon as well as thou hast done ; and if the clergy of our church, continued my father, addressing himself to Dr. Slop, would take part in what they deliver, as deeply as this poor fellow has done,—as their compositions are fine ;—[I deny it, quoth Dr. Slop]—I maintain it ;—that the eloquence of our pulpits, with such subjects to inflame it, would be a model for the whole world :—But, alas! continued my father, and I own it, sir, with sorrow, that, like

5

French politicians in this respect, what they gain in the cabinet they lose in the field. I know the author, for 'tis wrote, certainly, by the parson of the parish. The similitude of the style and manner of it with those my father had constantly heard preached in his parish-church was the ground of his conjecture,— proving it, as strongly as an argument *à priori* could prove such a thing to a philosophic mind, that it was Yorick's, and no one's else. —It was proved to be so *à posteriori*, the day after, when Yorick sent a servant to my uncle Toby's house to inquire after it.

It seems that Yorick, who was inquisitive about all kinds of knowledge, had borrowed Stevinus of my uncle Toby, and had carelessly popped his sermon, as soon as he had made it, into the middle of Stevinus ; and by an act of forgetfulness, to which he was ever subject, he had sent Stevinus home, and his sermon to keep him company.

CHAPTER VI.

I COME INTO THE WOBLD.

IT is now proper I think, quoth Dr. Slop (clearing up his looks), as we are in a condition to be of some service to Mrs. Shandy, to send upstairs to know how she goes on.

I have ordered, answered my father, the old midwife to come down to us upon the least difficulty;—for you must know, Dr. Slop, continued my father, with a perplexed kind of a smile upon his countenance, that by express treaty, solemnly ratified between me and my wife, you are no more than an auxiliary in this affair,—and not so much as that,—unless the lean old mother of a midwife above stairs cannot do without you. Women have their particular fancies, and in points of this nature, continued my father, where they bear the whole burden, and suffer so much acute pain for the advantage of our families, and the good of the species,—they claim the right of deciding, *en souveraines*, in whose hands, and in what fashion, they choose to undergo it.

They are in the right of it,—quoth my uncle Toby. But, sir, replied Dr. Slop, not taking notice of my uncle Toby's opinion, but turning to my father,—they had better govern in other points;—and a father of a family, who wished its perpetuity, in my opi-

5—2

nion, had better exchange this prerogative with them, and give up some other rights in lieu of it. I know not, quoth my father, answering a little too testily, to be quite dispassionate in what he said,—I know not, quoth he, what we have left to give up.   One would almost give up anything, replied Dr. Slop.   I beg your pardon, answered my uncle Toby.—Sir, replied Dr. Slop, it would astonish you to know what improvements we have made of late years in all branches of obstetrical knowledge,—which has received such lights that, for my part (holding up his hands), I declare I wonder how the world has....

I wish, Dr. Slop, quoth my uncle Toby, *you had seen what prodigious armies we had in Flanders.*
My uncle Toby's wish did Dr. Slop a disservice, which his heart never intended any man.— Sir, it confounded him—and thereby putting his ideas first into confusion, and then to flight, he could not rally them again for the soul of him.
In all disputes,—male or female,—whether for honour, for profit, or for love,—it makes no difference in the case ;—nothing is more dangerous, Madam, than a wish coming sideways in this unexpected manner upon a man : the safest way, in general, to take off the force of the wish is for the party wished at instantly to get upon his legs, — and wish the wisher something in return, of pretty near the same value ;—so, balancing the account upon the spot, you stand as you were,—nay, sometimes gain the advantage of the attack by it.

Bless my soul !—my poor mistress is ready to faint —and her pains are gone—and the drops are done— and the bottle of julap is broke—and the nurse has cut her arm—and, continued Susannah,—the midwife has fallen backwards upon the edge of the fender, and bruised her hip as black as your hat ;—but the midwife would gladly first give you an account how things are; so desires you would go upstairs and speak to her this moment.

Human nature is the same in all professions.

The midwife had just before been put over Dr. Slop's head;—he had not digested it.—No, replied Dr. Slop, 'twould be full as proper if the midwife came down to me.—I like subordination, quoth my uncle Toby,—and but for it, after the reduction of Lisle, I know not what might have become of the garrison of Ghent, in the mutiny for bread, in the year Ten.

It is two hours and ten minutes—and no more—cried my father, looking at his watch—since Dr. Slop and Obadiah arrived, and I know not how it happens, brother Toby—but to my imagination it seems almost an age.

Though my father said, "he knew not how it happened,"—yet he knew very well how it happened; —and at the instant he spoke it was predetermined in his mind to give my uncle Toby a clear account of the matter by a metaphysical dissertation upon the subject of duration and its simple modes; in order to show my uncle Toby by what mechanism and mensurations in the brain it came to pass, that the rapid succession of their ideas, and the eternal scampering of the discourse from one thing to another, since Dr. Slop had come into the room, had lengthened out so short a period to so inconceivable an extent.—I know not how it happens—cried my father—but it seems an age.

'Tis owing entirely, quoth my uncle Toby, to the succession of our ideas.

My father, who had an itch in common with all philosophers of reasoning upon everything which happened, and accounting for it too—proposed infinite pleasure to himself in this, of the succession of ideas, and had not the least apprehension of having it snatched out of his hands by my uncle Toby, who (honest man !) generally took everything as it happened ;—and who, of all things in the world, troubled his brain the least with abstruse thinking ; —the ideas of time and space—or how we came by those ideas—or of what stuff they were made—or whether they were born with us—or we picked them up afterwards as we went along—or whether we did it in frocks—or not till we had got into breeches—with a thousand other inquiries and disputes about infinity, prescience, liberty, necessity, and so forth, upon whose desperate and unconquerable theories so many fine heads have been turned and cracked—never did my uncle Toby's the least injury at all ; my father knew it —and was no less surprised, than he was disappointed, with my uncle's fortuitous solution.

Do you understand the theory of that affair ? replied my father.

Not I, quoth my uncle.

But you have some ideas, said my father, of what you talk about ?

No more than my horse, replied my uncle Toby.

Gracious heaven ! cried my father, looking upwards, and clasping his two hands together—there is a worth in thy honest ignorance, brother Toby—'twere almost a pity to exchange it for a knowledge.—But I'll tell thee.—

To understand what time is aright, without which we never can comprehend infinity, insomuch as one is a portion of the other—we ought seriously to sit down and consider what idea it is we have of duration, so as to give a satisfactory account how we came by it.— What is that to anybody ? quoth my uncle Toby.

Now, whether we observe it or no, continued my father, in every sound man's head, there is a regular succession of ideas of one sort or other, which follow each other in train just like—A train of artillery ? said my uncle Toby—A train of a fiddlestick !—quoth my father—which follow and succeed one another in our minds at certain distances, just like the images in the inside of a lanthorn turned round by the heat of a candle.—I declare, quoth my uncle Toby, mine are more like a smoke-jack.—Then, brother Toby, I have nothing more to say to you upon that subject, said my father.

What a conjuncture was here lost!—My father in one of his best explanatory moves—in eager pursuit of a metaphysic point into the very regions where clouds and thick darkness would soon have encompassed it about ;—my uncle Toby in one of the finest dispositions for it in the world ;—his head like a smoke-jack ;—the funnel unswept, and the ideas whirling round and round about in it, all obfuscated and darkened over with fuliginous matter !

Though my father persisted in not going on with the discourse—yet he could not get my uncle Toby's smoke-jack out of his head—piqued as he was at first with it :—there was something in the comparison at the bottom, which hit his fancy ; for which purpose, resting his elbow upon the table, and reclining the right side of his head upon the palm of his hand—but looking first steadfastly in the fire—he began to commune with himself and philosophize about it : but his spirits being wore out with the fatigues of investigating new tracts, and the constant exertion of his faculties upon that variety of subjects which had taken their turn in the discourse—the idea of the smoke-jack soon turned all his ideas upside down—so that he fell asleep almost before he knew what he was about.

As for my uncle Toby, his smoke-jack had not made a dozen revolutions, before he fell asleep also.— Peace be with them both !—Dr. Slop is engaged with the midwife and my mother above-stairs.—Trim is busy in turning an old pair of jack-boots into a couple of mortars to be employed in the siege of Messina next summer—and is this instant boring the touch-holes with the point of a hot poker.

—Every day for at least ten years together did my father resolve to have it mended—'tis not mended yet ;—no family but ours would have borne with it an hour—and what is most astonishing, there was not a subject in the world upon which my father was so eloquent, as upon that of door-hinges.—And yet at the same time, he was certainly one of the greatest bubbles to them, I think, that history can produce : his rhetoric and conduct were at perpetual handicuffs. —Never did the parlour door open—but his philosophy or his principles fell a victim to it ;—three drops of oil with a feather, and a smart stroke of a hammer, had saved his honour for ever.

When corporal Trim had brought his two mortars to bear, he was delighted with his handiwork above measure ; and knowing what a pleasure it would be to his master to see them, he was not able to resist the desire he had of carrying them directly into his parlour.

Had the parlour door opened and turned upon its hinges, as a door should do, in this case, I say, there had been no danger either to master or man, in corporal Trim's peeping in : the moment he had beheld my father and my uncle Toby fast asleep—the respectfulness of his carriage was such, he would have retired as silent as death, and left them both in their armchairs, dreaming as happy as he had found them : but the thing was, morally speaking, so very impracticable, that for the many years in which this hinge was suffered to be out of order, and amongst the hourly grievances my father submitted to upon its account—this was one ; that he never folded his arms to take his nap after dinner, but the thought of being unavoidably awakened by the first person who should open the door, was always uppermost in his imagination, and so incessantly stepped in betwixt

him and the first balmy presage of his repose, as to
rob him, as he often declared, of the whole sweets
of it.

Pray what's the matter? Who is there? cried my
father, waking, the moment the door began to creak.—
I wish the smith would give a peep at that confounded
hinge.—'Tis nothing, an' please your honour, said
Trim, but two mortars I am bringing in.—They shan't
make a clatter with them here, cried my father
hastily.—If Dr. Slop has any drugs to pound, let him
do it in the kitchen.—May it please your honour,
cried Trim, they are two mortar-pieces for a siege
next summer, which I have been making out of a pair
of jack-boots, which Obadiah told me your honour
had left off wearing.—By heaven! cried my father,
springing out of his chair, as he swore—I have not
one appointment belonging to me, which I set so
much store by, as I do by these jack-boots—they were
our great grandfather's, brother Toby—they were
hereditary. Then I fear, quoth my uncle Toby, Trim
has cut off the entail.—I have only cut off the tops,
an' please your honour, cried Trim.—I hate perpe-
tuities as much as any man alive, cried my father—
but these jack-boots, continued he (smiling, though
very angry at the same time) have been in the family,
brother, ever since the Civil Wars;—Sir Roger Shandy
wore them at the battle of Marston Moor.—I declare
I would not have taken ten pounds for them.—I'll
pay you the money, brother Shandy, quoth my uncle
Toby, looking at the two mortars with infinite pleasure, and putting his hand into his breeches pocket as
he viewed them—I'll pay you the ten pounds this
moment with all my heart and soul.

Brother Toby, replied my father, altering his tone,
you care not what money you dissipate and throw
away, provided, continued he, 'tis but upon a SIEGE.—
Have I not one hundred and twenty pounds a year,
besides my half-pay? cried my uncle Toby.—What is

that—replied my father, hastily—to ten pounds for a
pair of jack-boots ?—twelve guineas for your pontoons
—half as much for your Dutch drawbridge ?—to say
nothing of the train of little brass artillery you be-
spoke last week, with twenty other preparations for
the siege of Messina : believe me, dear brother Toby,
continued my father, taking him kindly by the hand
—these military operations of yours are above your
strength ;—you mean well, brother—but they carry you
into greater expenses than you were first aware of ;—
and take my word, dear Toby, they will in the end
quite ruin your fortune, and make a beggar of you.
—What signifies if they do, brother, replied my uncle
Toby, so long as we know 'tis for the good of the
nation ?—

My father could not help smiling for his soul—his
anger at the worst was never more than a spark ;—
and the zeal and simplicity of Trim—and the generous (though hobby-horsical) gallantry of my uncle
Toby, brought him into perfect good humour with
them in an instant.

Generous souls !—God prosper you both, and your
mortar-pieces, quoth my father to himself !

All is quiet and hush, cried my father, at least
above-stairs—I hear not one foot stirring.—Prithee,
Trim, who's in the kitchen ? There is no one soul in
the kitchen, answered Trim, making a low bow as he
spoke, except Dr. Slop—Confusion ! cried my father
(getting up upon his legs a second time)—not one
single thing has gone right this day ! had I faith in
astrology, brother (which by the by my father had), I
would have sworn some retrograde planet was hanging over this unfortunate house of mine, and turning
every individual thing in it out of its place.—Why, I
thought Dr. Slop had been above-stairs, and so said
you.—What can the fellow be puzzling about in the
kitchen ?—He is busy, an' please your honour, replied
Trim, in making a bridge.—'Tis very obliging in him,

quoth my uncle Toby ;—pray give my humble service
to Dr. Slop, Trim, and tell him I thank him heartily.

You must know my uncle Toby mistook the bridge
as widely as my father mistook the mortars.

When Trim came in and told my father that Dr.
Slop was in the kitchen, and busy in making a bridge
—my uncle Toby—the affair of the jack-boots having
just then raised a train of military ideas in his brain—
took it instantly for granted that Dr. Slop was making
a model of the marquis d'Hôpital's bridge.—'Tis very
obliging in him, quoth my uncle Toby ;—pray, give
my humble service to Dr. Slop, Trim, and tell him I
thank him heartily.

This unfortunate drawbridge of yours, quoth my
father—God bless your honour, cried Trim, 'tis a
bridge for young master's nose.—He has crushed his
nose, Susannah says, as flat as a pancake to his face,
and he is making a false bridge with a piece of cotton
and a thin piece of whalebone out of Susannah's stays,
to raise it up.—Lead me to my room, brother Toby,
cried my father, this instant !

Did ever man, brother Toby, cried my father, raising himself round to his elbow, and turning himself
round to the opposite side of the bed where my uncle
Toby was sitting in his old fringed chair, with his
chin resting upon his crutch—did ever a poor unfortunate man, brother Toby, cried my father, receive so
many lashes ?—The most I ever saw given, quoth my
uncle Toby, (ringing the bell at the bed's head for
Trim) was to a grenadier, I think in Makay's regiment.

Was it Makay's regiment, quoth my uncle Toby,
where the poor grenadier was so unmercifully whipped
at Bruges about the ducats ?—O Christ ! he was innocent ! cried Trim, with a deep sigh.—And he was
whipped, may it please your honour, almost to death's
door.—They had better have shot him outright, as he
begged, and he had gone directly to heaven, for he

was as innocent as your honour.—I thank thee, Trim, quoth my uncle Toby.—I never think of his, continued Trim, and my poor brother Tom's misfortunes, for we were all three schoolfellows, but I cry like a coward.—Tears are no proof of cowardice, Trim. I drop them ofttimes myself, cried my uncle Toby.—I know your honour does, replied Trim, and so am not ashamed of it myself.—But to think, may it please your honour, continued Trim, a tear stealing into a corner of his eye as he spoke—to think of two virtuous lads with hearts as warm in their bodies, and as honest as God could make them—the children of honest people, going forth with gallant spirits to seek their fortunes in the world—and fall into such evils I—poor Tom! to be tortured upon a rack for nothing—but marrying a Jew's widow who sold sausages—honest Dick Johnson's soul to be scourged out of his body, for the ducats another man put into his knapsack!— O!—these are misfortunes, cried Trim, pulling out his handkerchief—these are misfortunes, may it please your honour, worth lying down and crying over.

—My father could not help blushing.

—'Twould be a pity, Trim, quoth my uncle Toby, thou shouldst ever feel sorrow of thy own—thou feelest it so tenderly for others.—Alack-o-day, replied the corporal, brightening up his face—your honour knows I have neither wife nor child—I can have no sorrows in this world.—My father could not help smiling.—As few as any man, Trim, replied my uncle Toby; nor can I see how a fellow of thy light heart can suffer, but from the distress of poverty in thy old age—when thou art past all services, Trim—and hast outlived thy friends.—An' please your honour, never fear, replied Trim, cheerily.—But I would have thee never fear, Trim, replied my uncle; and therefore, continued my uncle Toby, throwing down his crutch, and getting up upon his legs as he uttered the word therefore—in recompense, Trim, of thy long fidelity to

me, and that goodness of thy heart I have had such
proofs of—whilst thy master is worth a shilling—thou
shalt never ask elsewhere, Trim, for a penny. Trim
attempted to thank my uncle Toby—but had not power
—tears trickled down his cheeks faster than he could
wipe them off—He laid his hands upon his breast—
made a bow to the ground, and shut the door.

—I have left Trim my bowling green, cried my
uncle Toby—My father smiled—I have left him moreover a pension, continued my uncle Toby—My father
looked grave.

Is this a fit time, said my father to himself, to talk
of pensions and grenadiers?

When I reflect, brother Toby, upon man; and take
a view of that dark side of him which represents his
life as open to so many causes of trouble—when I
consider, brother Toby, how oft we eat the bread of
affliction, and that we are born to it, as to the portion
of our inheritance—I was born to nothing, quoth my
uncle Toby, interrupting my father—but my commission.—Zooks! said my father, did not my uncle leave
you a hundred and twenty pounds a year?—What
could I have done without it? replied my uncle Toby.
—That's another concern, said my father, testily—
But I say, Toby, when one runs over the catalogue of
all the cross reckonings and sorrowful items with
which the heart of man is overcharged, 'tis wonderful
by what hidden resources the mind is enabled to stand
out and bear itself up, as it does against the imposi-
tions laid upon our nature.—Tis by the assistance of
Almighty God, cried my uncle Toby, looking up, and
pressing the palms of his hands close together—'tis
not from our own strength, brother Shandy—a senti-
nel in a wooden sentry-box might as well pretend to
stand it out against a detachment of fifty men,—we
are upheld by the grace and the assistance of the best
of beings.

—That is cutting the knot, said my father, instead

of untying it.—But give me leave to lead you, brother
Toby, a little deeper into the mystery.

With all my heart, replied my uncle Toby.—Though
man is of all others the most curious vehicle, said my
father, yet at the same time 'tis of so slight a frame,
and so totteringly put together, that the sudden jerks
and hard jostlings it unavoidably meets with in this
rugged journey, would overset and tear it to pieces a
dozen times a day—was it not, brother Toby, that
there is a secret spring within us—Which spring, said
my uncle Toby, I take to be religion.—Will that set
my child's nose on? cried my father, letting go his
finger, and striking one hand against the other.—It
makes everything straight for us, answered my uncle
Toby.—Figuratively speaking, dear Toby, it may, for
aught I know, said my father; but the spring I am
speaking of, is that great and elastic power within us
of counterbalancing evil, which like a secret spring in
a well-ordered machine, though it can't prevent the
shock—at least it imposes upon our sense of it.

Now, my dear brother, said my father, replacing his
forefinger, as he was coming closer to the point—had
my child arrived safe into the world, unmartyred in
that precious part of him—fanciful and extravagant
as I may appear to the world in my opinion of
Christian names, and of that magic bias which good
or bad names irresistibly impress upon our characters
and conducts—heaven is witness; that in the warmest
transports of my wishes for the prosperity of my child,
I never once wished to crown his head with more
glory and honour than what George or Edward would
have spread around it.

But alas! continued my father, as the greatest evil
has befallen him—I must counteract and undo it with -
the greatest good.

He shall be christened Trismegistus, brother.

I wish it may answer, replied my uncle Toby,
rising up.

CHAPTER VII.

THE CHRISTENING.

E shall bring all things to rights, said my
father, setting his foot upon the first step
from the landing—this Trismegistus, continued my father, drawing his leg back, and
turning to my uncle Toby—was the greatest (Toby) of
all earthly beings—he was the greatest king—the
greatest lawgiver, the greatest philosopher—and the
greatest priest—and engineer—said my uncle Toby.

—In course, said my father.

—And how does your mistress? cried my father,
taking the same step over again from the landing, and
calling to Susannah, whom he saw passing by the foot
of the stairs with a huge pincushion in her hand—
how does your mistress? As well, said Susannah,
tripping by, but without looking up, as can be expected.—What a fool am I, said my father, drawing
his leg back again--let things be as they will, brother
Toby, 'tis ever the precise answer.—And how is the
child, pray?—No answer. And where is doctor Slop?
added my father, raising his voice aloud, and looking
over the balusters—Susannah was out of hearing.

Of all the riddles of a married life, said my father,
crossing the landing, in order to set his back against
the wall, whilst he propounded it to my uncle Toby-
of all the puzzling riddles, said he, in a marriage

state,—of which you may trust me, brother Toby, there are more asses' loads than all Job's stock of asses could have carried—there is not one that has more intricacies in it than this—that from the very moment the mistress of the house is brought to bed, every female in it, from my lady's gentlewoman down to the cinder-wench, becomes an inch taller for it; and give themselves more airs upon that single inch, than all their other inches put together.

I think rather, replied my uncle Toby, that 'tis we who sink an inch lower.—If I meet but a woman with child—I do it—'Tis a heavy tax upon that half of our fellow creatures, brother Shandy, said my uncle Toby —'Tis a piteous burden upon them, continued he, shaking his head.—Yes, yes, 'tis a painful thing—said my father, shaking his head too—but certainly since shaking of heads came into fashion, never did two heads shake together in concert, from two such different springs.

God bless ⎱ 'em all—said my uncle Toby and my
Duce take ⎰ father, each to himself.

—So then, friend, you have got my father and my uncle Toby off the stairs, and seen them to bed?— And how did you manage it?—You dropped a curtain at the stair-foot.—I thought you had no other way for it.

'Tis even high time, for except a short nap, which they soon got whilst Trim was boring the jack boots— and which, by the bye, did my father no sort of good upon the score of the bad hinge—they have not else shut their eyes, since nine hours before.

Then reach me my breeches off the chair, said my father to Susannah. There is not a moment's time to dress you, sir, cried Susannah—the child is black in the face.—Bless me, sir, said Susannah, the child's in a fit.—And where's Mr. Yorick?—Never where he should be, said Susannah, but his curate's in the dressing-room, with the child upon his arm, waiting for the name—and my mistress bid me run as fast as

I could to know, as captain Shandy is the godfather,
whether it should not be called after him.

Were one sure, said my father to himself, scratching
his eyebrow, that the child was expiring, one might
as well compliment my brother Toby as not—and
'twould be a pity, in such a case, to throw away so
great a name as Trismegistus upon him.—But he may
recover.

No, no,—said my father to Susannah : I'll get up.—
There is no time, cried Susannah, the child's as black
as my shoe.—Trismegistus, said my father—but stay
—thou art a leaky vessel, Susannah, added my father ;
canst thou carry Trismegistus in thy head, the length
of the gallery without scattering?—Can I? cried
Susannah, shutting the door in a huff.—If she can,
I'll be shot, said my father, bouncing out of bed in
the dark, and groping for his breeches.

Susannah ran with all speed along the gallery.

My father made all possible speed to find his
breeches.

Susannah got the start, and kept it.—'Tis Tris—
something, cried Susannah.—There is no christian
name in the world, said the curate, beginning with
Tris—but Tristram. Then 'tis Tristram-gistus, quoth
Susannah.

There is no gistus to it, noodle !—'tis my own name,
replied the curate, dipping his hand as he spoke into
the bason — Tristram ! said he, &c. &c. &c. &c., so
Tristram was I called, and Tristram shall I be to the
day of my death.

My father followed Susannah with his nightgown
across his arm, with nothing more than his breeches
on, fastened through haste with but a single button,
and that button through haste thrust only half into
the button-hole.

She has not forgot the name, cried my father, half
opening the door.—No, no, said the curate, with a
tone of intelligence.—And the child is better, cried

6

Susannah.—And how does your mistress ?—As well, said Susannah, as can be expected.—Pish! said my father, the button of his breeches slipping out of the button-hole—So that whether the interjection was levelled at Susannah, or at the button-hole—whether pish was an interjection of contempt, or an interjection of modesty, was a doubt. All the light I am able to give the reader at present is this, that the moment my father cried pish! he whisked himself about—and with his breeches held up by one hand, and his night-gown thrown across the arm of the other, he returned along the gallery to bed, something slower than he came.

    *   *   *   *

If my wife will but venture him—brother Toby, Trismegistus shall be dressed and brought down to us, whilst you and I are getting our breakfast together.

Go, tell Susannah, Obadiah, to step here.

She has run upstairs, answered Obadiah, this very instant, sobbing and crying, and wringing her hands as if her heart would break.

We shall have a rare month of it, said my father, turning his head from Obadiah, and looking wistfully in my uncle Toby's face for some time — we shall have a devilish month of it, brother Toby, said my father, setting his arms a-kimbo, and shaking his head; fire, water, women—brother Toby!—'tis some misfortune, quoth my uncle Toby.—That it is, cried my father—to have so many jarring elements breaking loose, and riding triumph in every corner of a gentleman's house—little boots it to the peace of a family, brother Toby, that you and I possess ourselves, and sit here silent and unmoved—whilst such a storm is whistling over our heads.

And what's the matter, Susannah? they have called the child Tristram—and my mistress is just got out of an hysteric fit about it—no!—'tis not my fault, said Susannah—I told him it was Tristram-gistus.

Make tea for yourself, brother Toby, said my father, taking down his hat—but how different from the sallies and agitations of voice and members which a common reader would imagine!

For he spake in the sweetest modulation—and took down his hat with the gentlest movement of limbs, that ever affliction harmonized and attuned together.

Go to the bowling green for corporal Trim, said my uncle Toby, speaking to Obadiah, as soon as my father left the room.

Now, my father could not lie down with this affliction for his life—nor could he carry it upstairs like the other—He walked composedly out with it to the fish-pond.

Had my father leaned his head upon his hand, and reasoned an hour which way to have gone—reason, with all her force, could not have directed him to anything like it: there is something, sir, in fish-ponds—but what it is, I leave to system-builders and fish-pond diggers betwixt 'em to find out—but there is something, under the first disorderly transport of the humours, so unaccountably becalming in an orderly and a sober walk towards one of them, that I have often wondered that neither Pythagoras, nor Plato, nor Solon, nor Lycurgus, nor Mahomet, nor any one of your noted lawgivers, ever gave order about them.

Your honour, said Trim, shutting the parlour door before he began to speak, has heard, I imagine, of this unlucky accident.—O yes, Trim! said my uncle Toby, and it gives me great concern.—I am heartily concerned too, but I hope your honour, replied Trim, will do me the justice to believe, that it was not in the least owing to me.—To thee—Trim?—cried my uncle Toby, looking kindly in his face—'twas Susannah's and the curate's folly betwixt them.—What business could they have, an' please your honour, in the garden?—In the gallery, thou meanest, replied my uncle Toby.

6—2

Trim found he was upon a wrong scent, and stopped short with a low bow—Two misfortunes, quoth the corporal to himself, are twice as many at least as are needful to be talked over at one time ;—the mischief the cow has done in breaking into the fortifications, may be told his honour hereafter—Trim's casuistry and address, under the cover of his low bow, prevented all suspicion in my uncle Toby, so he went on with what he had to say to Trim as follows :

For my own part, Trim, though I can see little or no difference betwixt my nephew's being called Tristram or Trismegistus—yet as the thing sits so near my brother's heart, Trim—I would freely have given a hundred pounds rather than it should have happened.—A hundred pounds, an' please your honour, replied Trim,—I would not give a cherrystone to boot.—Nor would I, Trim, upon my own account, quoth my uncle Toby—but my brother, whom there is no arguing with in this case—maintains that a great deal more depends, Trim, upon christian names, than what ignorant people imagine ;—for he says there never was a great or heroic action performed since the world began by one called Tristram—nay he will have it, Trim, that a man can neither be learned, nor wise, nor brave.—'Tis all fancy, an' please your honour—I fought just as well, replied the corporal, when the regiment called me Trim, as when they called me James Butler.—And for my own part, said my uncle Toby, though I should blush to boast of myself, Trim, —yet had my name been Alexander, I could have done no more at Namur than my duty.—Bless your honour ! cried Trim, advancing three steps as he spoke, does a man think of his christian name when he goes upon the attack ?—Or when he stands in the trench, Trim ? cried my uncle Toby, looking firm.—Or when he enters a breach ? said Trim, pushing in between two chairs.—Or forces the lines ? cried my uncle, rising up, and pushing his crutch like a pike.—Or facing a platoon? cried Trim, presenting his stick like a firelock.—Or when he marches up the glacis? cried my uncle Toby, looking warm and setting his foot upon his stool.

My father was returned from his walk to the fish-pond—and opened the parlour door in the very height of the attack, just as my uncle Toby was marching up the glacis—Trim recovered his arms—never was my uncle Toby caught riding at such a desperate rate in his life! Alas! my uncle Toby! had not a weightier matter called forth all the ready eloquence of my father—how hadst thou then and thy poor hobby-horse too have been insulted!

My father hung up his hat with the same air he took it down; and after giving a slight look at the disorder of the room, he took hold of one of the chairs which had formed the corporal's breach, and placing it over against my uncle Toby, he sat down in it, and as soon as the tea things were taken away, and the door shut, he broke out in a lamentation as follows :

MY FATHER'S LAMENTATION.

It is in vain longer, said my father,—it is in vain longer, said my father, in the most querulous mono-tone imaginable, to struggle as I have done against this most uncomfortable of human persuasions—I see it plainly, that either for my own sins, brother Toby, or the sins and follies of the Shandy family, heaven has thought fit to draw forth the heaviest of its artillery against me ; and that the prosperity of my child is the point upon which the whole force of it is directed to play. Such a thing would batter the whole universe about our ears, brother Shandy, said my uncle Toby—if it was so—Unhappy Tristram! child of wrath! child of discrepitude! interruption! mis-take! and discontent!

Still, brother Toby, there was one cast of the dye left for our child after all—O Tristram! Tristram! Tristram!

We will send for Mr. Yorick, said my uncle Toby.

You may send for whom you will, replied my father.

Can the thing be undone, Yorick? said my father —for in my opinion, continued he, it cannot. I am a vile canonist, replied Yorick—but of all evils, holding suspense to be the most tormenting, we shall at least know the worst of this matter. I hate these great dinners—said my father. The size of the dinner is not the point, answered Yorick — we want, Mr. Shandy, to dive into the bottom of this doubt, whether the name can be changed or not—and as the beards of so many commissaries, officials, advocates, proctors, registers, and of the most eminent of our school divines, and others, are all to meet in the middle of one table, and Didius has so pressingly invited you— who in your distress would miss such an occasion? All that is requisite, continued Yorick, is to apprize Didius, and let him manage a conversation after dinner so as to introduce the subject. Then my brother Toby, cried my father, clapping his two hands together, shall go with us.

Let my old tye-wig, quoth my uncle Toby, and my laced regimentals, be hung to the fire all night, Trim.

We'll go in the coach, said my father—prithee, have the arms been altered, Obadiah?—It would have made my story much better to have begun with telling you, that at the time my mother's arms were added to the Shandys', when the coach was repainted upon my father's marriage, it had so fallen out, that the coach-painter, whether by performing all his works with the left hand, like Turpilius the Roman, or Hans Holbein of Basil—or whether 'twas more from the blunder of his head than hand — or whether, lastly, it was from the sinister turn, which everything relating to

our family was apt to take—it so fell out, however, to
our reproach, that instead of the bend dexter, which
since Harry the Eighth's reign was honestly our due—
a bend sinister, by some of these fatalities, had been
drawn quite across the field of the Shandy arms. 'Tis
scarce credible that the mind of so wise a man as my
father was, could be so much incommoded with so
small a matter. The word coach—let it be whose it
would—or coachman, or coach-horse, or coach-hire,
could never be named in the family, but he constantly
complained of carrying this vile mark of illegitimacy
upon the door of his own ; he never once was able
to step into the coach, or out of it, without turning
round to take a view of the arms, and making a vow
at the same time, that it was the last time he would
ever set his foot in it again, till the bend-sinister was
taken out—but like the affair of the hinge, it was one
of the many things which the destinies had set down
in their books—ever to be grumbled at (and in wiser
families than ours)—but never to be mended.

Has the bend-sinister been brushed out, I say?
said my father.—There has been nothing brushed out,
sir, answered Obadiah, but the lining. We'll go o'
horseback, said my father, turning to Yorick.

—Now, quoth Didius, rising up, and laying his right
hand with his fingers spread upon his breast—had
such a blunder about a christian name happened
before the reformation—[It happened the day before
yesterday, quoth my uncle Toby to himself] and when
baptism was administered in Latin—['Twas all in
English, said my uncle]—many things might have
coincided with it, and upon the authority of sundry
decreed cases, to have pronounced the baptism null,
with the power of giving the child a new name—had
a priest, for instance, which was no uncommon thing,
through ignorance of the Latin tongue, baptised a
child of Tom-o'-Stiles, *in nomine patriæ & filia &
spiritum sanctos*—the baptism was held null.—I beg

your pardon, replied Kysarcius—in that case, as the mistake was only the terminations, the baptism was valid—and to have rendered it null the blunder of the priest should have fallen upon the first syllable of each noun—and not, as in your case, upon the last.

My father delighted in subtleties of this kind, and listened with infinite attention.

Gastripheres, for example, continued Kysarcius, baptizes a child of John Stradling's *in Gomine gatris*, &c. &c., instead of *in Nomine patris*, &c.—Is this a baptism? No—say the ablest canonists; inasmuch as the radix of each word is hereby torn up, and the sense and meaning of them removed and changed quite to another object; for Gomine does not signify a name, nor gatris a father.—What do they signify? said my uncle Toby.—Nothing at all, quoth Yorick. —Ergo, such a baptism is null, said Kysarcius.—In course, answered Yorick, in a tone two parts jest and one part earnest.

But in the case cited, continued Kysarcius, where *patrim* is put for *patris*, *filia* for *filii*, and so on—as it is a fault only in the declension, and the roots of the words continue untouched, the inflexions of their branches, either this way or that, does not in any sort hinder the baptism, inasmuch as the same sense continues in the words as before.—But then, said Didius, the intention of the priest's pronouncing them grammatically, must have been proved to have gone along with it.—Right, answered Kysarcius; and of this, brother Didius, we have an instance in a decree of the decretals of Pope Leo III.—But my brother's child, cried my uncle Toby, has nothing to do with the pope—'tis the plain child of a protestant gentleman, christened Tristram against the wills and wishes both of his father and mother, and all who are a kin to it.

If the wills and wishes, said Kysarcius, interrupting my uncle Toby, of those only who stand related to Mr. Shandy's child, were to have weight in this matter, Mrs. Shandy, of all people, has the least to do in it. My uncle Toby laid down his pipe, and my father drew his chair still closer to the table, to hear the conclusion of so strange an introduction.

It has not only been a question, captain Shandy, amongst the best lawyers and civilians in this land, continued Kysarcius, "Whether the mother be of kin to her child,"—but, after much dispassionate enquiry and jactitation of the arguments on all sides —it has been adjudged for the negative—namely, "That the mother is not of kin to her child." My father instantly clapped his hand upon my uncle Toby's mouth, under colour of whispering in his ear ; —the truth was, he was alarmed for Lillibullero—and having a great desire to hear more of so curious an argument—he begged my uncle Toby, for heaven's sake, not to disappoint him in it.—My uncle Toby gave a nod—resumed his pipe, and contenting himself with whistling Lillibullero inwardly—Kysarcius, Didius, and Triptolemus went on with the discourse as follows.

This determination, considered Kysarcius, how contrary soever it may seem to run to the stream of vulgar ideas, yet had reason strongly on its side ; and has been put out of all manner of dispute from the famous case, known commonly by the name of the Duke of Suffolk's case, where the judges, with the master of the faculties, were all unanimously of opinion, that the mother was not of kin to her child.

And what said the Duchess of Suffolk to it? said my uncle Toby.

The unexpectedness of my uncle Toby's question confounded Kysarcius more than the ablest advocate —he stopped a full minute, looking in my uncle Toby's face without replying. The company broke up.

And pray, said my uncle Toby, leaning upon Yorick,

as he and my father were helping him leisurely down stairs—don't be terrified, madam, this staircase conversation is not so long as the last—And pray, Yorick, said my uncle Toby, which way is this said affair of Tristram at length settled by these learned men? Very satisfactorily, replied Yorick ; no mortal, sir, has any concern with it—for Mrs. Shandy the mother is nothing at all akin to him—and as the mother's is the surest side—Mr. Shandy, in course, is still less than nothing—in short, he is not as much akin to him, sir, as I am.

That may well be, said my father, shaking his head.

Let the learned say what they will, there must certainly, quoth my uncle Toby, have been some sort of consanguinity betwixt the Duchess of Suffolk and her son.—

The vulgar are of the same opinion, quoth Yorick, to this hour.—

Though my father was hugely tickled with the subtleties of these learned discourses—'twas still but like the anointing of a broken bone—The moment he got home, the weight of his afflictions returned upon him but so much the heavier, as is ever the case when the staff we lean on slips from under us—He became pensive—walked frequently forth to the fish-pond—let down one loop of his hat—sighed often—forbore to snap—and as the hasty sparks of temper, which occasion snapping, so much assist perspiration and digestion, as Hippocrates tells us—he had certainly fallen ill with the extinction of them, had not his thoughts been critically drawn off, and his health rescued by a fresh train of disquietudes left him, with a legacy of a thousand pounds by my aunt Dinah.—

My father had scarce read the letter, when taking the thing by the right end, he instantly began to plague and puzzle his head how to lay it out mostly to the honour of his family.—A hundred and fifty odd

projects took possession of his brains by turns—he
would do this, and that, and t'other—he would go to
Rome—he would go to law—he would buy stock—he
would buy John Hobson's farm—he would new fore-
front his house, and add a new wing to make it even
—there was a fine water-mill on this side, and he
would build a wind-mill on the other side of the river
in full view to answer it—But above all things in the
world, he would enclose the great *Ox-moor*, and send
out my brother Bobby immediately upon his travels.

But as the sum was finite, and consequently could
not do everything—and in truth very few of these to
any purpose—of all the projects which offered themselves upon this occasion, the two last seemed to make
the deepest impression ; and he would infallibly
have determined upon both at once, but for the small
inconvenience hinted at above, which absolutely put
him under a necessity of deciding in favour either of
the one or the other.—

People may laugh as they will—but the case was this.

It had ever been the custom of the family, and by
length of time was almost become a matter of common
right, that the eldest son of it should have free ingress,
egress, and regress, into foreign parts before marriage
not only for the sake of bettering himself by the benefit
of exercise and change of so much air—but simply for
the mere delectation of his fancy, by the feather put
into his cap, of having been abroad—*tantum valet*,
my father would say, *quantum sonat*.

Now as this was a reasonable, and in course a most
christian indulgence—to deprive him of it, without
why or wherefore—and thereby make an example of
him, as the first Shandy unwhirled about Europe in a
post-chaise, and only because he was a heavy lad
—would be using him ten times worse than a Turk.

On the other hand, the case of the Ox-moor was
full as hard.

Exclusive of the original purchase money, which

was eight hundred pounds—it had cost the family
eight hundred pounds more in a law-suit about fifteen
years before—besides the Lord knows what trouble
and vexation.

I think there must certainly have been a mixture of
ill-luck in it, that the reasons on both sides should
happen to be so equally balanced by each other ; for
though my father weighed them in all humours and
conditions—spent many an anxious hour in the most
profound and abstracted meditation upon what was
best to be done—reading books of farming one day—
books of travels another—laying aside all passion
whatever—viewing the arguments on both sides in all
their lights and circumstances—communing every
day with my uncle Toby—arguing with Yorick, and
talking over the whole affair of the Ox-moor with
Obadiah—yet nothing in all that time appeared so
strongly in behalf of the one, which was not either
strictly applicable to the other, or at least so far
counterbalanced by some consideration of equal
weight, as to keep the scales even.

In point of interest—the contest, I own, at first
sight, did not appear so undecisive betwixt them ;
for whenever my father took pen and ink in hand,
and set about calculating the simple expense of paring
and burning, and fencing in the Ox-moor, &c. &c.—
with the certain profit it would bring him in return—
the latter turned out so prodigiously in his way of
working the account, that you would have sworn the
Ox-moor would have carried all before it.   For it
was plain he should reap a hundred lasts of
rape, at twenty pounds a last, the very first year—
besides an excellent crop of wheat the year following
—and the year after that, to speak within bounds,
a hundred—but, in all likelihood, a hundred and fifty
—if not two hundred quarters of peas and beans—
besides potatoes without end—But then, to think
he was all this while breeding up my brother like a

hog to eat them—knocked all on the head again, and generally left the old gentleman in such a state of suspense—that, as he often declared to my uncle Toby—he knew no more than his heels what to do.

Nobody, but he who has felt it, can conceive what a plaguing thing it is to have a man's mind torn asunder by two projects of equal strength, both obstinately pulling in a contrary direction at the same time. My father had certainly sunk under this evil, as certainly as he had done under that of my Christian name—had he not been rescued out of it, as he was out of that, by a fresh evil—the misfortune of my brother Bobby's death.

What is the life of man! Is it not to shift from side to side?—from sorrow to sorrow?—to button up one cause of vexation?—and unbutton another?

When my father received the letter which brought him the melancholy account of my brother Bobby's death, he was busy calculating the expense of his riding post from Calais to Paris, and so on to Lyons.

'Twas a most inauspicious journey; my father having had every foot of it to travel over again, and his calculation to begin afresh, when he had almost got to the end of it, by Obadiah's opening the door to acquaint him the family was out of yeast—and to ask whether he might not take the great coach-horse early in the morning, and ride in search of some.—With all my heart, Obadiah, said my father, (pursuing his journey)—take the coach-horse, and welcome.—But he wants a shoe, poor creature! said Obadiah.—Poor creature! said my uncle Toby, vibrating the note back again, like a string in unison.—He cannot bear a saddle upon his back, quoth Obadiah, for the whole world.—Then go on foot for your pains, cried my father.—I had much rather walk than ride, said Obadiah, shutting the door.

What plagues! cried my father, going on with his

calculation.—But the waters are out, said Obadiah,—opening the door again.

Till that moment, my father, who had a map of Sanson's and a book of the post roads before him, had kept his hand upon the head of the compasses, with one foot of them fixed upon Nevers, the last stage he had paid for—purposing to go on from that point with his journey and calculation, as soon as Obadiah quitted the room ; but this second attack of Obadiah's in opening the door and laying the whole country under water, was too much.—He let go his compasses—or rather with a mixed motion betwixt accident and anger, he threw them upon the table ; and then there was nothing for him to do, but to return back to Calais (like many others) as wise as he had set out.

When the letter was brought into the parlour, which contained the news of my brother's death, my father had got forwards again upon his journey to within a stride of the compasses of the very same stage of Nevers.—By your leave, Monsieur Sanson, cried my father, striking the point of his compasses through Nevers into the table,—and nodding to my uncle Toby, to see what was in the letter,—twice of one night is too much for an English gentleman and his son, Monsieur Sanson, to be turned back from so lousy a town as Nevers,—what thinkest thou, Toby ? added my father, in a sprightly tone.—Unless it be a garrison town, said my uncle Toby,—for then—I shall be a fool, said my father, smiling to himself, as long as I live.—So giving a second nod—and keeping his compasses still upon Nevers with one hand, and holding his book of the post roads in the other—half calculating and half listening, he leaned forwards upon the table with both elbows, as my uncle Toby hummed over the letter.

—— —— —— —— ——
—— —— —— —— he's gone !
said my uncle Toby.—Where—who ? cried my father.

My nephew, said my uncle Toby.—What—without leave—without money—without governor? cried my father in amazement. No:—he is dead, my dear brother, quoth my uncle Toby.—Without being ill? cried my father again.—I daresay not, said my uncle Toby, in a low voice, and fetching a deep sigh from the bottom of his heart, he has been ill enough, poor lad! I'll answer for him—for he is dead.

My father was proud of his eloquence as Marcus Tullius Cicero could be for his life, and for aught I am convinced of the contrary at present, with as much reason: it was indeed his strength—and his weakness too.—A blessing which tied up my father's tongue, and a misfortune which set it loose with a grace, were pretty equal: sometimes, indeed, the misfortune was the better of the two; for instance, where the pleasure of the harangue was as ten, and the pain of the misfortune but as five—my father gained half-in-half, and consequently was as well again off, as it never had befallen him.

This clue will unravel what otherwise would seem very inconsistent in my father's domestic character; and it is this, that in the provocations arising from the neglects and blunders of servants, or other mishaps unavoidable in a family, his anger, or rather the duration of it, eternally ran counter to all conjecture.

Now let us go back to my brother's death.

Philosophy has a fine saying for everything.—For death it has an entire set; the misery was, they all at once rushed into my father's head, that 'twas difficult to string them together, so as to make anything of a consistent show out of them.—He took them as they came.

"'Tis an inevitable chance—the first statute in Magna Charta—it is an everlasting act of parliament, my dear brother,—All must die.

" If my son could not have died, it had been a matter of wonder,—not that he is dead.

" Monarchs and princes dance in the same ring with us.

" To die is the great debt and tribute due unto .nature : tombs and monuments, which should perpetuate our memories, pay it themselves ; and the proudest pyramid of them all, which wealth and science have erected, has lost its apex, and stands obtruncated in the traveller's horizon." (My father found he got great ease, and went on)—" Kingdoms and provinces, and towns, and cities, have they not their periods ? and when those principles and powers, which at first cemented and put them together, have performed their several evolutions, they fall back." —Brother Shandy, said my uncle Toby, laying down his pipe at the word evolutions—Revolutions, I mean, quoth my father,—by heaven ! I meant revolutions, brother Toby—evolutions is nonsense.—'Tis not nonsense—said my uncle Toby—But is it not nonsense to break the thread of such a discourse, upon such an occasion ? cried my father— Do not—dear Toby, continued he, taking him by the hand, do not—do not, I beseech thee, interrupt me at this crisis.—My uncle Toby put his pipe into his mouth.

" Where is Troy and Mycenæ, and Thebes, and Delos, and Persepolis, and Agrigentum ?"—continued my father, taking up his book of post roads, which he had laid down.—" What is become, brother Toby, of Nineveh and Babylon, of Cizicum and Mitylenæ ? Returning out of Asia, when I sailed from Ægina towards Megara," (when can this have been ? thought my uncle Toby) " I began to view the country round about. Ægina was behind me, Megara was before, Pyræus on the right hand, Corinth on the left.—What flourishing towns now prostrate upon the earth ! Alas ! said I to myself, that man should disturb his soul for the loss of a child, when so much as this lies awfully buried in his presence—Remember, said I to myself again—remember thou art a man.

Now my uncle Toby knew not that this last paragraph was an extract of Servius Sulpicius's consolatory letter to Tully.—He had as little skill, honest man, in the fragments, as he had in the whole pieces of antiquity.—And as my father, whilst he was concerned in the Turkey trade, had been three or four different times in the Levant, in one of which he had stayed a whole year and a half at Zant, my uncle Toby naturally concluded, that in some one of these periods he had taken a trip across the Archipelago into Asia ; and that all this sailing affair with Ægina behind, and Megara before, and Pyræus on the right hand, &c. &c. was nothing more than the true course of my father's voyage and reflections.—'Twas certainly in his manner and many an undertaking critic would have built two stories higher upon worse foundations. —And pray, brother, quoth my uncle Toby, laying the end of his pipe upon my father's hand in a kindly way of interruption—but waiting till he had finished the account—what year of our Lord was this ?—'Twas no year of our Lord, replied my father.—That's impossible, cried my uncle Toby.—Simpleton ! said my father,—'twas forty years before Christ was born.

My uncle Toby had but two things for it ; either to suppose his brother to be the wandering Jew, or that his misfortunes had disordered his brain.—" May the Lord God of heaven and earth protect him and restore him," said my uncle Toby, praying silently for my father, and with tears in his eyes.

My father placed the tears to a proper account, and went on with his harangue with great spirit.

" There is not such great odds, brother Toby, betwixt good and evil, as the world imagines "—(this way of setting off, by-the-bye, was not likely to cure my uncleToby's suspicions).—" Labour, sorrow, grief, sick-

7

ness, want, and woe, are the sauces of life."—Much
good may it do them.—said my uncle Toby to himself.

" My son is dead !—so much the better ;—'tis a
shame in such a tempest to have but one anchor.

" But he is gone for ever from us !—be it so. He is
got from under the hands of his barber before he was
bald—he is but risen from a feast before he was sur-
feited—from a banquet before he had got drunken.

" The Thracians wept when a child was born"—
(and we were very near it, quoth my uncle Toby)—
" and feasted and made merry when a man went out
of the world ; and with reason.—Death opens the gate
of 'fame, and shuts the gate of envy after it,—it un-
looses the chain of the captive, and puts the bonds-
man's task into another man's hands.

"Show me the man, who knows what life is,
who dreads it, and I'll show thee a prisoner who
dreads his liberty."

Is it not better, my dear brother Toby, (for mark—
our appetites are but diseases)—is it not better not to
hunger at all, than to eat ?—not to thirst, than to take
physic to cure it ?

Is it not better to be freed from cares and agues,
from love and melancholy, and the other hot and cold
fits of life, than like a galled traveller, who comes
weary to his inn, to be bound to begin his journey
afresh ?

There is no terror, brother Toby, in its looks, but
what it borrows from groans and convulsions—and
the blowing of noses, and the wiping away of tears
with the bottoms of curtains in a dying man's room.
—Strip it of these, what is it ?—'Tis better in battle
than in bed, said my uncle Toby.—Take away its
hearses, its mutes and its mourning,—its plumes,
scutcheons, and other mechanic aids—What is it !—
Better in battle ! continued my father, smiling, for he
had absolutely forgot my brother Bobby—'tis terrible no
way—for consider, brother Toby,—when we *are*—

death is *not ;*—and when death *is*—we are *not*. My
uncle Toby laid down his pipe to consider the proposition ; my father's eloquence was too rapid to stay for
any man—away it went,—and hurried my uncle Toby's
ideas along with it.

For this reason, continued my father, 'tis worthy
to recollect, how little alteration in great men the
approaches of death have made—Vespasian died in a
jest—Galba with a sentence—Septimus Severus in a
despatch—and Cæsar Augustus in a compliment. I
hope 'twas a sincere one, quoth my uncle Toby.—
'Twas to his wife, said my father.

My mother was going very gingerly in the dark
along the passage which led to the parlour, as my
uncle Toby pronounced the word *wife.*—'Tis a shrill
penetrating sound of itself, so that my mother heard
enough of it to imagine herself the subject of the conversation : so laying the edge of her finger across her
two lips, holding in her breath, and bending her head
a little downwards, with a twist of her neck—she listened with all her powers.—She listened with com-
posed intelligence, and would have done so to the end
of the chapter, had not my father plunged (which he
had no occasion to have done) into that part of the
pleading where the great philosopher reckons up his
connexions, his alliances, and children ; but renounces
a security to be so won by working upon the passions
of his judges.—"I have friends—I have relations,—I
have three desolate children,"—says Socrates.

Then, cried my mother, opening the door,—you have
one more, Mr. Shandy, than I know of.

By heaven ! I have one less,—said my father, getting up, and walking out of the room.

They are Socrates' children, said my uncle Toby.
He has been dead a hundred years ago, replied my
mother.

My uncle Toby was no chronologer—so not caring
to advance a step but upon safe ground, he laid down

7—2

his pipe deliberately upon the table, and rising up, and taking my mother most kindly by the hand, without saying another word, either good or bad to her, he led her out after my father, that he might finish the eclaircissement himself.

Now whenever an extraordinary message, or letter, was delivered in the parlour,—or a discourse suspended till a servant went out—or the lines of discontent were observed to hang upon the brows of my father or mother—or, in short, when anything was supposed to be upon the tapis worth knowing or listening to, 'twas the rule to leave the door, not absolutely shut, but somewhat ajar, which under covert of the bad hinge (and that possibly might be one of the many reasons why it was never mended), it was not difficult to manage ; by which means, in all these cases, a passage was generally left, not indeed as wide as the Dardanelles, but wide enough, for all that, to carry on as much of this windward trade as was sufficient to save my father the trouble of governing his house. My mother at this moment stands profiting by it— Obadiah did the same thing, as soon as he had left the letter upon the table which brought the news of my brother's death ; so that before my father had well got over his surprise, and entered upon his harangue, —had Trim got upon his legs, to speak his sentiments upon the subject.

My young master in London is dead ! said Obadiah—

A green satin nightgown of my mother's which had been twice scoured, was the first idea which Obadiah's exclamation brought into Susannah's head.—Well might Locke write a chapter upon the imperfections of words.—Then, quoth Susannah, we must all go into mourning.—But note a second time : the word mourning, notwithstanding Susannah made use of it herself —failed also of doing its office ; it excited not one single idea, tinged either with grey or black,—all was green.—The green satin nightgown hung there still.

O ! 'twill be the death of my poor mistress, cried Susannah.—My mother's whole wardrobe followed.— What a procession ! her red damask, — her orange-tawny,—her white and yellow lustrings,—her brown taffata, — her bone-laced caps, her bedgowns, and comfortable under petticoats.—Not a rag was left behind.—" No, — she will never look up again," said Susannah.

We had a fat foolish scullion—my father, I think, kept her for her simplicity ;—she had been all autumn struggling with a dropsy.—He is dead, said Obadiah, —he is certainly dead !—So am not I, said the foolish scullion.

Here is sad news, Trim ! cried Susannah, wiping her eyes as Trim stepped into the kitchen,—master Bobby is dead and buried—the funeral was an interpolation of Susannah's—we shall have all to go into mourning, said Susannah.

I hope not, said Trim !— You hope not ! cried Susannah earnestly.—The mourning ran not in Trim's head, whatever it did in Susannah's.—I hope, said Trim, explaining himself, I hope in God the news is not true.—I heard the letter read with my own ears, answered Obadiah ; and we shall have a terrible piece of work of it in stubbing the ox-moor. — Oh ! he's dead, said Susannah.—As sure, said the scullion, as I am alive.

I lament for him, from my heart and my soul, said Trim, fetching a sigh.—Poor creature !—poor boy ! poor gentleman !

He was alive last Whitsuntide, said the coachman. —Whitsuntide ! alas ! cried Trim, extending his right arm, and falling instantly into the same attitude in which he read his sermon, — what is Whitsuntide, Jonathan (for that was the coachman's name,) or Shrovetide, or any tide or time past, to this ? Are we not here now, continued the corporal, (striking the end of his stick perpendicularly upon the floor, so as

to give an idea of health and stability)—and are we
not—(dropping his hat upon the ground) gone ! in a
moment !—'Twas infinitely striking ! Susannah burst
into a flood of tears. We are not stocks and stones.
—Jonathan, Obadiah, the cook-maid, all melted.—The
foolish fat scullion herself, who was scouring a fish-
kettle upon her knees, was roused with it. The whole
kitchen crowded about the corporal.

—" Are we not here now ;"—continued the corporal,
" and are we not "—(dropping his hat plump upon the
ground—and pausing before he pronounced the word)
—" gone ! in a moment ?" The descent of the hat was
as if a heavy lump of clay had been kneaded into
the crown of it.—Nothing could have expressed the
sentiment of mortality, of which it was the type and
forerunner, like it,—his hand seemed to vanish from
under it,—it fell dead,—the corporal's eye fixed upon
it, as upon a corpse,—and Susannah burst into a flood
of tears.

—To us, Jonathan, who know not what want or care
is—who live here in the service of two of the best of
masters—(bating in my own case his majesty King
William the Third, whom I had the honour to serve
both in Ireland and Flanders)—I own it, that from
Whitsuntide to within three weeks of Christmas,—
'tis not long—'tis like nothing ;—but to those, Jonathan,
who knew what death is, and what havoc and destruction he can make, before a man can wheel about
—'tis like a whole age. O Jonathan ! 'twould make
a good-natured man's heart bleed, to consider, continued the corporal (standing perpendicularly), how
low many a brave and upright fellow has been laid
since that time ! And trust me, Susy, added the
corporal, turning to Susannah, whose eyes were swimming in water,—before that time comes round again,—
many a bright eye will be dim. Susannah placed it
to the right side of the page—she wept—but she
curtseyed too. Are we not, continued Trim, looking

still at Susannah,—are we not like a flower of the
field—a tear of pride stole in betwixt every two tears
of humiliation—else no tongue could have described
Susannah's affliction—is not all flesh grass? 'Tis clay
—'tis dirt. They all looked directly at the scullion,—
the scullion had just been scouring a fish-kettle. It
was not fair.

What is the finest face that ever man looked at!—I
could hear Trim talk so for ever, cried Susannah,—
what is it! (Susannah laid her hand upon Trim's
shoulder)—but corruption?—Susannah took it off.

For my own part, I declare it, that out of doors, I
value not death at all :—not this...added the corporal,
snapping his fingers,—but with an air which no one
but the corporal could have given to the sentiment.
In battle I value death not this.........and let him not
take me cowardly, like poor Joe Gibbons, in scouring
his gun. What is he? A pull of a trigger—a push of
a bayonet an inch this way or that—makes the difference. Look along the line—to the right—see! Jack's
down! well—'tis worth a regiment of horse to him.
No—'tis Dick. Then Jack's no worse.—Never mind
which,—we pass on,—in hot pursuit the wound itself
which brings him is not felt,—the best way is to stand
up to him,—the man who flies, is in ten times more
danger than the man who marches up into his jaws.
I've looked him, added the corporal, an hundred times
in the face,—and know what he is.—He's nothing,
Obadiah, at all in the field.—But he's very frightful in
a house, quoth Obadiah.—I never mind it myself, said
Jonathan, upon a coach-box.—It must, in my opinion,
be most natural in bed, replied Susannah.—And could
I escape him by creeping into the worst calf's-skin
that ever was made into a knapsack, I would do it
there—said Trim—but that is nature.

—Nature is nature, said Jonathan.—And that is the
reason, cried Susannah, I so much pity my mistress.
She will never get the better of it.—Now I pity the

captain the most of any one in the family, answered
Trim.—Madam will get ease of heart in weeping—and
the squire in talking about it,—but my poor master
will keep it all in silence to himself.—I shall hear him
sigh in his bed for a whole month together, as he did
for lieutenant Le Fever. An' please your honour, do not
sigh so piteously, I would say to him as I lay beside
him.   I cannot help it, Trim, my master would say,—
'tis so melancholy an accident—I cannot get it off my
heart.—Your honour fears not death yourself.—I hope,
Trim, I fear nothing, he would say, but the doing a
wrong thing.—Well, he would add, whatever betides,
I will take care of Le Fever's boy—And with that, like
a quieting draught, his honour would fall asleep.

I like to hear Trim's stories about the captain, said
Susannah.—He is a kindly-hearted gentleman, said
Obadiah, as ever lived.—Aye—and as brave a one too,
said the corporal, as ever stepped before a platoon.—
There never was a better officer in the king's army,—
or a better man in God's world ; for he would march
up to the mouth of a cannon, though he saw the lighted
match at the very touchhole,—and yet, for all that, he
has a heart as soft as a child for other people.—He
would not hurt a chicken.—I would sooner, quoth
Jonathan, drive such a gentleman for seven pounds a-
year—than some for eight.   Thank thee, Jonathan !
for thy twenty shillings,—as much, Jonathan, said the
corporal, shaking him by the hand, as if thou hadst put
the money into my own pocket.—I would serve him
to the day of my death out of love.   He is a friend
and a brother to me—and could I be sure my poor
brother Tom was dead,—continued the corporal, taking
out his handkerchief, — was I worth ten thousand
pounds, I would leave every shilling of it to the captain.   Trim could not refrain from tears at this testa-
mentary proof he gave of his affection to his master.
The whole kitchen was affected.

CHAPTER VIII.

MY FATHER'S GRAND TRISTRA-PÆDIA.

THE first thing which entered my father's head, after affairs were a little settled in the family, and Susannah had got possession of my mother's green satin nightgown,—was to sit down coolly, after the example of Xenophon, and write a Tristra-pædia, or system of education for me ; collecting first for that purpose his own scattered thoughts, counsels, and notions ; and binding them together, so as to form an institute for the government of my childhood and adolescence. I was my father's last stake—he had lost my brother Bobby entirely,—he had lost, by his own computation, full three-fourths of me—that is, he had been unfortunate in his three first great casts for me—my geniture, nose, and name,—there was but this one left ; and accordingly my father gave himself up to it with as much devotion as ever my uncle Toby had done to his doctrine of projectiles.

In about three years, or something more, my father had got advanced almost into the middle of his work. —Like all other writers, he met with disappointments. —He imagined he should be able to bring whatever he had to say into so small a compass, that when it was finished and bound it might be rolled up in my mother's housewife.

This is the best account I am determined to give of

the slow progress my father made in his *Tristra-pœdia;* at which (as I said) he was three years, and something more, indefatigably at work, and, at last, had scarce completed, by his own reckoning, one half of his undertaking : the misfortune was that I was all that time totally neglected and abandoned to my mother : and what was almost as bad, by the very delay, the first part of the work, upon which my father had spent the most of his pains, was rendered entirely useless—every day a page or two became of no consequence—

—No—I think I have advanced nothing, replied my father, making answer to a question which Yorick had taken the liberty to put to him—I have advanced nothing in the *Tristra-pœdia,* but what is as clear as any one proposition in Euclid.—Reach me, Trim, that book from off the scrutoire.—It has oftentimes been in my mind, continued my father, to have read it over, both to you, Yorick, and to my brother Toby ; and I think it a little unfriendly in myself, in not having done it long ago.—Shall we have a short chapter or two now,—and a chapter or two hereafter, as occasions serve ; and so on, till we get through the whole ? My uncle Toby and Yorick made the obeisance which was proper ; and the corporal, though he was not included in the compliment, laid his hand upon his breast, and made his bow at the same time.—The company smiled. Trim, quoth my father, has paid the full price for staying out the entertainment.

My uncle Toby never felt the consciousness of his existence with more complacency than what the corporal's and his own reflections made him do at that moment :—he lighted his pipe.—Yorick drew his chair closer to the table,—Trim snuffed the candle,—my father stirred up the fire,—took up the book,—coughed twice, and began.

I enter upon this speculation, said my father carelessly, and half shutting the book, as he went on,—

merely to show the foundation of the natural relation
between a father and his child ; the right and juris-
diction over whom he acquires these several ways—

1st, by marriage.

2nd, by adoption.

3rd, by legitimation.

And 4th, by creation ; all which I consider in their
order.

I lay a slight stress upon one of them ; replied
Yorick—the last, especially where it ends there, in my
opinion lays as little obligation upon the child, as it
conveys power to the father.— You are wrong,—said
my father argutely. I own that the offspring, upon
this account, is not so under the power and jurisdic-
tion of the mother.—But the reason, replied Yorick,
equally holds good for her.—She is under authority
herself, said my father.—In what ? quoth my uncle
Toby.—Though by all means, added my father (not
attending to my uncle Toby), *"The son ought to pay
her respect ;"* as you may read, Yorick, at large in the
first book of the Institutes of Justinian, at the eleventh
title and the tenth section...I can read it as well, replied Yorick, in the catechism.

Trim can repeat every word of it by heart, quoth
my uncle Toby.—

Pugh ! said my father, not caring to be interrupted
with Trim's saying his catechism. He can, upon my
honour, replied my uncle Toby.—Ask him, Mr. Yorick,
any question you please.—

The fifth commandment, Trim,—said Yorick, speaking mildly, and with a gentle nod, as to a modest
catechumen. The corporal stood silent.—You don't
ask him right, said my uncle Toby, raising his voice,
and giving it rapidly, like the word of command ;—
The fifth——cried my uncle Toby.—I must begin
with the first, an' please your honour, said the corporal.—

Yorick could not forbear smiling.—Your reverence does not consider, said the corporal, shouldering his stick like a musket, and marching into the middle of the room, to illustrate his position,—that 'tis exactly the same thing, as doing one's exercise in the field.—

"Join your right hand to your firelock," cried the corporal, giving the word of command, and performing the motion. —

"Poise your firelock," cried the corporal, doing the duty still of both adjutant and private man.—

"Rest your firelock,"—one motion, an' please your reverence, you see, leads into another.— If his honour will begin but with the first.—

The first—cried my uncle Toby, setting his hand upon his side—

The second—cried my uncle Toby, waving his tobacco-pipe, as he would have done his sword at the head of a regiment.—The corporal went through his manual with exactness ; and having *honoured his father and mother*, made a low bow, and fell back to the side of the room.

Everything in the world, said my father, is big with jest,—and has wit in it, and instruction too,—if we can but find it out.

—Here is the scaffold work of instruction, its true point of folly, without the building behind it—

—Sciences may be learned by rote, but Wisdom not.

Yorick thought my father inspired.—I will enter into obligations this moment, said my father, to lay out all my aunt Dinah's legacy, in charitable uses (of which, by the bye, my father had no high opinion) if the corporal has any one determinate idea annexed to any one word he has repeated.—Prithee, Trim, quoth my father, turning round to him,—What do'st thou mean, by "honouring thy father and mother ?"

Allowing them, an' please your honour, three half-pence a day out of my pay, when they grew old.— And didst thou do that, Trim ? said Yorick.—He did indeed, replied my uncle Toby.—Then, Trim, said Yorick, springing out of his chair, and taking the corporal by the hand, thou art the best commentator upon that part of the Decalogue ; and I honour thee more for it, corporal Trim, than if thou hadst had a hand in the Talmud itself.

O blessed health ! cried my father, making an exclamation, as he turned over the leaves to the next chapter,—thou art above all gold and treasure ; 'tis thou who enlargest the soul,—and openest all its powers to receive instruction and to relish virtue.—He that has thee, has little more to wish for ;—and he that is so wretched as to want thee,—wants everything with thee.

I have concentrated all that can be said upon this important head, said my father, into a very little room, therefore we'll read the chapter quite through.

My father read as follows.

" The whole secret of health depending upon the due contention for mastery betwixt the radical heat and the radical moisture "—you have proved that matter of fact, I suppose, above, said Yorick. Sufficiently, replied my father.

In saying this, my father shut the book,—not as if he resolved to read no more of it, for he kept his forefinger in the chapter :—nor pettishly,—for he shut the book slowly ; his thumb resting, when he had done it, upon the upper side of the cover, as his three fingers supported the lower side of it, without the least compressive violence.

I have demonstrated the truth of that point, quoth my father, nodding to Yorick, most sufficiently in the preceding chapter.

The description of the siege of Jericho itself, could not have engaged the attention of my uncle Toby more powerfully ;—his eyes were fixed upon my father throughout it ;—he never mentioned radical heat and radical moisture, but my uncle Toby took his pipe out of his mouth, and shook his head ; and as soon as the chapter was finished, he beckoned to the corporal to come close to his chair, to ask him a question.

It was at the siege of Limerick, an' please your honour, replied the corporal, making a bow.

The poor fellow and I, quoth my uncle Toby, addressing himself to my father, were scarce able to crawl out of our tents, at the time the siege of Limerick was raised, upon the very account you mention.—Now what can have got into that precious noddle of thine, my dear brother Toby? cried my father, mentally.—By heaven! continued he, communing still with himself, it would puzzle an Œdipus to bring it in point.—

I believe, an' please your honour, quoth the corporal, that if it had not been for the quantity of brandy we set fire to every night, and the claret and cinnamon with which I plied your honour off ;—And the geneva, Trim, added my uncle Toby, which did us more good than all—I verily believe, continued the corporal, we had both, an' please your honour, left our lives in the trenches, and been buried in them too.—The noblest grave, corporal! cried my uncle Toby, his eyes sparkling as he spoke, that a soldier could wish to lie down in.—But a pitiful death for him! an' please your honour, replied the corporal.

All this was as much Arabic to my father, as the rites of Colchi and Troglodites had been before to my uncle Toby ; my father could not determine whether he was to frown or smile--

My uncle Toby, turning to Yorick, resumed the case at Limerick, more intelligibly than he had begun it,—and so settled the point for my father at once.

It was undoubtedly, said my uncle Toby, a great happiness for myself and the corporal, that we had all along a burning fever, attended with a most raging thirst, during the whole five and twenty days the flux was upon us in the camp ; otherwise what my brother calls the radical moisture, must, as I conceive it, inevitably have got the better.—My father drew in his lungs top full of air, and looking up, blew it forth again, as slowly as he possibly could—

It was heaven's mercy to us, continued my uncle Toby, which put it into the corporal's head to maintain that due contention betwixt the radical heat and the radical moisture, by re-inforcing the fever, as he did all along, with hot wine and spices.

—Well,—said my father, with a full aspiration, and pausing awhile after the word—Was I judge, and the laws of the country which made me one permitted it, I would condemn some of the worst malefactors, provided they had had their clergy——Yorick, foreseeing the sentence was likely to end with no sort of mercy, laid his hand upon my father's breast, and begged he would respite it for a few minutes, till he had asked the corporal a question.—Prithee, Trim, said Yorick, without staying for my father's leave,—tell us honestly —what is thy opinion concerning this self-same radical heat and radical moisture?

With humble submission to his honour's better judgment, quoth the corporal, making a bow to my uncle Toby.—Speak thy opinion freely, corporal, said my uncle Toby.—The poor fellow is my servant,—not my slave,—added my uncle Toby, turning to my father.

The corporal put his hat under his left arm, and with his stick hanging upon the wrist of it, by a black thong split into a tassel about the knot, he marched up to the ground where he had performed his catechism; then touching his under jaw with the thumb and fingers of his right hand before he opened his mouth, —he delivered his notion thus.

Just as the corporal was humming to begin, in waddled Dr. Slop.

The city of Limerick, the siege of which was begun under his Majesty King William himself, the year after I went into army—lies, an' please your honours,

in the middle of a devilish wet, swampy country.—
'Tis quite surrounded, said my uncle Toby, with the
Shannon, and is, by its situation, one of the strongest
fortified places in Ireland.

I think this is a new fashion, quoth Dr. Slop, of
beginning a medical lecture.—'Tis all true, answered
Trim.—Then I wish the faculty would follow the cut
of it, said Yorick.—'Tis all cut through, an' please
your reverence, said the corporal, with drains and bogs;
and besides, there was such a quantity of rain fell during the siege, the whole country was like a puddle,—
'twas that, and nothing else, which brought on the flux,
and which had liked to have killed both his honour and
myself; now there was no such thing, after the first
ten days, continued the corporal, for a soldier to lie
dry in his tent, without cutting a ditch round it, to
draw off the water;—nor was that enough, for those
who could afford it, as his honour could, without
setting fire every night to a pewter dish full of brandy,
which took off the damp of the air, and made the inside of the tent as warm as a stove.

And what conclusion dost thou draw, corporal Trim,
cried my father, from all these premises?

I infer, an' please your worship, replied Trim, that
the radical moisture is nothing in the world but ditch-
water—and that the radical heat, of those who can go
to the expense of it, is burnt brandy—and a dram of
geneva—and give us but enough of it, with a pipe of
.tobacco, to give us spirits, and drive away the vapours
—we know not what it is to fear death.

I am at a loss, Captain Shandy, quoth Dr. Slop, to
determine in which branch of learning your servant
shines most, whether in physiology, or divinity.—Slop
had not forgot Trim's comment upon the sermon.

It is but an hour ago, replied Yorick, since the corporal was examined in the latter, and passed muster
with great honour.

The radical heat and moisture, quoth Dr. Slop,

turning to my father, you must know, is the basis and foundation of our being,—as the root of a tree is the source and principle of its vegetation.—It is inherent in the seeds of all animals, and may be preserved sundry ways, but principally in my opinion by consubstantials, impriments, and occludents.—Now this poor fellow, continued Dr. Slop, pointing to the corporal, has had the misfortune to have heard some superficial empiric discourse upon this nice point.—That he has,—said my father.—Very likely, said my uncle. I'm sure of it—quoth Yorick.

Dr. Slop being called out, it gave my father an opportunity of going on with another chapter in the *Tristra-pœdia.*

Five years with a bib under his chin ;

A year and a half in learning to write his own name ;

Seven long years and more τυπτω-ing it, at Greek and Latin ;

Four years at his *probations* and his *negations ;*—the fine statue still lying in the middle of the marble block,—and nothing done but his tools sharpened to hew it out !—'Tis a piteous delay !—Was not the great Julius Scaliger within an ace of never getting his tools sharpened at all ?—Forty-four years old was he before he could manage his Greek ;—and Peter Damianus, Lord Bishop of Ostia, as all the world knows, could not so much as read, when he was of man's estate :— and Baldus himself, eminent as he turned out after, entered upon the law so late in life that everybody imagined he intended to be an advocate in the other world.

Yorick listened to my father with great attention ; there was a seasoning of wisdom unaccountably mixed up with his strangest whims ; and he had sometimes such illuminations in the darkest of his eclipses as almost atoned for them.

I am convinced, Yorick, continued my father, half reading and half discoursing, that there is a north-

8

west passage to the intellectual world ; and that the
soul of man has shorter ways of going to work, in
furnishing itself with knowledge and instruction, than
we generally take with it.—But, alack ! all fields have
not a river or a spring running beside them ;—every
child, Yorick, has not a parent to point it out.

—The whole entirely depends, added my father, in a
low voice, upon the *auxiliary verbs*, Mr. Yorick.

Now the use of the *Auxiliaries* is at once to set the
soul a-going by herself upon the materials as they are
brought her ; and, by the versability of this great
engine, round which they are twisted, to open new
tracts of enquiry, and make every idea engender
millions.

You excite my curiosity greatly, said Yorick.

For my own part, quoth my uncle Toby, I have
given it up....The Danes, an' please your honour, quoth
the corporal, who were on the left at the siege of
Limerick, were all auxiliaries....And very good ones,
said my uncle Toby....And your honour roul'd with
them—captains with captains—very well, said the
corporal....But the auxiliaries, Trim, my brother is
talking about, answered my uncle Toby, I conceive to
be different things.—

My father took a single turn across the room, then
sat down and finished the chapter.

The verbs auxiliary we are concerned in here, continued my father, are am ; was ; have ; had ; do ;
did ; make ; made ; suffer ; shall ; should ; will ;
would ; can ; could ; owe ; ought ; used ; or is wont.
—And these varied with tenses, present, past, future,
conjugated with the verb see—or with these questions
added to them ;—Is it ? was it ? will it be ? would it
be ? may it be ? might it be ?   And these again put
negatively, is it not ? was it not ? ought it not ?—Or
affirmatively,—it is ; it was ; it ought to be.—Or
chronologically,—has it been always ? lately ? how
long ago ?—Or hypothetically—if it was ; if it was

not ? What would follow ?—If the French should
beat the English ? If the sun go out of the Zodiac ?

Now by the right use and application of these, continued my father, in which a child's memory should
be exercised, there is no one idea can enter his brain
how barren soever, but a magazine of conceptions and
conclusions may be drawn forth from it.—Did'st thou
ever see a white bear ? cried my father, turning his
head round to Trim, who stood at the back of his
chair :—No, an' please your honour, replied the corporal.—But thou could'st discourse about one, Trim,
said my father, in case of need ?—How is it possible,
brother, quoth my uncle Toby, if the corporal never
saw one ?—'Tis the fact I want, replied my father,—
and the possibility of it, is as follows.

A white bear ! Very well. Have I ever seen one ?
Might I ever have seen one ? Am I ever to see
one ? Ought I ever to have seen one ? Or can I ever
see one ?

Would I had seen a white bear ? (for how can I
imagine it ?)

If I should see a white bear, what should I say? If
I should never see a white bear, what then ?

If I never have, can, must, or shall see a white bear
alive ; have I ever seen the skin of one ? Did I ever
see one painted ?—described ? Have I never dreamed
of one ?

Did my father, mother, uncle, aunt, brothers or
sisters, ever see a white bear ? What would they
give ? How would they behave ? How would the
white bear have behaved ? Is he wild ? tame ?
terrible ? rough ? smooth ?

— Is the white bear worth seeing ?—

Is there no sin in it ?

—Is it better than a BLACK ONE ?—

When my father had danced his white bear backwards and forwards through half a dozen pages,
he closed the book for good an' all—and in a kind of

8—2

triumph redelivered it into Trim's hand with a nod to lay it upon the 'scrutoire where he found it.—Tristram, said he, shall be made to conjugate every word in the dictionary, backwards and forwards the same way ;—every word, Yorick, by this means, you see, is converted into a thesis or an hypothesis ; —every thesis and hypothesis have an offspring of propositions ;—and each proposition has its own consequences and conclusions ; every one of which leads the mind on again into fresh tracks of inquiries and doubtings.—The force of this engine, added my father, is incredible, in opening a child's head.—'Tis enough, brother Shandy, cried my uncle Toby, to burst it into a thousand splinters.

There are a thousand resolutions, sir, both in church and state, as well as in matters, madam, of a more private concern ;—which, though they have carried all the appearance in the world of being taken, and entered upon in a hasty, hair-brained, and unadvised manner, were, notwithstanding this, weighed, poised, and perpended—argued upon—canvassed through—entered into, and examined on all sides with so much coolness, that the goddess of coolness herself (I do not take upon me to prove her existence) could neither have wished it, nor done it better.

Of the number of these was my father's resolution of putting me into breeches ; which, though determined at once, in a kind of huff, and a defiance of all mankind, had, nevertheless, been pro'd and con'd, and judicially talked over betwixt him and my mother about a month before, in two several beds of justice, which my father had held for that purpose.

We should begin, said my father, turning himself half round in bed, and shifting his pillow a little towards my mother's, as he opened the debate—we should begin to think, Mrs. Shandy, of putting this boy into breeches.—

We should so—said my mother.—We defer it, my dear, quoth my father, shamefully.

I think we do, Mr. Shandy—said my mother.

—Not but the child looks extremely well, said my father, in his vests and tunics.—

He does look very well in them,—replied my mother.—

And for that reason it would be almost a sin, added my father, to take him out of 'em.

It would so—said my mother :—But indeed he is growing a very tall lad—rejoined my father.

He is very tall for his age, indeed—said my mother.

I can not (making two syllables of it) imagine, quoth my father, who the deuce he takes after.

I cannot conceive, for my life—said my mother.

Humph!—said my father.

(The dialogue ceased for a moment.)

I am very short myself—continued my father, gravely.

You are very short, Mr. Shandy,—said my mother.

Humph! quoth my father to himself, a second time : in muttering which, he plucked his pillow a little further from my mother's—and turning about again, there was end of the debate for three minutes and a half.

When he gets these breeches made, cried my father, in a higher tone, he'll look like a beast in 'em.

He will be very awkward in them at first, replied my mother.

And 'twill be lucky, if that's the worst on't, added my father.

It will be very lucky, answered my mother.

I suppose, replied my father,—making some pause first—he'll be exactly like other people's children.

Exactly, said my mother.—

Though I should be sorry for that, added my father: and so the debate stopped again.

They should be of leather, said my father, turning him about again.—

They will last him, said my mother, the longest.

But he can have no linings to 'em, replied my father.—

He cannot, said my mother.

'Twere better to have them of fustian, quoth my father.

Nothing can be better, quoth my mother.

—Except dimity—replied my father :—'Tis best of all—replied my mother.

One must not give him his death, however—interrupted my father.

By no means, said my mother :—and so the dialogue stood still again.

I am resolved, however, quoth my father, breaking silence the fourth time, he shall have no pockets in them.

There is no occasion for any, said my mother.

I mean in his coat and waistcoat,—cried my father.

I mean so too—replied my mother.

Though if he gets a gig or a top—poor souls ! it is a crown and a sceptre to them—they should have where to secure it.

Order it as you please, Mr. Shandy, replied my mother.

But don't you think it right ? added my father, pressing the point home to her.

Perfectly, said my mother, if it pleases you, Mr. Shandy.

There's for you ! cried my father, losing temper—Pleases me !—You never will distinguish, Mrs. Shandy, nor shall I ever teach you to do it, betwixt a point of pleasure and a point of convenience.—This was on the Sunday night ; and further this chapter sayeth not.

After my father had debated the affair of the breeches with my mother, he consulted Albertus

Rubenius upon it ; and Albertus Rubenius used my father ten times worse in the consultation (if possible) than even my father had used my mother : for as Rubenius had wrote a quarto express, De re Vestiaria Veterum—it was Rubenius's business to have given my father some lights. On the contrary, my father might as well have thought. of extracting the seven cardinal virtues out of a long beard, as of extracting a single word out of Rubenius upon the subject.

Upon every other article of ancient dress, Rubenius was very communicative to my father ;—gave him a full and satisfactory account of

The Toga, or loose gown,

The Chlamys.
The Ephod.
The Tunica, or jacket.
The Synthesis.
The Pænula.
The Lacema, with its Cucullus.

—But what are all these to the breeches ? said my father.

Rubenius threw him down, upon the counter, all kinds of shoes which had been in fashion with the Romans :—

There was, The open shoe.
The close shoe.
The slip shoe.
The wooden shoe.
The sock.
The buskin.
And The military shoe, with hob nails in it, which Juvenal takes notice of.

There were, The clogs.
The pattens.
The pantoufles.
The brogues.
The sandals, with latchets to them.

There was, The felt shoe.
      The linen shoe.
 .   The laced shoe.
      The braided shoe.
      The calceus insisus.
 And The calceus rostratus.

Rubenius showed my father how well they all fitted,—-in what manner they laced on,—with what points, straps, thongs, latchets, ribands, jaggs, and ends.—

—But I want to be informed about the breeches, said my father.

Albertus Rubenius informed my father that the Romans manufactured stuffs of various fabrics :—some plain,—some striped,—others diapered throughout the whole contexture of the wool with silk and gold—That linen did not begin to be in common use till towards the declension of the empire, when the Egyptians, coming to settle amongst them, brought it into vogue.

That persons of quality and fortune distinguished themselves by the fineness and whiteness of their clothes ; which colour (next to purple, which was appropriated to the great offices) they most affected, and wore on their birth-days and public rejoicings.—that it appeared, from the best historians of those times, that they frequently sent their clothes to the fuller, to be cleaned and whitened :—but that the inferior people, to avoid that expense, generally wore brown clothes, and of a something coarser texture,—till towards the beginning of Augustus's reign, when the slave dressed like his master, and almost every distinction of habiliment was lost, but the *Latus clavus.*

And what was the *Latus clavus?* said my father.

Rubenius told him that the point was still litigating amongst the learned :—that Egnatius, Sigonius, Bossius Ticinensis, Baysius, Budæus, Salmasius, Lipsius Lazius, Isaac Causabon, and Joseph Scaliger, all differed from each other,—and he from them : that some took it to be the button —some the coat itself —others only the colour of it :—that the great Baysius, in his " Wardrobe of the Ancients," chap. 12,—honestly said he knew not what it was,—whether a tibula,—a stud,—a button,—a loop,—a buckle,—or clasps and keepers.—

My father lost the horse, but not the saddle.—They are hooks and eyes, said my father—and with hooks and eyes he ordered my breeches to be made.

CHAPTER IX.

OU see 'tis high time, said my father, addressing himself equally to my uncle Toby and Yorick, to take this young creature out of these women's hands, and put him into those of a private governor. Marcus Antonius provided fourteen governors all at once to superintend his son Commodus's education,—and in six weeks he cashiered five of them.

I will have him, continued my father, cheerful, faceté, jovial ; at the same time prudent, attentive to business, vigilant, acute, argute, inventive, quick in resolving doubts and speculative questions ;—he shall be wise and judicious, and learned.—And why not humble, and moderate, and gentle tempered, and good ? said Yorick.—And why not, cried my uncle Toby, free, and generous, and bountiful, and brave ?—He shall, my dear Toby, replied my father, getting up and shaking him by his hand.—Then, brother Shandy, answered my uncle Toby, raising himself off the chair, and laying down his pipe to take hold of my father's other hand,—I humbly beg I may recommend poor Le Fever's son to you ;—a tear of joy of the first water sparkled in my uncle Toby's eye, and another, the fellow to it, in the corporal's, as the proposition was made :—you will see why when you read Le Fever's story.

It was some time in the summer of that year in which Dendermond was taken by the allies,—which was about seven years before my father came into the country,—and about as many after the time that my uncle Toby and Trim had privately decamped from my father's house in town, in order to lay some of the finest sieges to some of the finest fortified cities in Europe—when my uncle Toby was one evening getting his supper, with Trim sitting behind him at a small sideboard,—I say, sitting—for in consideration of the corporal's lame knee (which sometimes gave him exquisite pain)—when my uncle Toby dined or supped alone, he would never suffer the corporal to stand ; and the poor fellow's veneration for his master was such, that, with a proper artillery, my uncle Toby could have taken Dendermond itself with less trouble than he was able to gain this point over him ; for many a time when my uncle Toby supposed the corporal's leg was at rest, he would look back, and detect him standing behind him with the most dutiful respect : this bred more little squabbles betwixt them, than all other causes for five-and-twenty years together ; but this is neither here nor there—why do I mention it ? Ask my pen,—it governs me,—I govern not it.

He was one evening sitting thus at his supper, when the landlord of a little inn in the village came into the parlour with an empty phial in his hand, to beg a glass or two of sack ; 'Tis for a poor gentleman, I think, of the army, said the landlord, who has been taken ill at my house four days ago, and has never held up his head since, or had a desire to taste anything, till just now, that he has a fancy for a glass of sack and a thin toast—I think, says he, taking his hand from his forehead, it would comfort me.

If I could neither beg, borrow, or buy such a thing, —added the landlord,—I would almost steal it for the poor gentleman, he is so ill. I hope in God he will still mend, continued he,—we are all of us concerned for him.

Thou art a good-natured soul, I will answer for thee, cried my uncle Toby ; and thou shalt drink the poor gentleman's health in a glass of sack thyself,— and take a couple of bottles with my service, and tell him he is heartily welcome to them, and to a dozen more if they will do him good.

Though I am persuaded, said my uncle Toby, as the landlord shut the door, he is a very compassionate fellow,—Trim,—yet I cannot help entertaining a high opinion of his guest too ; there must be something more than common in him, that in so short a time should win so much upon the affections of his host.— And of his whole family, added the corporal, for they are all concerned for him.—Step after him, said my uncle Toby,—do Trim,—and ask if he knows his name.

—I have quite forgot it, truly, said the landlord, coming back into the parlour with the corporal,—but I can ask his son again. Has he a son with him then ? said my uncle Toby. A boy, replied the landlord, of about eleven or twelve years of age ;—but the poor creature has tasted almost as little as his father ; he does nothing but mourn and lament for him night and day :—He has not stirred from the bedside these two days.

My uncle Toby laid down his knife and fork, and thrust his plate from before him, as the landlord gave him the account ; and Trim, without being ordered, took away without saying one word, and in a few minutes after brought him his pipe and tobacco.

Stay in the room a little, said my uncle Toby.

Trim !—said my uncle Toby, after he lighted his pipe, and smoked about a dozen whiffs. Trim came in front of his master and made his bow ;—my uncle Toby smoked on, and said no more.—Corporal ! said my uncle Toby—the corporal made his bow.—My uncle Toby proceeded no further, but finished his pipe.

Trim! said my uncle Toby, I have a project in my head, as it is a bad night, of wrapping myself up warm in my roquelaure, and paying a visit to this poor gentleman.—Your honour's roquelaure, replied the corporal, has not once been had on since the night before your honour received your wound, when we mounted guard in the trenches before the gate of St. Nicholas;—and besides it is so cold and rainy a night, that what with the roquelaure, and what with the weather, 'twill be enough to give your honour your death, and bring on your honour's torment in your groin. I fear so, replied my uncle Toby; but I am not at rest in my mind, Trim, since the account the landlord has given me. I wish I had not known so much of this affair, added my uncle Toby,—or that I had known more of it :—How shall we manage it? Leave it, an't please your honour, to me, quoth the corporal;—I'll take my hat and stick, and go to the house and reconnoitre, and act accordingly; and I will bring your honour a full account in an hour. Thou shalt go, Trim, said my uncle Toby, and here's a shilling for thee to drink with his servant.--I shall get it all out of him, said the corporal, shutting the door.

My uncle Toby filled his second pipe; and had it not been, that he now and then wandered from the point, with considering whether it was not full as well to have the curtain of the tenaille a straight line, as a crooked one,—he might be said to have thought of nothing else but poor Le Fever and his boy the whole time he smoked it.

It was not till my uncle Toby had knocked the ashes out of his third pipe, that corporal Trim returned from the inn, and gave him the following account.

I despaired at first, said the corporal, of being able to bring back your honour any kind of intelligence concerning the poor sick lieutenant.—Is he in the army then? said my uncle Toby.—He is, said the corporal. —And in what regiment? said my uncle Toby.—I'll tell your honour, replied the corporal, everything straight forwards, as I learnt it.—Then, Trim, I'll fill another pipe, said my uncle Toby, and not interrupt thee till thou hast done ; so sit down at thy ease, Trim, in the window-seat, and begin thy story again. The corporal made his old bow, which generally spoke as plain as a bow could speak it—Your honour is good :— and having done that, he sat down, as he was ordered, —and began the story to my uncle Toby over again in pretty near the same words.

I despaired at first, said the corporal, of being able to bring back any intelligence to your honour about the lieutenant and his son ; for when I asked where his servant was, from whom I made myself sure of knowing everything which was proper to be asked— That's a right distinction, Trim, said my uncle Toby— I was answered, an' please your honour, that he had no servant with him ;—that he had come to the inn with hired horses, which, upon finding himself unable to proceed (to join, I suppose the regiment) he had dis- missed the morning after he came.—If I get better, my dear, said he, as he gave his purse to his son to pay the man, we can hire horses from hence.—But alas ! the poor gentleman will never get from hence, said the landlady to me,—for I heard the death-watch all night long ;—and when he dies, the youth, his son, will certainly die with him ; for he is broken-hearted already.

I was hearing this account, continued the corporal, when the youth came into the kitchen, to order the thin toast the landlord spoke of ;—but I will do it for my father myself, said the youth.—Pray let me save you the trouble, young gentleman, said I, taking up a fork for the purpose, and offering him my chair to sit down upon by the fire, whilst I did it.—I believe, sir, said he, very modestly, I can please him best myself.—I am sure, said I, his honour will not like the toast the worse for being toasted by an old soldier.

—The youth took hold of my hand, and instantly burst into tears.—Poor youth! said my uncle Toby, he has been bred up from an infant in the army, and the name of a soldier, Trim, sounded in his ears like the name of a friend ;—I wish I had him here.

— I never in the longest march, said the corporal, had so great a mind to my dinner, as I had to cry with him for company : what could be the matter with me, an' please your honour ? Nothing in the world, Trim, said my uncle Toby, blowing his nose—but that thou art a good-natured fellow.

When I gave him the toast, continued the corporal, I thought it was proper to tell him I was Captain Shandy's servant, and that your honour (though a stranger) was extremely concerned for his father ;— and that if there was anything in your house or cellar —(and thou might'st have added my purse too, said my uncle Toby)—he was heartily welcome to it :—he made a very low bow (which was meant to your honour) but no answer,—for his heart was full—so he went upstairs with the toast :—I warrant you, my dear, said I, as I opened the kitchen door, your father will be well again.—Mr. Yorick's curate was smoking a pipe by the kitchen fire,—but said not a word good or bad to comfort the youth.—I thought it wrong, added the corporal.—I think so too, said my uncle Toby.

When the lieutenant had taken his glass of sack and toast, he felt himself a little revived, and sent down into the kitchen to let me know, that in about ten minutes he should be glad if I would step upstairs. —I believe, said the landlord, he is going to say his prayers,—for there was a book laid upon the chair by his bedside, and as I shut the door, I saw his son take up a cushion.

I thought, said the curate, that you gentlemen of the army, Mr. Trim, never said your prayers at all. —I heard the poor gentleman say his prayers last night, said the landlady, very devoutly, and with my own ears, or I could not have believed it.—Are you sure of it? replied the curate. — A soldier, an' please your reverence, said I, prays as often (of his own accord) as a parson ;—and when he is fighting for his king, and for his own life, and for his honour too, he has the most reason to pray to God of any one in the whole world.—'Twas well said of thee, Trim, said my uncle Toby.—But when a soldier, said I, an' please your reverence, has been standing for twelve hours together in the trenches, up to his knees in cold water, —or engaged, said I, for months together in long and dangerous marches ;—harassed, perhaps, in his rear to-day ;—harassing others to-morrow ;—detached here ; —countermanded there ;—resting this night out upon his arms ;—beat up in his shirt the next ;—benumbed in his joints ;—perhaps without straw in his tent to kneel on ;—must say his prayers how and when he can.—I believe, said I,—for I was piqued, quoth the corporal, for the reputation of the army,—I believe, an' please your reverence, said I, that when a soldier gets time to pray,—he prays as heartily as a parson,— though not with all his fuss and hypocrisy.—Thou should'st not have said that, Trim, said my uncle Toby, —for God only knows who is a hypocrite, and who is not : — At the great and general review of us all, corporal, at the day of judgment (and not till then) it will be seen who has done their duties in this world, and who has not ; and we shall be advanced, Trim, accordingly.—I hope we shall, said Trim.—It is in the Scripture, said my uncle Toby ; and I will show it thee to-morrow :—In the meantime we may depend upon it, Trim, for our comfort, said my uncle Toby, that God Almighty is so good and just a governor of the world, that if we have but done our duties in it, - it will never be inquired into, whether we have done them in a red coat or a black one.—I hope not ; said the corporal.—But go on, Trim, said my uncle Toby, with thy story.

When I went up, continued the corporal, into.the lieutenant's room, which I did not do till the expiration of the ten minutes, he was lying in his bed with his head raised upon his hand, with his elbow upon the pillow, and a clean white cambric handkerchief beside it :— The youth was just stooping down to take up the cushion, upon which I supposed he had been kneeling, —the book was laid upon the bed,—and as he rose, in taking up the cushion with one hand, he reached out his other to take it away at the same time.—Let it remain there, my dear, said the lieutenant.

He did not offer to speak to me, till I had walked up close to his bedside :—If you are Captain Shandy's servant, said he, you must present my thanks to your master, with my little boy's thanks along with them, for his courtesy to me ;—if he was of Leven's—said the lieutenant.—I told him your honour was—Then, said he, I served three campaigns with him in Flanders, and remember him,—but 'tis most likely, as I had not the honour of any acquaintance with him, that he knows nothing of me. You will tell him, however, that the person his good nature has laid under obligations to him, is one Le Fever, a lieutenant in Angus's —but he knows me not, — said he, a second time, musing ; possibly he may my story—added he—pray tell the captain, I was the ensign at Breda, whose wife was most unfortunately killed with a musket shot, as she lay in my arms in my tent.—I remember the story, an't please your honour, said I, very well.—Do you so? said he, wiping his eyes with his handkerchief,—then well may I.—In saying this he drew a little ring out of his bosom, which seemed tied with a black ribband about his neck, and kissed it twice.—Here, Billy, said he,—the boy flew across the room to the bedside,—and falling down upon his knee, took the ring in his hand, and kissed it too—then kissed his father, and sat down upon the bed and wept.

9

I wish, said my uncle Toby, with a deep sigh—I wish, Trim, I was asleep.

Your honour, replied the corporal, is too much concerned ;—shall I pour your honour out a glass of sack to your pipe ?—Do, Trim, said my uncle Toby.

I remember, said my uncle Toby, sighing again, the story of the ensign and his wife, with a circumstance his modesty omitted :—and particularly well that he, as well as she, upon some account or other (I forgot what) was universally pitied by the whole regiment ; —but finish the story thou art upon :—'tis finished already, said the corporal—for I could stay no longer —so wished his honour a good night; young Le Fever rose from off the bed, and saw me to the bottom of the stairs ; and as we went down together, told me, they had come from Ireland, and were on their route to join the regiment in Flanders.—But alas ! said the corporal—the lieutenant's last day's march is over.— Then what is to become of his poor boy? cried my uncle Toby.

It was to my uncle Toby's eternal honour--though I tell it only for the sake of those who, when cooped in betwixt a natural and positive law, know not for their souls which way in the world to turn themselves —that notwithstanding my uncle Toby was warmly engaged at that time in carrying on the siege of Dendermond, parallel with the allies, who pressed theirs on so vigorously, that they scarce allowed him time to get his dinner—that nevertheless he gave up Dendermond, though he had already made a lodgment upon the counterscarp ;—and bent his whole thoughts towards the private distress at the inn ; and, except that he ordered the garden gate to be bolted up, by which he might be said to have turned the siege of Dendermond into a blockade,—he left Dendermond to itself—to be relieved or not by the French king, as the French king thought good ; and only considered how he himself should relieve the poor lieutenant and his son.

—That kind Being, who is a friend to the friendless, shall recompense thee for this.

Thou has left this matter short, said my uncle Toby, to the corporal, as he was putting him to bed—and I will tell thee in what, Trim.—In the first place, when thou mad'st an offer of my services to Le Fever—as sickness and travelling are both expensive, and thou knowest he was but a poor lieutenant, with a son to subsist as well as himself, out of his pay—that thou did'st not make an offer to him of my purse ; because, had he stood in need, thou knowest, Trim, he had been as welcome to it as myself.—Your honour knows, said the corporal, I had no orders. True, quoth my uncle Toby—thou didst very right, Trim, as a soldier—but certainly very wrong as a man.

In the second place, for which, indeed, thou hast the same excuse, continued my uncle Toby—when thou offeredst him whatever was in my house—thou shouldst have offered him my house too :—A sick brother officer should have the best quarters, Trim ; and if we had him with us—we could tend and look to him:—Thou art an excellent nurse thyself, Trim—and what with thy care of him, and the old woman's, and his boy's, and mine together, we might recruit him again at once, and set him upon his legs.—

—In a fortnight or three weeks, added my uncle Toby, smiling—he might march.—He will never march, an' please your honour, in this world, said the corporal :— He will march, said my uncle Toby, rising up from the side of the bed, with one shoe off :—An' please your honour, said the corporal, he will never march but to his grave :—He shall march, cried my uncle Toby, marching the foot which had a shoe on, though without advancing an inch—he shall march to his regiment. —He cannot stand it, said the corporal ;—He shall be supported, said my uncle Toby ;—He'll drop at last,

9—2

said the corporal, and what will become of his boy?
—He shall not drop, said my uncle Toby, firmly.—
A-well-o'-day,—do what we can for him, said Trim,
maintaining his point,—the poor soul will die :—He
shall not die, by G——, cried my uncle Toby.

—The accusing spirit which flew up to heaven's chan-
cery with the oath, blushed as he gave it in—and the
recording angel as he wrote it down, dropped a tear
upon the word, and blotted it out for ever.

My uncle Toby went to his bureau—put his purse
into his breeches pocket, and having ordered the corporal to go early in the morning for a physician—he
went to bed, and fell asleep.

The sun looked bright the morning after, to every
eye in the village but Le Fever's and his afflicted son's;
the hand of death pressed heavy upon his eyelids—and
hardly could the wheel at the cistern turn round its
circle,—when my uncle Toby, who had rose up an
hour before his wonted time, entered the lieutenant's
room, and without preface or apology, sat himself
down upon the chair by the bedside, and, independ-
ently of all modes and customs, opened the curtain in
the manner an old friend and brother officer would
have done it, and asked him how he did—how he had
rested in the night—what was his complaint—where
was his pain—and what he could do to help him :—and,
without giving him time to answer any one of the
inquiries, went on and told him of the little plan which
he had been concerting with the corporal the night
before for him.

You shall go home directly, Le Fever, said my uncle
Toby, to my house,—and we'll send for a doctor to see
what's the matter—and we'll have an apothecary—and
the corporal shall be your nurse ;—and I'll be your
servant, Le Fever.

There was a frankness in my uncle Toby—not the
effect of familiarity—but the cause of it—which let
you at once into his soul, and showed you the good-

ness of his nature ; to this, there was something in his
looks, and voice, and manner, superadded, which eternally beckoned to the unfortunate to come and take
shelter under him ; so that before my uncle Toby had
half finished the kind offers he was making to the
father, had the son insensibly pressed up close to his
knees, and had taken hold of the breast of his coat,
and was pulling it towards him.—The blood and spirits
of Le Fevre, which were waxing cold and slow within
him, and were retreating to their last citadel, the heart
—rallied back,—the film forsook his eyes for a moment
—he looked up wistfully in my uncle Toby's face—then
cast a look upon his boy—and that ligament, fine as it
was—was never broken.

Nature instantly ebbed again—the film returned to
its place—the pulse fluttered—stopped—went on—
throbbed—stopped again—moved—stopped—shall I
go on ?—No.

CHAPTER X.

MY UNCLE TOBY'S FORTIFICATIONS.

EAVE we then the breeches in the tailor's hands, with my father standing over him with his cane, reading him as he sat at work a lecture upon the *latus clavus*, and pointing to the precise part of the waistband where he was determined to have it sewed on.

Leave we my mother—(truest of all the *Pococurantes* of her sex!)—careless about it, as about everything else in the world which concerned her; that is,—indifferent whether it was done this way or that,—provided it was but done at all.

Leave we Slop likewise.

Let us leave, if possible, *myself*:—but, 'tis impossible;—I must go along with you to the end of the work.

If the reader has not a clear conception of the rood and a half of ground which lay at the bottom of my uncle Toby's kitchen garden, and which was the scene of so many of his delicious hours—the fault is not in me—but in his imagination : for I am sure I gave him so minute a description, I was almost ashamed of it.

My uncle Toby came down, as the reader has been

informed, with plans along with him of almost every fortified town in Italy and Flanders ; so let the Duke of Marlborough, or the allies, have set down before what town they pleased, my uncle Toby was prepared for them.

His way, which was the simplest one in the world, was this ; as soon as ever a town was invested—(but sooner when the design was known)—to take the plan of it (let it be what town it would) and enlarge it upon a scale to the exact size of his bowling green ; upon the surface of which, by means of a large roll of packthread and a number of small piquets driven into the ground, at the several angles and redans, he transferred the lines from his paper ; then taking the profile of the place, with its works, to determine the depths and slopes of the ditches, the talus of the glacis, and the precise height of the several banquets, parapets, &c., he set the corporal to work, and sweetly went it on :—The nature of the soil—the nature of the work itself—and above all, the good nature of my uncle Toby sitting by from morning to night, and chatting kindly with the corporal upon past-done deeds—left Labour little else but the ceremony of the name.

When the place was finished in this manner, and put into a proper posture of defence—it was invested —and my uncle Toby and the corporal began to run their first parallel. I beg I may not be interrupted in my story, by being told That the first parallel should be at least three hundred toises distant from the main body of the place, and that I have not left a single inch for it ; for my uncle Toby took the liberty of encroaching upon his kitchen garden, for the sake of enlarging his works on the bowling-green, and for that reason generally ran his first and second parallels betwixt two rows of his cabbages and his cauliflowers.

When the town, with its works, was finished, my

uncle Toby and the corporal began to run their first
parallel, not at random, or anyhow, but from the
same points and distances the allies had begun to
run theirs; and regulating their approaches and attacks, by the accounts my uncle Toby received from
the daily papers, they went on, during the whole
siege, step by step with the allies.

When the Duke of Marlborough made a lodgment,
my uncle Toby made a lodgment too—And when the
face of a bastion was battered down, or a defence
ruined, the corporal took his mattock and did as
much, and so on ; gaining ground, and making themselves masters of the works one after another, till the
town fell into their hands.

To one who took pleasure in the happy state of
others, there could not have been a greater sight in
the world, than on a post-morning, in which a practicable breach had been made by the Duke of Marlborough in the main body of the place—to have
stood behind the horn-beam hedge, and observed the
spirit with which my uncle Toby, with Trim behind
him, sallied forth ; the one with the Gazette in his
hand—the other with a spade on his shoulder to execute the contents. What an honest triumph in my
uncle Toby's looks as he marched up to the ramparts !
What intense pleasure swimming in his eye as he
stood over the corporal, reading the paragraph ten
times over to him as he was at work, lest, peradventure, he should make the breach an inch too wide—or
leave it an inch too narrow. But when the chamade
was beat, and the corporal helped my uncle up it,
and followed with the colours in his hand, to fix them
upon the ramparts—Heaven ! Earth ! Sea !—but
what avails apostrophes ?—with all your elements,-
wet or dry, ye never compounded so intoxicating a
draught.

In this track of happiness for many years, without
one interruption to it, except now and then when the

wind continued to blow due west for a week or ten
days together, which detained the Flanders mail,
and kept them so long in torture—but still 'twas
the torture of the happy—In this track, I say, did
my uncle Toby and Trim move for many years,
every year of which, and sometimes every month,
from the invention of either one or the other of them,
adding some new conceit or quirk of improvement to
their operations, which always opened fresh springs
of delight in carrying them on.

The first year's campaign was carried on from beginning to end in the plain and simple method I've
related.

In the second year, in which my uncle Toby took
Liege and Ruremond, he thought he might afford the
expense of four handsome draw-bridges, of two of which
I have given an exact description in the former part
of my work.

At the latter end of the same year he added a
couple of gates with portcullises:—these last were
converted afterwards in orgues, as the better thing;
and during the winter of the same year, my uncle
Toby, instead of a new suit of clothes, which he
always had at Christmas, treated himself with a
handsome sentry-box, to stand at the corner of the
bowling-green, betwixt which point and the foot of
the glacis there was left a little kind of an esplanade
for him and the corporal to confer and hold councils
of war upon.

—The sentry-box was in case of rain.

All these were painted white three times over the
ensuing spring, which enabled my uncle Toby to take
the field with great splendour.

My father would often say to Yorick, that if any
mortal in the whole universe had done such a thing,
except his brother Toby, it would have been looked
upon by the world as one of the most refined satires
upon the parade and prancing manner in which

Louis XIV. from the beginning of the war, but particularly that very year, had taken the field.—But 'tis not my brother Toby's nature, kind soul ! my father would add, to insult any one.

I must observe, that although in the first year's campaign the word town is often mentioned—yet there was no town at that time within the polygon ; that addition was not made till the summer following the spring in which the bridges and sentry-box were painted, which was the third year of my uncle Toby's campaigns,—when upon his taking Amberg, Bonn, and Rhinberg, and Huy and Limbourg, one after another, a thought came into the corporal's head, that to talk of taking so many towns, without one town to show for it, was a very nonsensical way of going to work ; and so proposed to my uncle Toby, that they should have a little model of a town built for them, to be run up together of slit deals, and then painted, and clapped within the interior polygon to serve for all.

My uncle Toby felt the good of the project instantly, and instantly agreed to it, but with the addition of two singular improvements, of which he was almost as proud, as if he had been the original inventor of the project itself.

The one was ; to have the town built exactly in the style of those of which it was most likely to be the representative :—with great windows, and the gable ends of the houses facing the streets, &c., &c.— as those in Ghent and Bruges, and the rest of the towns in Brabant and Flanders.

The other was, not to have the houses run up together, as the corporal proposed, but to have every house independent, to hook on, or off, so as to form into the plan of whatever town they pleased. This was put directly into hand, and many and many a look of mutual congratulation was exchanged between my uncle Toby and the corporal, as the carpenter did the work.

It answered prodigiously the next summer—the town was a perfect Proteus—It was Landen, and Trerebach, and Santlivet, and Drusen, and Hagenau —and then it was Ostend and Menin, and Aeth and Dendermond.

Surely never did any town act so many parts, as my uncle Toby's town did.

In the fourth year, my uncle Toby, thinking a town looked foolishly without a church, added a very fine one with a steeple. Trim was for having bells in it; my uncle Toby said, the metal had better be cast into cannon.

This led the way to the next campaign for half-a-dozen brass field-pieces—to be planted three and three on each side of my uncle Toby's sentry-box ; and in a short time these led the way for a train of somewhat larger—and so on—(as must always be the case in hobby-horsical affairs) from pieces of half an inch bore, till it came at last to my father's jack-boots.

The next year, which was that in which Lisle was besieged, and at the close of which both Ghent and Bruges fell into our hands—my uncle Toby was sadly put to it for proper ammunition ; I say proper ammunition, because his great artillery would not bear powder ; and 'twas well for the Shandy family they would not. For so full were the papers, from the beginning to the end of the siege, of the incessant firings kept up by the besiegers, and so heated was my uncle Toby's imagination with the accounts of them, that he had infallibly shot away all his estate.

Something therefore was wanting, as a succedaneum, especially in one or two of the more violent paroxysms of the siege, to keep up something like a continual firing in the imagination — and this something, the corporal, whose principal strength lay in invention, supplied by an entire new system of battering of his own, without which this had been objected to by mi-

litary critics to the end of the world, as one of the
great desiderata of my uncle Toby's apparatus.

With two or three other trinkets, small in themselves,
but of great regard, which poor Tom, the corporal's
unfortunate brother, had sent him over, with the
account of his marriage with the Jew's widow—there
was

A Montero cap and two Turkish tobacco-pipes.

The Montero cap I shall describe by-and-bye. The
Turkish tobacco-pipes had nothing particular in them,
they were fitted up and ornamented as usual, with
flexible tubes of Morocco leather and gold wire, and
mounted at their ends, the one of them with ivory—
the other with black ebony, tipped with silver.

My father, who saw all things in lights different from
the rest of the world, would say to the corporal, that
he ought to look upon these two presents more as
tokens of his brother's nicety, than his affection. Tom
did not care, Trim, he would say, to put on the cap,
or to smoke in the tobacco-pipe of a Jew. God bless
your honour, the corporal would say (giving a strong
reason to the contrary)—how can that be?

The Montero cap was scarlet, of a superfine Spanish
cloth, dyed in grain, and mounted all round with fur,
except about four inches in the front, which was faced
with a light blue, slightly embroidered, and seemed to
have been the property of a Portuguese quarter-master,
not of foot, but of horse, as the word denotes.

The corporal was not a little proud of it, as well for
its own sake, as the sake of the giver, so seldom or
never put it on but upon gala days ; and yet never
was a Montero cap put to so many uses ; for in all
controverted points, whether military or culinary, provided the corporal was sure he was in the right—it
was either his oath, his wager, or his gift.

'Twas his gift in the present case.

I'll be bound, said the corporal, speaking to himself,
to give away my Montero cap to the first beggar who

comes to the door if I do not manage this matter to his honour's satisfaction.

The completion was no further off than the very next morning; which was that of the storm of the counterscarp betwixt the Lower Deule, to the right, and the gate of St. Andrew—and on the left, between St. Magdalen's and the river.

As this was the most memorable attack in the whole war--the most gallant and obstinate on both sides—and I must add the most bloody too, for it cost the allies themselves that morning above eleven hundred men—my uncle Toby prepared himself for it with a more than ordinary solemnity.

The eve which preceded, as my uncle Toby went to bed, he ordered his Ramallie wig, which had laid inside out for many years in the corner of an old campaigning trunk, which stood by his bedside, to be taken out and laid upon the lid of it, ready for the morning; and the very first thing he did in his shirt, when he had stepped out of bed, my uncle Toby, after he had turned the rough side outwards—put it on :—this done, he proceeded next to his breeches, and having buttoned the waistband, he forthwith buckled on his sword and belt, and had got his sword half way in, when he considered he should want shaving, and that it would be very inconvenient doing it with his sword on—so took it off :—In essaying to put on his regimental coat and waistcoat, my uncle Toby found the same objection in his wig—so that went off too : So that what with one thing, and what with another, as always falls out when a man is in the most haste, 'twas ten o'clock, which was half an hour later than his usual time, before my uncle Toby sallied out.

My uncle Toby had scarce turned the corner of his yew hedge, which separated his kitchen garden from his bowling-green, when he perceived the corporal had begun the attack without him.—

Let me stop and give you a picture of the corporal's

apparatus; and of the corporal himself in the height of this attack, just as it struck my uncle Toby, as he turned towards the sentry-box.

The corporal had slipped out about ten minutes before my uncle Toby, in order to fix his apparatus, and just give the enemy a shot or two before my uncle Toby came.

He had drawn the six field-pieces for this end, all close up together in front of my uncle Toby's sentry-box, leaving only an interval of about a yard and a half betwixt the three, on the right and left, for the convenience of charging, &c. and the sake possibly of two batteries, which he might think double the honour of one.

In the rear, and facing this opening, with his back to the door of the sentry-box, for fear of being flanked, had the corporal wisely taken his post.—He held the ivory pipe, appertaining to the battery on the right, betwixt the finger and thumb of his right hand — and the ebony pipe, tipped with silver, which appertained to the battery on the left, betwixt the finger and thumb of the other—and with his right knee fixed firm upon the ground, as if in the front rank of his platoon, was the corporal, with his Montero cap upon his head, furiously playing off his two cross batteries at the same time against the counterguard which faced the counterscarp, where the attack was to be made that morning. His first intention, as I said, was no more than giving the enemy a single puff or two; but the pleasure of the puffs, as well as the puffing, had insensibly got hold of the corporal, and drawn him on from puff to puff, into the very height of the attack, by the time my uncle Toby joined him.

'Twas well for my father, that my uncle Toby had not his will to make that day.

My uncle Toby took the ivory pipe out of the corporal's hand — looked at it for half a minute, and returned it.

In less than two minutes my uncle Toby took the pipe from the corporal again, and raised it half way to his mouth—then hastily gave it back a second time.

The corporal redoubled the attack—my uncle Toby smiled—then looked grave—then smiled for a moment —then looked serious for a long time. Give me hold of the ivory pipe, Trim, said my uncle Toby—my uncle Toby put it to his lips, drew it back directly, gave a peep over the horn-beam hedge ; never did my uncle Toby's mouth water so much for a pipe in his life. My uncle Toby retired into the sentry-box with the pipe in his hand.

There was, madam, in my uncle Toby a singleness of heart which misled him so far out of the little serpentine tracks in which things of this nature usually go on ; you can—you can have no conception of it : with this, there was a plainness and simplicity of thinking, with such an unmistrusting ignorance of the plies and foldings of the heart of woman—and so naked and defenceless did he stand before you (when a siege was out of his head) that you might have stood behind any one of your serpentine walks, and shot my uncle Toby ten times in a day through his liver, if nine times in a day, madam, had not served your purpose.

With all this, madam—and what confounded everything as much on the other hand, my uncle Toby had that unparalleled modesty of nature I once told you of, and which, by-the-bye, stood eternal sentry upon his feelings, that you might as soon—But where am I going ? these reflections crowd in upon me ten pages at least too soon, and take up that time which I ought to bestow upon facts.

Amongst the many ill consequences of the treaty of Utrecht, it was within a point of giving my uncle Toby a surfeit of sieges ; and though he recovered his appetite afterwards, yet Calais itself left not a deeper scar in Mary's heart, than Utrecht upon my ¯uncle Toby's. To the end of his life he never could hear Utrecht mentioned upon any account whatever, or so much as read an article of news extracted out of the Utrecht Gazette, without fetching a sigh, as if his heart would break in twain.

My father, who was a great motive-monger, and consequently a very dangerous person for a man to sit by, either laughing or crying—for he generally knew your motive for doing both much better than you knew it yourself—would always console my uncle Toby upon these occasions in a way which showed plainly he imagined my uncle Toby grieved for nothing in the whole affair so much as the loss of his hobby-horse. Never mind, brother Toby, he would say—by God's blessing we shall have another war break out again some of these days ; and when it does, the belligerent powers, if they would hang themselves, cannot keep us out of play. I defy 'em, my dear Toby, he would add, to take countries without taking towns—or towns without sieges.

My uncle Toby never took this backstroke of my father's at his hobby-horse kindly. He thought the stroke ungenerous ; and the more so, because in striking the horse he hit the rider too, and in the most dishonourable part a blow could fall ; so that upon these occasions, he always laid down his pipe upon the table with more fire to defend himself than common.

I told the reader, this time two years, that my uncle Toby was not eloquent ; and in the very same page gave an instance to the contrary : I repeat the observation, and a fact which contradicts it again. He was not eloquent—it was not easy to my uncle Toby to make long harangues—and he hated florid ones ; but there were occasions where the stream overflowed the man, and ran so counter to its usual course, that in some parts my uncle Toby, for a time, was at least equal to Tertullus—but in others, in my opinion, infinitely above him.

My father was so highly pleased with one of these apologetical orations of my uncle Toby's, which he had delivered one evening before him and Yorick, that he wrote it down before he went to bed. I have had the good fortune to meet with it amongst my father's papers, with here and there an insertion of his own, two crooks, thus [ ], and is endorsed,

My brother Toby's justification of his own principles and conduct in wishing to continue the war.

I may safely say, I have read over this apologetical oration of my uncle Toby's a hundred times, and think it so fine a model of defence, and shows so sweet a temperament of gallantry and good principles in him, that I give it to the world, word for word (interlineations and all) as I find it.

I am not insensible, brother Shandy, that when a man, whose profession is arms, wishes, as I have done, for war—it has an ill aspect to the world; and that how just and right soever his motives and intentions may be, he stands in an uneasy posture in vindicating himself, from private views in doing it.

For this cause, if a soldier is a prudent man, which he may be, without being a jot the less brave, he will be sure not to utter his wish in the hearing of an enemy; for, say what he will, an enemy will not believe him. He will be cautious of doing it even to a friend, lest he may suffer in his esteem :—but if his heart is overcharged, and a secret sigh for arms must have its vent, he will reserve it for the ear of a brother, who knows his character to the bottom, and what his true notions, dispositions, and principles of honour are; What, I hope, I have been in all these,

10

brother Shandy, would be unbecoming in me to say;
much worse, I know, have I been than I ought—and
something worse, perhaps, than I think : but such as
I am, you, my dear brother Shandy, who have sucked
the same breasts with me—and with whom I have
been brought up from my cradle—and from whose
knowledge, from the first hours of our boyish pas-
times down to this, I have concealed no one action of
my life, and scarce a thought in it—Such as I am,
brother, you must by this time know me with all
my vices, and with all my weaknesses, too, whether
of my age, my temper, my passions, or my understanding.

Tell me then, my dear brother Shandy, upon which
of them it is, that when I condemned the peace of
Utrecht, and grieved the war was not carried on with
vigour a little longer, you should think your brother
did it upon unworthy views ; or that in wishing for
war, he should be bad enough to wish more of his
fellow creatures slain—more slaves made, and more
families driven from their peaceful habitations, merely
for his own pleasure? Tell me, brother Shandy, upon
what one deed of mine do you ground it? [The
devil a deed do I know of, dear Toby, but one for a
hundred pounds, which I lent thee to carry on these
cursed sieges.]

O brother! 'tis one thing for a soldier to gather
laurels, and 'tis another to scatter cypress. [Who
told thee, my dear Toby, that cypress was used by the
ancients on mournful occasions?]

'Tis one thing, brother Shandy, for a soldier to
hazard his own life—to leap first down into the trench,
where he is sure to be cut to pieces :—'Tis one thing,
from public spirit and a thirst of glory, to enter the
breach the first man—to stand in the foremost rank,
and march bravely on with drums and trumpets, and
colours flying about his ears :—'Tis one thing, I say,
brother Shandy, to do this, and 'tis another thing to

reflect on the miseries of war ; to view the desolation of whole countries, and consider the intolerable fatigues and hardships which the soldier himself, the instrument who works them, is forced (for sixpence a day, if he can get it) to undergo.

The Peace created, I say, a sort of shyness betwixt my uncle Toby and his hobby-horse. He had no occasion for him from the month of March to November, which was the summer after the articles were signed, except it was now and then to take a short ride out, just to see that the fortifications and harbour of Dunkirk were demolished, according to stipulation.

The French were so backward all that summer in setting about the affair, that Monsieur Tugghe, the deputy from the magistrates of Dunkirk, presented so many affecting petitions to the queen, beseeching her majesty to cause only her thunderbolts to fall upon the martial works, which might have incurred her displeasure—but to spare—to spare the mole, for the mole's sake ; which, in its situation, could be no more than an object of pity, and the queen (who was but a woman) being of a pitiful disposition—and her ministers also, they not wishing in their hearts to have the town dismantled ; so that the whole went heavily on with my uncle Toby ; insomuch, that it was not within three full months, after he and the corporal had constructed the town, and put it in a condition to be destroyed, that the several commandants, commissaries, deputies, negotiators, and intendants, would permit him to set about it. Fatal interval of inactivity !

The corporal was for beginning the demolition, by making a breach in the ramparts, or main fortifications of the town.—No, that will never do, corporal, said my uncle Toby, for in going that way to work with the town, the English garrison will not be safe in it an hour ; because if the French are treacherous

—They are as treacherous as devils, an' please your honour, said the corporal—It gives me concern always when I hear it, Trim, said my uncle Toby—for they don't want personal bravery ; and if a breach is made in the ramparts, they may enter it, and make themselves masters of the place when they please.—Let them enter it, said the corporal, lifting up his pioneer's spade in both his hands, as if he was going to lay about him with it—let them enter, an'please your honour, if they dare.—In cases like this, corporal, said my uncle Toby, slipping his right hand down to the middle of his cane, and holding it afterwards truncheon-wise, with his forefinger extended—'tis no part of the consideration of a commandant what the enemy dare, or what they dare not do ; he must act with prudence. We will begin with the outworks both towards the sea and the land, and particularly with Fort Louis, the most distant of them all, and demolish it first—and the rest, one by one, both on our right and left, as we retreat towards the town ; then we'll demolish the mole—next fill up the harbour, then retire into the citadel, and blow it up into the air ; and, having done that, corporal, we'll embark for England. We are there, quoth the corporal, recollecting himself. Very true, said my uncle Toby— looking at the church.

A delusive, delicious consultation or two of this kind, betwixt my uncle Toby and Trim, upon the demolition of Dunkirk—for a moment rallied back the ideas of those pleasures which were slipping from under him : still—still all went on heavily—the magic left the mind the weaker—Stillness, with Silence at her back, entered the solitary parlour, and drew their gauzy mantle over my uncle Toby's head ; and Listlessness, with her lax fibre and undirected eye, sat quietly down beside him in his arm-chair. No longer Amberg, and Rhinberg, and Limbourg, and Huy, and Bonn, in one year—and the prospect of Landen, and

Trerebach, and Drusen, and Dendermond, the next—
hurried on the blood : no longer did saps, and mines,
and blinds, and gabions, and palisadoes, keep out
this fair enemy of man's repose—No more could my
uncle Toby, after passing the French lines, as he eat
his egg at supper, from thence break into the heart of
France—cross over the Oyes, and with all Picardy
open behind him, march up to the gates of Paris, and
fall asleep with nothing but ideas of glory :—no more
was he to dream, he had fixed the royal standard upon
the tower of the Bastille, and awake with it stream-
ing in his head.

Softer visions—gentler vibrations stole sweetly in
upon his slumbers ; the trumpet of war fell out of
his hands—he took up the lute, sweet instrument ! of
all others the most delicate ! the most difficult !—how
wilt thou touch it, my dear uncle Toby !

CHAPTER XI.

THE WIDOW WADMAN.

S Susannah was informed by an express from Mrs. Bridget, of my uncle Toby's falling in love with her mistress fifteen days before it happened—the contents of which express Susannah communicated to my mother the next day —it has just given me an opportunity of entering upon my uncle Toby's amours a fortnight before their existence.

I have an article of news to tell you, Mr. Shandy, quoth my mother, which will surprise you greatly.

Now my father was then holding one of his second beds of justice, and was musing within himself about the hardships of matrimony, as my mother broke silence.

—My brother Toby, quoth she, is going to be married to Mrs. Wadman.

—Then he will never, quoth my father, be able to lie diagonally in his bed again as long as he lives.

It was a consuming vexation to my father, that my mother never asked the meaning of a thing she did not understand.

—That she is not a woman of science, my father would say—is her misfortune—but she might ask a question.

My mother never did. In short, she went out of the

world at last without knowing whether it turned round, or stood still. My father had officiously told her above a thousand times which way it was — but she always forgot.

For these reasons a discourse seldom went on much further betwixt them, than a proposition—a reply—and a rejoinder; at the end of which, it generally took breath for a few minutes (as in the affair of the breeches) and then went on again.

If he marries, 'twill be the worse for us, quoth my mother.

Not a cherrystone, said my father—he may as well batter away his means upon that, as anything else.

To be sure, said my mother : so here ended the proposition, the reply, and the rejoinder, I told you of.

Though the corporal had been as good as his word in putting my uncle Toby's great ramallie-wig into pipes, yet the time was too short to produce any great effects from it : it had lain many years squeezed up in the corner of his old campaign trunk ; and as bad forms are not so easy to be got the better of, and the use of candle-ends not so well understood, it was not so pliable a business as one would have wished. The corporal, with cheery eye and both arms extended, had fallen back perpendicular from it a score times, to inspire it, if possible, with a better air—had spleen given a look at it, 'twould have cost her ladyship a smile—it curled everywhere but where the corporal would have it ; and where a buckle or two, in his opinion, would have done it honour, he could as soon have raised the dead.

Such it was, or rather such would it have seemed upon any other brow ; but the sweet look of goodness which sat upon my uncle Toby's, assimilated everything around it so sovereignly to itself, and nature had moreover wrote Gentleman with so fair a hand in every line of his countenance, that even his tarnished gold-laced hat and huge cockade of flimsy taffeta became him; and though not worth a button in themselves, yet the moment my uncle Toby put them on, they became serious objects, and altogether seemed to have been picked up by the hand of science to set him off to advantage.

Nothing in this world could have co-operated more powerfully towards this, than my uncle Toby's blue and gold—had not Quantity in some measure been necessary to Grace; in a period of fifteen or sixteen years since they had been made, by a total inactivity in my uncle Toby's life—for he seldom went further than the bowling-green—his blue and gold had become so miserably too straight for him, that it was with the utmost difficulty the corporal was able to get him into them; the taking them up at the sleeves, was of no advantage. They were laced however down the back, and at the seams of the sides, &c., in the mode of King William's reign; and to shorten all description, they shone so bright against the sun that morning, and had so metallic, and doughty an air with them, that had my uncle Toby thought of attacking in armour, nothing could have so well imposed upon his imagination.

As for the thin scarlet breeches, they had been unripped by the tailor between the legs, and left at sixes and sevens.—

It is enough they were held impracticable the night before, and as there was no alternative in my uncle Toby's wardrobe, he sallied forth in the red plush.

The corporal had arrayed himself in poor Le Fever's regimental coat; and with his hair tucked up under his Montero cap, which he had furbished up for the occasion, marched three paces distance from his master: a whiff of military pride had puffed out his shirt at the wrist; and upon that in a black leather thong clipped into a tassel beyond the knot, hung the corporal's stick—My uncle Toby carried his cane like a pike.

It looks well at least; quoth my father to himself.

My uncle Toby turned his head more than once behind him, to see how he was supported by the corporal: and the corporal as oft as he did it, gave a slight flourish with his stick—but not vapouringly; and with the sweetest accent of most respectful encouragement, bid his honour "never fear."

Now my uncle Toby did fear; and grievously too: and was never altogether at his ease near any one of the sex, unless in sorrow or distress; then infinite was his pity; nor would the most courteous knight of romance have gone any further, at least upon one leg, to have wiped away a tear from a woman's eye; and yet excepting once that he was beguiled into it by Mrs. Wadman, he had never looked stedfastly into one.

She cannot, quoth my uncle Toby, halting, when they had marched up to within twenty paces of Mrs. Wadman's door—she cannot, corporal, take it amiss.

—She will take it, an' please your honour, said the corporal, just as the Jew's widow at Lisbon took it of my brother Tom.

And how was that? quoth my uncle Toby, facing quite about to the corporal.

Your honour, replied the corporal, knows of Tom's misfortunes; but this affair has nothing to do with them any further than this, that if Tom had not married the widow—or had it pleased God after their marriage, that they had but put pork into their sausages, the honest soul had never been taken out of his warm bed, and dragged to the inquisition,—'Tis a cursed place, added the corporal, shaking his head,—when once a poor creature is in, he is in, an' please your honour, for ever.

'Tis very true; said my uncle Toby, looking gravely at Mrs. Wadman's house, as he spoke.

Nothing, continued the corporal, can be so sad as confinement for life, or so sweet, an' please your honour, as liberty.

Nothing, Trim, said my uncle Toby, musing.

Whilst a man is free—cried the corporal, giving a flourish with his stick.—

A thousand of my father's most subtle syllogisms could not have said more for celibacy.

My uncle Toby looked earnestly towards his cottage and his bowling-green.

The corporal had unwarily conjured up the spirit of calculation with his wand : and he had nothing to do, but to conjure him down again with his story, and in this form of exorcism, most unecclesiastically did the corporal do it.

As Tom's place, an' please your honour, was easy, and the weather warm, it put him upon thinking seriously of settling himself in the world ; and as it fell out about that time, that a Jew who kept a sausage-shop in the same street, had the ill luck to die of a strangury, and leave his widow in possession of a rousing trade, Tom thought (as everybody in Lisbon was doing the best he could devise for himself) there could be no harm in offering her his service to carry it on : so without any introduction to the widow, except that of buying a pound of sausages at her shop, Tom set out, counting the matter thus within himself, as he walked along ; that let the worst come of it that could, he should at least get a pound of sausages for their worth—but, if things went well, he should be set up; inasmuch as he should get not only a pound of sausages, but a wife, and a sausage-shop, an' please your honour, into the bargain.

Every servant in the family, from high to low, wished Tom success ; and I can fancy, an' please your honour, I see him this moment with his white dimity waistcoat and breeches, and hat a little o' one side, passing jollily along the street swinging his stick, with a smile and a cheerful word for everybody he met :— But alas ! Tom ! thou smilest no more, cried the corporal, looking on one side of him upon the ground, as if he apostrophised him in his dungeon.

Poor fellow ! said my uncle Toby, feelingly.

He was an honest, light-hearted lad, an' please your honour, as ever blood warmed.—

Then he resembled thee, Trim, said my uncle Toby, rapidly.

The corporal blushed down to his fingers' ends—a tear of sentimental bashfulness—another of gratitude to my uncle Toby, and a tear of sorrow for his brother's misfortunes, started into his eye and ran sweetly down his cheek together ; my uncle Toby's kindled as one lamp does at another ; and taking hold of the breast of Trim's coat (which had been that of Le Fever's) as if to ease his lame leg, but in reality to gratify a finer feeling, he stood silent for a minute and a half ; at the end of which he took his hand away, and the corporal making a bow, went on with his story of his brother and the Jew's widow.

When Tom, an' please your honour, got to the shop, there was nobody in it, but a poor negro girl, with a bunch of white feathers slightly tied to the end of a long cane, flapping away flies, not killing them.—'Tis a pretty picture ! said my uncle Toby—she had suffered persecution, Trim, and had learnt mercy.

She was good, an' please your honour, from nature as well as from hardships : and there are circumstances in the story of that poor friendless slut that would melt a heart of stone, said Trim ; and some dismal winter's evening, when your honour is in the humour, they shall be told you with the rest of Tom's story, for it makes a part of it.

Then do not forget, Trim, said my uncle Toby.

A Negro has a soul ? an' please your honour, said the corporal (doubtingly).

I am not much versed, Corporal, quoth my uncle Toby, in things of that kind ; but I suppose, God would not leave him without one, any more than thee or me.

It would be putting one sadly over the head of another, quoth the corporal.

It would so ; said my uncle Toby. Why then, an' please your honour, is a black wench to be used worse than a white one ?

I can give no reason, said my uncle Toby.

Only, cried the corporal, shaking his head, because she has no one to stand up for her.

'Tis that very thing, Trim, quoth my uncle Toby, which recommends her to protection, and her brethren with her ; 'tis the fortune of war which has put the whip into our hands now—where it may be hereafter, heaven knows ! but be it where it will, the brave, Trim ! will not use it unkindly.

God forbid, said the corporal.

Amen, responded my uncle Toby, laying his hand upon his heart.

The corporal returned to his story, and went on, but with an embarrassment in doing it, which here and there a reader in this world will not be able to comprehend ; for by the many sudden transitions all along, from one kind and cordial passion to another, in getting thus far on his way, he had lost the sportable key of his voice which gave sense and spirit to his tale : he attempted twice to resume it, but could not please himself ; so giving a stout hem ! to rally back the retreating spirits, and aiding nature at the same time with his left arm a-kimbo on one side, and with his right a little extended, supporting her on the other—the corporal got as near the note as he could ; and in that attitude, continued his story.

As Tom, an' please your honour, had no business at that time with the Moorish girl, he passed on into the room beyond to talk to the Jew's widow about love, and his pound of sausages ; and being, as I have told your honour, an open, cheery hearted lad, with his character wrote in his looks and carriage, he took a chair, and without much apology, but with great civility at the same time, placed it close to her at the table, and sat down.

There is nothing so awkward, as courting a woman, an' please your honour, whilst she is making sausages. So Tom began a discourse upon them ; first gravely, —" as how they were made—with what meats, herbs and spices " and so on—taking care only as he went along, to season what he had to say upon sausages, rather under, than over.

It was owing to the neglect of that very precaution, said my uncle Toby, laying his hand upon Trim's shoulder, that Count de la Motte lost the battle of Wynendale : he pressed too speedily into the wood ; which if he had not done, Lisle had not fallen into our hands, nor Ghent and Bruges, which both followed her example ; it was so late in the year, continued my uncle Toby, and so terrible a season came on, that if things had not fallen out as they did, our troops must have perished in the open field.

Why, therefore, may not battles, an' please your honour, as well as marriages, be made in heaven? My uncle Toby mused.

Religion inclined him to say one thing, and his high idea of military skill tempted him to say another ; so not being able to frame a reply exactly to his mind, my uncle Toby said nothing at all ; and the corporal finished his story.

As Tom perceived, an' please your honour, that he gained ground, and all that he had said upon the subject of sausages was kindly taken, he went on to help her a little in making them, first by cutting strings into proper lengths, and holding them in his hand, whilst she took them out one by one ; then by putting them across her mouth that she might take them out as she wanted them—and so on from little to more.— Now a widow, an' please your honour, always chooses

a second husband as unlike the first as she can : so
the affair was more than half settled in her mind
before Tom mentioned it.—O Sir ! the story will make
your heart bleed,—as it has made mine a thousand
times ; but it is too long to be told now ;—your
honour shall hear it from first to last some day when
I am working beside you in our fortifications ;—but
the short of the story is this :—when he married the
Jew's widow, who kept the small shop, somehow or
other it was the cause of his being taken in the
middle of the night out of his bed, where he was
lying with his wife and two small children, and
carried directly to the Inquisition, where, God help
him, continued Trim, fetching a sigh from the bottom
of his heart,—the poor honest lad lies confined at this
hour ;—he was as honest a soul, added Trim (pulling
out his handkerchief), as ever blood warmed.—

—The tears trickled down Trim's cheeks faster
than he could well wipe them away.—A dead silence
ensued for some minutes.—Certain proof of pity !

All womankind, continued Trim (commenting upon
his story,) from the highest to the lowest, an' please
your honour, love jokes ; the difficulty is to know
how they choose to have them cut ; and there is no
knowing that, but by trying as we do with our
artillery in the field.

I like the comparison, said my uncle Toby.

Because your honour, quoth the corporal, loves
glory more than pleasure.

I hope, Trim, answered my uncle Toby, I love
mankind more than either ; and as the knowledge of
arms tends so apparently to the good and quiet of
the world, and particularly that branch of it which we
have practised together in our bowling-green, has no
object but to shorten the strides of ambition, and
intrench the lives and fortunes of the few, from the
plunderings of the many—whenever that drum beats
in our ears, I trust, corporal, we shall neither of us

want so much humanity and fellow-feeling as to face about and march.

In pronouncing this, my uncle Toby faced about and marched firmly as at the head of his company—and the faithful corporal shouldering his stick, and striking his hand upon his coat-skirt as he took his first step, marched close behind him down the avenue.

Now what can their two noddles be about? cried my father to my mother—My mother had gone with her left arm twisted in my father's right, till they had got to the angle of the old garden wall; as this was directly opposite to the front of Mrs. Wadman's house, when my father came to it, he gave a look across; and seeing my uncle Toby and the corporal within ten paces of the door, he turned about—"Let us just stop a moment," quoth my father, "and see with what ceremonies my brother Toby and his man Trim make their first entry—it will not detain us," added my father, "a single minute:"—No matter, if it be ten minutes, quoth my mother.

It will not detain us half a one; said my father.

The corporal was just then setting in with the story of his brother Tom and the Jew's widow: the story went on, and on—it had episodes in it—it came back, and went on,—and on again; there was no end of it.

My father stood it out as well as he could to the end of Trim's story; and from thence to the end of my uncle Toby's panegyric upon arms, in the chapter following it; when seeing that instead of marching up to Mrs. Wadman's door, they both faced about and marched down the avenue diametrically opposite to his expectation, he broke out at once with that little subacid soreness of humour which, in certain situations, distinguished his character from that of all other men.

"Now what can their two noddles be about?" cried my father, &c.

I dare say, said my mother, they are making forti-fications.

Not on Mrs. Wadman's premises ! cried my father, stepping back.

I suppose not : quoth my mother.

I wish, said my father, raising his voice, the whole science of fortification at the devil, with all its trum-pery of saps, mines, blinds, gabions, fausse-brays and cuvetts.—

They are foolish things—said my mother.

Now she had a way, which by the bye, I would this moment give away my purple jerkin, and my yellow slippers into the bargain, if some of your reverences would imitate—and that was never to refuse her assent and consent to any proposition my father laid before her, merely because she did not understand it, or had no ideas to the principal word or term of art, upon which the tenet or proposition rolled. She con-tented herself with doing all that her godfathers and godmothers promised for her, but no more ; and so would go on using a hard word twenty years together, and replying to it too, if it was a verb, in all its moods and tenses, without giving herself any trouble to inquire about it.

This was an eternal source of misery to my father, and broke the neck, at the first setting out, of more dialogues between them, than could have done the most petulant contradiction—the few which survived were the better for the cuvetts—

" They are foolish things ;" said my mother.

Particularly the cuvetts ; replied my father.

'Twas enough—he tasted the sweet of triumph and went on.

Not that they are, properly speaking, Mrs. Wad-man's premises, said my father, partly correcting him-self—because she is but tenant for life.

That makes a great difference—said my mother.

In a fool's head, replied my father.

Unless she should happen to have a child—said my mother.

Though if it comes to that—said my father—Lord have mercy upon them.

Amen : said my mother, *piano.*

Amen : cried my father, *fortissimè.*

Amen: said my mother again—but with such a sighing cadence of personal pity at the end of it, as discomfited every fibre about my father—he instantly took out his almanack ; but before he could untie it, Yorick's congregation coming out of church, became a full answer to one half of his business with it—and my mother telling him it was a sacrament day, left him as little in doubt, as to the other part—he put his almanac into his pocket.

When my uncle Toby and the corporal had marched down to the bottom of the avenue, they recollected their business lay the other way ; so they faced about and marched up straight to Mrs. Wadman's door.

I warrant your honour ; said the corporal, touching his Montero-cap, with his hand, as he passed him in order to give a knock at the door—My uncle Toby, contrary to his invariable way of treating his faithful servant, said nothing good or bad : the truth was, he had not altogether marshalled his ideas ; he wished for another conference, and as the corporal was mounting up the three steps before the door, he hemmed twice— a portion of my uncle Toby's most modest spirits fled, at each expulsion, towards the corporal ; he stood with the rapper of the door suspended for a full minute in his hand, he scarce knew why. Bridget stood perdue within, with her finger and her thumb upon the latch, benumbed with expectation ; and Mrs. Wadman, with an eye ready to be deflowered again, sat breathless behind the window-curtain of her bedchamber, watching their approach.

Trim ! said my uncle Toby—but as he articulated the word, the minute expired, and Trim let fall the rapper.

11

My unclè Toby perceiving that all hopes of a conference were knocked on the head by it,—whistled Lillabullero.

As Mrs. Bridget opened the door before the corporal had well given the rap, the interval betwixt that and my uncle Toby's introduction into the parlour, was so short, that Mrs. Wadman had but just time to get from behind the curtain, lay a bible upon the table, and advance a step or two towards the door to receive him.

My uncle Toby saluted Mrs. Wadman, after the manner in which women were saluted by men in the year of our Lord God one thousand seven hundred and thirteen—then facing about, he marched up abreast with her to the sofa, and in three plain words —though not before he was sat down—nor after he was sat down—but as he was sitting down, told her, "he was in love"—so that my uncle Toby strained himself more in the declaration than he needed.

Mrs. Wadman naturally looked down—she had been darning her apron—in expectation every moment, that my uncle Toby would go on ; but having no talents for amplification, and love moreover of all others being a subject of which he was the least a master, when he had told Mrs. Wadman once that he loved her, he let it alone, and left the matter to work after its own way.

My father was always in raptures with this system of my uncle Toby's, as he falsely called it, and would often say, that could his brother Toby to his process have added but a pipe of tobacco—he had wherewithal to have found his way, if there was faith in a Spanish proverb, towards the hearts of half the women upon the globe.

My uncle Toby never understood what my father meant ; nor will I presume to extract more from it, than a condemnation of an error which the bulk of the world lie under—but the French, every one of 'em to a man, who believe in it. "That talking of love, is making it."

Let us go on : Mrs. Wadman sat in expectation my uncle Toby would do so, to almost the first pulsation of that minute, wherein silence on one side or the other, generally becomes indecent : so edging herself a little more towards him, and raising up her eyes, sub-blushing, as she did it, she took up the gauntlet, or the discourse (if you like it better) and communed with my uncle Toby, thus.

The cares and disquietudes of the marriage state, quoth Mrs. Wadman, are very great, I suppose so— said my uncle Toby : and therefore when a person, continued Mrs. Wadman, is so much at his case as you are, so happy, Captain Shandy, in yourself, your friends and your amusements—I wonder, what reasons can incline you to the state.

—They are written, quoth my uncle Toby, in the Common Prayer Book.

Thus far my uncle Toby went on warily, and kept within his depth, leaving Mrs. Wadman to sail upon the gulf as she pleased.

As for children—said Mrs. Wadman—though a principal end perhaps of the institution, and the natural wish, I suppose, of every parent, yet do not we all find, they are certain sorrows, and very uncertain comforts ? and what is there, dear sir, to pay one for the heartaches—what compensation for the many tender and disquieting apprehensions of a suffering and defenceless mother who brings them into life ? I declare, said my uncle Toby, smit with pity, I know of none ; unless it be that it has pleased God—Feeling within himself that he had somehow or other got beyond his depth, he stopped short ; and without entering further either into the pains or pleasures of matrimony, he laid his hand upon his heart, and

11—2

made an offer to take them as they were, and share
them along with her.

When my uncle Toby had said this, he did not care
to say it again ; so casting his eye upon the bible which
Mrs. Wadman had laid upon the table, he took it up ;
and popping, dear soul ! upon a passage in it, of all
others the most interesting to him—which was the
siege of Jericho—he set himself to read it over,
leaving his proposal of marriage, as he had done his
declaration of love, to work with her after its own
way.—But there is an accent of humanity—how shall
I describe it ?—So tenderly spoke to, and so directed
towards my uncle Toby's heart, that every item sank
ten times deeper into it than the evils themselves—
but when Mrs. Wadman went round about by
Namut ; and engaged him to attack the point of the
advanced Counterscarp, and *pêle mêle* with the Dutch
to take the counterguard of St. Roch sword in hand,
and then with tender notes playing upon his ear, led
him all bleeding by the hand out of the trench, wiping
her eye, as he was carried to his tent—Heaven ! earth !
sea ! all was lifted up—the springs of nature rose
above their levels—an angel of mercy sat beside him
on the sofa—his heart glowed with fire—and had he
been worth a thousand, he had lost every heart of
them to Mrs. Wadman.

My uncle Toby and the corporal had gone on separ-
ately with their operations the greatest part of the
campaign, and as effectually cut off from all communication of what either the one or the other had
been doing, as if they had been separated from each
other by the Maes or the Sambre.

My uncle Toby, on his side, had presented himself
every afternoon in his red and silver, and blue and
gold alternately, and sustained an infinity of attacks
in them, without knowing them to be attacks, and so
had nothing to communicate.

The corporal, on his side, in taking Bridget, by it

had gained considerable advantages, and consequently had much to communicate—Best of honest and gallant servants !

Now my uncle Toby had one evening laid down his pipe upon the table, and was counting over to himself upon his finger ends (beginning at his thumb), all Mrs. Wadman's perfections one by one ; and happening two or three times together, either by omitting some, or counting others twice over to puzzle himself sadly before he could get beyond his middle finger.— Prithee, Trim ! said he, taking up his pipe again.— bring me a pen and ink : Trim brought paper also.

Take a full sheet, Trim ! said my uncle Toby, making a sign with his pipe at the same time to take a chair and sit down close by him at the table. The corporal obeyed, placed the paper directly before him, took a pen and dipped it in the ink.

She has a thousand virtues, Trim ! said my uncle Toby.

Am I to set them down, an' please your honour ? quoth the corporal.

But they must be taken in their ranks, replied my uncle Toby ; for of them all, Trim, that which wins me most, and which is a security for all the rest, is the compassionate turn and singular humanity of her character.

The corporal dipped the pen a second time into the inkhorn ; and my uncle Toby, pointing with the end of his pipe as close to the top of the sheet, at the left hand corner of it, as he could get it, the corporal wrote down the word Humanity...thus.

I wish my uncle Toby had been a water-drinker ; for then the thing had been accounted for, that the first moment widow Wadman saw him, she felt something stirring within her in his favour. My uncle Toby's head at that time was full of other matters, so that it was not till the demolition of Dunkirk, when all the other civilities of Europe were settled, that he found leisure to return this.

This made an armistice (that is speaking with regard to my uncle Toby—but with respect to Mrs. Wadman, a vacancy) of almost eleven years. But in all cases of this nature, as it is the second blow, happen at what distance of time it will, which makes the fray, I choose for that reason to call these the amours of my uncle Toby with Mrs. Wadman, rather than the amours of Mrs. Wadman with my uncle Toby. Now, as widow Wadman did love my uncle Toby, and my uncle Toby did not love widow Wadman, there was nothing for widow Wadman to do, but to go on and love my uncle Toby, or let it alone.

Widow Wadman would do neither the one nor the other.

The fates, who certainly all foreknew of these amours of widow Wadman and my uncle Toby, had, from the first creation of matter and motion (and with more courtesy than they usually do things of this kind) established such a chain of causes and effects hanging so fast to one another, that it was scarce possible for my uncle Toby to have dwelt in any other house in the world, or to have occupied any other garden in Christendom, but the very house and garden which joined and laid parallel to Mrs. Wadman's ; this, with the advantage of a thickset arbour in Mrs. Wadman's garden, but planted in the hedge-row of my uncle Toby's, put all the occasions into her hands which love-militancy wanted ; she could observe my uncle Toby's motions, and was mistress likewise of his councils of war ; and as his unsuspecting heart had given leave to the corporal, through the mediation of Bridget, to make her a wicker gate of communication to enlarge her walks, it enabled her to carry on her approaches to the very door of the sentry-box ; and sometimes out of gratitude, to make an attack, and endeavour to blow my uncle Toby up in the very sentry-box itself.

Now, through all the lumber-rooms of military furniture, including both of horse and foot, from the great arsenal of Venice to the Tower of London (exclusive) if Mrs. Wadman had been rummaging for seven years together, and with Bridget to help her, she could not have found any one blind or mantelet so fit for her purpose, as that which the expediency of my uncle Toby's affairs had fixed up ready to her hands.

I believe I have not told you—but I don't know—possibly I have—be it as it will, 'tis one of the number of those many things, which a man had better do over again, than dispute about it—that whatever town or fortress the corporal was at work upon, during the course of their campaign, my uncle Toby always took care on the inside of his sentry-box, which was towards his left hand, to have a plan of the place, fastened up with two or three pins at the top, but loose at the bottom, for the conveniency of holding it up to the eye, &c.......as occasions required ; so that when an attack was resolved upon, Mrs. Wadman had nothing more to do, when she had got advanced to the door of the sentry-box, but to extend her right hand ; and edging in her left foot at the same movement, to take hold of the map or plan, or upright, or whatever it was, and with outstretched neck meeting it halfway, to advance it towards her ; on which my uncle Toby's passions were sure to catch fire, for he would instantly take hold of the other corner of the map in his left hand, and with the end of his pipe, in the other, begin an explanation.

When the attack was advanced to this point, the world will naturally enter into the reasons of Mrs. Wadman's next stroke of generalship, which was, to take my uncle Toby's tobacco-pipe out of his hand as soon as she possibly could ; which, under one pre-

tence or other, but generally that of pointing more
distinctly at some redoubt or breast-work in the map,
she would effect before my uncle Toby (poor soul!)
had well marched above half-a-dozen toises with it.

This, though slight skirmishing, and at a distance
from the main body, yet drew on the rest; for here,
the map usually falling with the back of it, close to
the side of the sentry-box, my uncle Toby, in the
simplicity of his soul, would lay his hand flat upon
it, in order to go on with his explanation; and Mrs.
Wadman, by a manœuvre as quick as thought, would
as certainly place hers close beside it; this at once
opened a communication, large enough for any sentiment to pass or repass, which a person skilled in the
elementary and practical part of love-making, has
occasion for—

By bringing up her forefinger parallel (as before)
to my uncle Toby's, it unavoidably brought the whole
hand. Thine, dear uncle Toby! was never now in
its right place—Mrs. Wadman had it ever to take up,
or, with the gentlest pushings and compressions, that
a hand to be removed is capable of receiving, to
get it pressed a hair breadth of one side out of her
way.

So that my uncle Toby being thus attacked and
sore pushed on both his wings, was it a wonder, if
now and then, it put his centre into disorder?

The deuce take it! said my uncle Toby.—

I think, an' please your honour, quoth Trim, the
fortifications are quite destroyed—and the bason is
upon a level with the mole—I think so too; replied
my uncle Toby with a sigh half suppressed—but step
into the parlour, Trim, for the stipulation, it lies upon
the table.

It has lain there, these six weeks, replied the corporal, till this very morning that the old woman kindled the fire with it.

Then, said my uncle Toby, there is no further

occasion for our services. The more, an' please your honour, the pity, said the corporal ; in uttering which he cast his spade into the wheelbarrow, which was beside him, with an air the most expressive of disconsolation that can be imagined, and was heavily turning about to look for his pickaxe, his pioneer's shovel, his pickets, and other little military stores, in order to carry them off the field—when a heigh ho! from the sentry-box, which, being made of thin slit deal, reverberated the sound more sorrowfully to his ear, forbad him.

No ; said the corporal to himself, I'll do it before his honour rises to-morrow morning ; so taking his spade out of the wheelbarrow again, with a little earth in it, as if to level something at the foot of the glacis, but with a real intent to approach nearer to his master, in order to divert him, he loosened a sod or two, pared their edges with his spade, and having given them a gentle blow or two with the back of it, he sat himself down close by my uncle Toby's feet, and began as follows.

It was a thousand pities, though I believe, an' please your honour, I am going to say but a foolish kind of a thing for a soldier— '

A soldier, cried my uncle Toby, interrupting the corporal, is no more exempt from saying a foolish thing, Trim, than a man of letters.—But not so often ; an' please your honour, replied the corporal.—My uncle Toby gave a nod.

It was a thousand pities then, said the corporal, casting his eye upon Dunkirk, and the mole, as Servius Sulpicius, in returning out of Asia (when he sailed from Ægina towards Megara) did upon Corinth and Pyreus—

" It was a thousand pities, an' please your honour, to destroy these works— and a thousand pities to have let them stood."

Thou art right, Trim, in both cases : said my uncle

Toby.—This, continued the corporal, is the reason, that from the beginning of their demolition to the end, I have never once whistled, or sung, or laughed, or cried, or talked of passed done deeds, or told your honour one story good or bad.

Thou hast many excellences, Trim, said my uncle Toby, and I hold it not the least of them, as thou happenest to be a story-teller, that of the number thou hast told me, either to amuse me in my painful hours, or divert me in my grave ones, thou hast seldom told me a bad one.

Because, an' please your honour, except one of a King of Bohemia and his seven castles,—they are all true ; for they are about myself.

I do not like the subject the worse, Trim, said my uncle Toby, on that score ; but prithee what is this story? thou hast excited my curiosity.

I'll tell it your honour, quoth the corporal directly —Provided, said my uncle Toby, looking earnestly towards Dunkirk and the mole again—provided it is not a merry one ; to such, Trim, a man should ever bring one half of the entertainment along with him ; and the disposition I am in at present would wrong both thee, Trim, and thy story.—It is not a merry one by any means, replied the corporal.—Nor would I have it altogether a grave one, added my uncle Toby. —It is neither the one nor the other, replied the corporal, but will suit your honour exactly.—Then I'll thank thee for it with all my heart, cried my uncle Toby, so prithee begin it, Trim.

The Story of the King of Bohemia and his Seven Castles.

There was a certain king of Bo—he——

As the corporal was entering the confines of Bohemia, my uncle Toby obliged him to halt for a single moment; he had set out bare-headed, having since he pulled off

his Montero cap in the latter end of the last chapter,
left it lying beside him on the ground.

The eye of goodness espieth all things — so that
before the corporal had well got through the first five
words of his story, had my uncle Toby twice touched
his Montero cap with the end of his cane, interrogatively, as much as to say, why don't you put it on,
Trim? Trim took it up with the most respectful
slowness, and casting a glance of humiliation as he
did it, upon the embroidery of the forepart, which
being dismally tarnished and frayed moreover in some
of the principal leaves and boldest parts of the pattern,
he laid it down again betwixt his two feet, in order
to moralize upon the subject.

'Tis every word of it but too true, cried my uncle
Toby, that thou art about to observe—

"Nothing in this world, Trim, is made to last for
ever."

But when tokens, dear Tom, of thy love and remem-
brance wear out, said Trim, what shall we say?

There is no occasion, Trim, quoth my uncle Toby,
to say anything else; and was a man to puzzle his
brains till doomsday, I believe, Trim, it would be
impossible.

The corporal perceiving my uncle Toby was in the
right, and that it would be in vain for the wit of man
to think of extracting a purer moral from his cap,
without further attempting it, he put it on; and
passing his hand across his forehead to rub out a
pensive wrinkle, which the text and the doctrine
between them had engendered, he returned, with the
same look and tone of voice, to his story of the king
of Bohemia and his seven castles.

There was a certain king of Bohemia, but in whose
reign, except his own, I am not able to inform your
honour.—

I do not desire it of thee, Trim, by any means, cried
my uncle Toby.

It was a little before the time, an' please your honour, when giants were beginning to leave off breeding; but in what year of our Lord that was,—

I would not give a halfpenny to know, said my uncle Toby.

Only, an' please your honour, it makes a story look the better in the face.

'Tis thy own, Trim, so ornament it after thy own fashion; and take any date, continued my uncle Toby, looking pleasantly upon him — take any date in the whole world thou choosest, and put it to — thou art heartily welcome.

The corporal bowed.

In the year of our Lord, one thousand seven hundred and twelve, there was, an' please your honour—

—To tell thee truly, Trim, quoth my uncle Toby, any other date would have pleased me much better, not only on account of the sad stain upon our history that year, in marching off our troops, and refusing to cover the siege of Quesnoi, though Fagel was carrying on the works with such incredible vigour—but likewise on the score, Trim, of thy own story; because if there are—and which, from what thou hast dropped I partly suspect to be the fact—if there are giants in it—

There is but one, an' please your honour.

'Tis as bad as twenty, replied my uncle Toby—thou should'st have carried him back some seven or eight hundred years out of harm's way, both of critics and other people; and therefore I would advise thee, if ever thou tellest it again—

If I live, an' please your honour, but once to get through it, I will never tell it again, quoth Trim, either to man, woman, or child—Poo, poo! said my uncle Toby, but with accents of such sweet encouragement did he utter it, that the corporal went on with his story with more alacrity than ever.

There was, an' please your honour, said the corporal,

raising his voice and rubbing the palms of his two hands cheerily together as he began, a certain king of Bohemia—

Leave out the date entirely, Trim, quoth my uncle Toby, leaning forwards, and laying his hand gently upon the corporal's shoulder to temper the interruption —leave it out entirely, Trim ; a story passes very well without these niceties, unless one is pretty sure of 'em—Sure of 'em! said the corporal, shaking his head.

Right ; answered my uncle Toby, it is not easy, Trim, for one, bred up as thou and I have been to arms, who seldom looks further forward than to the end of his musket, or backwards beyond his knapsack, to know much about this matter.—God bless your honour! said the corporal, won by the manner of my uncle Toby's reasoning, as much as by the reasoning itself, he has something else to do ; if not on action, or a march, or upon duty in his garrison, he has his firelock, an' please your honour, to furbish, his accoutrements to take care of, his regimentals to mend, himself to shave and keep clean, so as to appear always like what he is upon the parade ; what business, added the corporal triumphantly, has a soldier, an' please your honour, to know anything at all of geography.

—Thou would'st have said chronology, Trim, said my uncle Toby ; for as for geography, 'tis of absolute use to him ; he must be acquainted intimately with every country and its boundaries where his profession carries him ; he should know every town and city, and village and hamlet, with the canals, the roads, and hollow ways which lead up to them ; there is not a river or a rivulet he passes, Trim, but he should be able at first sight to tell thee what is its name—in what mountain it takes its rise—what is its course—how far it is navigable— where fordable—where not ; he should know the fertility of every valley, as well as the hind who ploughs it ; and be able to describe, or if it is required, to give thee an exact map of all the plains and defiles, the forts, the acclivities, the woods and morasses, through and by which his army is to march.

Is it else to be conceived, corporal, continued my uncle Toby, rising up in his sentry-box, as he began to warm in this part of his discourse, how Marlborough could have marched his army from the banks of the Maes to Belburg ; from Belburg to Kerpenord—(here the corporal could sit no longer) from Kerpenord, Trim, to Kalsaken ; from Kalsaken to Newdorf ; from Newdorf to Landenbourg : from Landenbourg to Mildenheim ; from Mildenheim to Elchingen ; from Elchingen to Gingen ; from Gingen to Balmerchoffen ; from Balmerchoffen to Skellenburg, where he broke in upon the enemy's works ; forced his passage over the Danube ; crossed the Lech—pushed on his troops into the heart of the empire, marching at the head of them through Friburg, Hokenwert, and Schonevelt, to the plains of Blenheim and Hochstet ?—Great as he was, corporal, he could not have advanced a step or made one single day's march without the aid of geography. As for chronology, I own, Trim, continued my uncle Toby, sitting down again coolly in his sentry-box, that of all others, it seems a science which the soldier might best spare, was it not for the lights which that science must one day give him, in determining the invention of powder ? and the Chinese, added my uncle Toby, embarrass us, and all accounts of it, still more, by boasting of the invention some hundreds of years even before him.

They are a pack of liars, I believe, cried Trim.

They are somehow or other deceived, said my uncle Toby, in this matter, as is plain to me from the present miserable state of military architecture amongst them ; which consists of nothing more than a fosse with a brick wall without flanks—and for what they give us as a bastion at each angle of it, 'tis so barbarously constructed, that it looks for all the world—Like one of my seven castles, an' please your honour, quoth Trim.

My uncle Toby, though in the utmost distress for a comparison, most courteously refused Trim's offer, till Trim telling him, he had half-a-dozen more in Bohemia, which he knew not how to get off his hands, my uncle Toby was so touched with the pleasantry of heart of the corporal, that he discontinued his dissertation upon gunpowder, and begged the corporal forthwith to go on with his story of the King of Bohemia and his seven castles.

This unfortunate King of Bohemia, said Trim—Was he unfortunate then? cried my uncle Toby, for he had been so wrapped up in his dissertation upon gunpowder and other military affairs, that though he had desired the corporal to go on, yet the many interruptions he had given, dwelt not so strong upon his fancy, as to account for the epithet—Was he unfortunate then, Trim? said my uncle Toby, pathetically— The corporal, wishing first the word and all its synonimas at the devil, forthwith began to run back in his mind the principal events in the King of Bohemia's story; from every one of which, it appearing that he was the most fortunate man that ever existed in the world—it put the corporal to a stand: for not caring to retract his epithet, and less to explain it, and least of all, to twist his tale (like men of lore) to serve a system, he looked up in my uncle Toby's face for assistance—but seeing it was the very thing, my uncle Toby sat in expectation of himself, after a hum and a haw, he went on—

The King of Bohemia, an' please your honour, replied the corporal, was unfortunate, as thus—that taking great pleasure and delight in navigation and all sort of sea affairs, and there happening throughout the whole kingdom of Bohemia, to be no seaport town whatever—

How the deuce should there, Trim? cried my uncle Toby; for Bohemia being totally inland, it could have happened no otherwise—It might; said Trim, if it had pleased God.

My uncle Toby never spoke of the being and natural attributes of God, but with diffidence and hesitation.

I believe not, replied my uncle Toby, after some pause—for being inland, as I said, and having Silesia and Moravia to the east ; Lusatia and Upper Saxony to the north ; Franconia to the west ; and Bavaria to the south : Bohemia could not have been propelled to the sea without ceasing to be Bohemia—nor could the sea, on the other hand, have come up to Bohemia, without overflowing a great part of Germany, and destroying millions of unfortunate inhabitants who could make no defence against it—Scandalous ! cried Trim—Which would bespeak, added my uncle Toby, mildly, such a want of compassion in him who is the father of it, that, I think, Trim, the thing could have happened no way.

The corporal made a bow of unfeigned conviction ; and went on.

Now the King of Bohemia with his queen and courtiers happening one fine summer's evening to walk out—Aye ! there the word happening is right, Trim, cried my uncle Toby ; for the King of Bohemia and his queen might have walked out, or let it alone ; 'twas a matter of contingency, which might happen, or not, just as chance ordered it.

King William was of opinion, an' please your honour, quoth Trim, that everything was predestined for us in this world ; insomuch that he would often say to his soldiers, that "every ball had its billet." He was a great man, said my uncle Toby—And I believe, continued Trim, to this day, that the shot which disabled me at the battle of Landen, was pointed at my knee for no other purpose, but to take me out of his service, and place me in your honour's, where I should be taken so much better care of in my old age—It shall never, Trim, be construed otherwise, said my uncle Toby.

The heart, both of the master and the man, were alike subject to sudden overflowings ;—a short silence ensued.

Besides, said the corporal, resuming the discourse, but in a gayer accent—if it had not been for that single shot, I had never, an' please your honour, been in love. So, thou wast once in love, Trim ! said my uncle Toby, smiling.

Souse ! replied the corporal—over head and ears, an' please your honour. Prithee when ? where ? and how came it to pass ? I never heard one word of it before, quoth my uncle Toby : I daresay, answered Trim, that every drummer and serjeant's son in the regiment knew of it.—It's high time I should—said my uncle Toby.

Your honour remembers with concern, said the corporal, the total rout and confusion of our camp and army at the affair of Landen ; everyone was left to shift for himself ; and if it had not been for the regiments of Wyndham, Lumley, and Galway, which covered the retreat over the bridge of Neerspecken, the king himself could scarce have gained it—he was pressed hard, as your honour knows, on every side of him.

Gallant mortal ! cried my uncle Toby, caught up with enthusiasm—this moment, now that all is lost, I see him galloping across me, corporal, to the left, to bring up the remains of the English horse along with him to support the right, and tear the laurel from Luxembourg's brows, if yet 'tis possible—I see him with the knot of his scarf just shot off, infusing fresh spirits into poor Galway's regiment, riding along the line, then wheeling about, and charging Conti at the head of it. Brave ! brave by heaven ! cried my uncle Toby—he deserves a crown—As richly, as a thief a halter ; shouted Trim.

My uncle Toby knew the corporal's loyalty ;—otherwise the comparison was not at all to his mind—it did

12

not altogether strike the corporal's fancy when he had
made it, but it could not be recalled, so he had nothing
to do but proceed.

As the number of wounded was prodigious, and no
one had time to think of anything, but his own safety.
—Though Talmash, said my uncle Toby, brought off
the foot with great prudence—But I was left upon
the field, said the corporal.—Thou wast so ; poor
fellow ! replied my uncle Toby—So that it was noon
the next day, continued the corporal, before I was
exchanged, and put into a cart with thirteen or fourteen more, in order to be conveyed to our hospital.

There is no part of the body, an' please your honour,
where a wound occasions more intolerable anguish
than upon the knee.—

Except the groin ; said my uncle Toby. An' please
your honour, replied the corporal, the knee, in my
opinion, must certainly be the most acute, there being
so many tendons and what-d'ye-call-'ems all about it.

The dispute was maintained with amicable and
equal force betwixt my uncle Toby and Trim for some
time ; till Trim at length recollecting that he had
often cried at his master's sufferings, but never shed a
tear at his own, was for giving up the point, which
my uncle Toby would not allow—'Tis a proof of
nothing, Trim, said he, but the generosity of thy
temper.

So that whether the pain of a wound in the groin
(cæteris paribus) is greater than the pain of a wound
in the knee—or

Whether the pain of a wound in the knee is not
greater than the pain of a wound in the groin—are
points which to this day remain unsettled.

The anguish of my knee, continued the corporal,
was excessive in itself ; and the uneasiness of the
cart, with the roughness of the roads, which were
terribly cut up, making bad still worse, every step

was death to me : so that with the loss of blood, and
the want of care-taking of me, and a fever I felt
coming on besides—(Poor soul! said my uncle Toby)
all together, an' please your honour, was more than I
could sustain.

I was telling my sufferings to a young woman at a
peasant's house, where our cart, which was the last of
the line, had halted ; they had helped me in, and the
young woman had taken a cordial out of her pocket
and dropped it upon some sugar, and seeing it had
cheered me, she had given it me a second and a third
time—So I was telling her, an' please your honour,
the anguish I was in, and saying it was so intolerable
to me, that I had much rather lie down upon the bed,
turning my face towards one which was in the corner
of the room, and die, than go on, when, upon her
attempting to lead me to it, I fainted away in her
arms. She was a good soul! as your honour, said the
corporal, wiping his eyes, will hear.

I thought love had been a joyous thing, quoth my
uncle Toby.

'Tis the most serious thing, an' please your honour
(sometimes) that is in the world.

By the persuasion of the young woman, continued
the corporal, the cart with the wounded men set off
without me : she assured them I should expire immediately if I was put into the cart. So when I came
to myself, I found myself in a still quiet cottage, with
no one but the young woman, and the peasant and
his wife. I was laid across the bed in a corner of the
room, with my wounded leg upon a chair, and the
young woman beside ne, holding the corner of her
handkerchief dipped in vinegar to my nose with one
hand, and rubbing my temples with the other.

I took her at first for the daughter of the peasant
(for it was no inn)—so had offered her a little purse
with eighteen florins, which my poor brother Tom

12—2

(here Trim wiped his eyes) had sent me as a token, by a recruit, just before he set out for Lisbon.

The young woman called the old man and his wife into the room, to show them the money, in order to gain me credit for a bed and what little necessaries I should want, till I should be in a condition to be got to the hospital—Come then ! said she, tying up the little purse—I'll be your banker—but as that office alone will not keep me employed, I'll be your nurse too.

I thought by her manner of speaking this, as well as by her dress, which I then began to consider more attentively, that the young woman could not be the daughter of the peasant.

She was in black down to her toes, with her hair concealed under a cambric border, laid close to her forehead : she was one of those kind of nuns, an' please your honour, of which, your honour knows, there are a good many in Flanders which they let go loose—By thy description, Trim, said my uncle Toby, I daresay she was a young Beguine, of which there are none to be found anywhere but in the Spanish Netherlands—except at Amsterdam—they differ from nuns in this, that they can quit their cloister if they choose to marry ; they visit and take care of the sick by profession—I had rather, for my own part, they did it out of good nature.

She often told me, quoth Trim, she did it for the love of Christ—I did not like it.—I believe, Trim, we are both wrong, said my uncle Toby—we'll ask Mr. Yorick about it to-night at my brother Shandy's, so put me in mind ; added my uncle Toby.

The young Beguine, continued the corporal, had scarce given herself time to tell me "she would be my nurse," when she hastily turned about to begin the office of one, and prepare something for me, and in a short time, though I thought it a long one, she came back with flannels, &c., &c., and having fomented

my knee soundly for a couple of hours, &c., and
made me a thin basin of gruel for my supper, she
wished me rest, and promised to be with me early in
the morning. She wished me, an' please your honour,
what was not to be had. My fever ran very high
that night—her figure made sad disturbance within
me—I was every moment cutting the world in two,
to give her half of it—and every moment was I crying, that I had nothing but a knapsack and eighteen
florins to share with her. The whole night long was
the fair Beguine, like an angel, close by my bed side,
holding back my curtain and offering me cordials, and
I was only awakened from my dream by her coming
there at the hour promised, and giving them in
reality. In truth, she was scarce ever from me,
and so accustomed was I to receive life from her
hands, that my heart sickened, and I lost colour when
she left.

But 'tis no marvel, continued the corporal, seeing
my uncle Toby musing upon it—for love, an' please
your honour, is exactly like war, in this; that a
soldier, though he has escaped three weeks complete
o' Saturday night, may nevertheless be shot through
his heart on Sunday morning. It happened so here,
an' please your honour, with this difference only, that
it was on Sunday in the afternoon, when I fell
in love all at once with a sisserara—it burst upon me,
an' please your honour, like a bomb, scarce giving me
time to say "God bless me."

I thought, Trim, said my uncle Toby, a man never
fell in love so very suddenly.

Yes, an' please your honour, if he is in the way of
it—replied Trim.

I prithee, quoth my uncle Toby, inform me how
this matter happened.

With all pleasure, said the corporal, making a bow.

I had escaped, continued the corporal, all that time
from falling in love, and had gone on to the end of

the chapter had it not been predestined otherwise—
there is no resisting our fate.

It was on a Sunday, in the afternoon, as I told your
honour—

The old man and his wife had walked out—

Everything was still and hush as midnight about
the house—

There was not so much as a duck or a duckling
about the yard—

When the fair Beguine came in to see me.

My wound was then in a fair way of doing well
—the inflammation had been gone off for some time,
but it was succeeded with an itching both above and
below my knee, so insufferable, that I had not shut
my eyes the whole night for it.

Let me see it, said she, kneeling down upon the
ground parallel to my knee, and laying her hand upon
the part below it.—It only wants rubbing a little,
said the Beguine; so covering it with the bed
clothes, she began with the forefinger of her right
hand to rub under my knee.

She continued rubbing for a good while; it then
came into my head, that I should fall in love. I
blushed when I saw how white a hand she had—I
shall never, an' please your honour, behold another
hand so white whilst I live.

The young Beguine, continued the corporal, perceiving it was of great service to me, then rubbed
with her whole hand: I will never say another word,
an' please your honour, upon hands again, but it
was softer than satin.

Prithee Trim, commend it as much as thou wilt,
said my uncle Toby; I shall hear thy story with
more delight.—The corporal thanked his master most
unfeignedly; but having nothing to say upon the
Beguine's hand, but the same over again, he proceeded
to the effects of it.

The fair Beguine, said the corporal, continued rubbing till I feared her zeal would weary her—"I would do a thousand times more," said she, "for the love of Christ."—I perceived, then, I was beginning to be in love.—I seized her hand.—

And then, thou clappedst it to thy lips, Trim, said my uncle Toby—and madest a speech.

Whether the corporal's amour terminated in the way my uncle Toby described it, is not material ; it is enough that it contained in it the essence of all the love romances which ever have been wrote since the beginning of the world.

CHAPTER XII.

THE SENTRY-BOX.

S soon as the corporal had finished the story of his amour, or rather my uncle Toby for him, Mrs. Wadman silently sallied forth, passed the wicker gate, and advanced slowly towards my uncle Toby's sentry-box: the disposition which Trim had made in my uncle Toby's mind, was too favourable a crisis to be let slipped.

The attack was to be determined upon: it was facilitated still more by my uncle Toby's having ordered the corporal to wheel off the pioneer's shovel, the spade, the pickaxe, the pickets, and other military stores which lay scattered upon the ground where Dunkirk stood—The corporal had marched—the field was clear.

Now if ever plan, independent of all circumstances, deserved registering in letters of gold (I mean in the archives of Gotham)—it was certainly the plan of Mrs. Wadman's attack of my uncle Toby in his sentry-box, by plan—Now the plan hanging up in it at this juncture, being the plan of Dunkirk, and the tale of Dunkirk a tale of relaxation, it opposed every impression she could make.

O! let woman alone for this. Mrs. Wadman had scarce opened the wicker-gate, when she formed a new attack in a moment.

I am half distracted, Captain Shandy, said Mrs. Wadman, holding up her cambric handkerchief to her left eye, as she approached the door of my uncle Toby's sentry-box—a mote, or sand, or something, I know not what, has got into this eye of mine—do look into it—it is not in the white—

In saying which, Mrs. Wadman edged herself close in beside my uncle Toby, and squeezing herself down upon the corner of his bench, she gave him an opportunity of doing it without rising up.—Do look into it —said she.

Honest soul! thou didst look into it with as much innocency of heart as ever child looked into a raree show-box: and 'twere as much a sin to have hurt thee.

If a man will be peeping of his own accord into things of that nature—I've nothing to say to it.

My uncle Toby never did; and I will answer for him, that he would have sat quietly upon a sofa from June to January, with an eye as fine as the Thracian Rodope's beside him, without being able to tell, whether it was a black or a blue one.

The difficulty was to get my uncle Toby, to look at one at all.

'Tis surmounted. And

I see him yonder with his pipe pendulous in his hand, and the ashes falling out of it, looking, and looking, then rubbing his eyes, and looking again, with twice the good nature that ever Galileo looked for a spot in the sun.

In vain! for by all the powers which animate the organ, widow Wadman's left eye shines this moment as lucid as her right—there is neither mote, or sand, or dust, or chaff, or speck, or particle of opaque matter

floating in it—there is nothing, my dear paternal
uncle ! but one lambent delicious fire, furtively shooting out from every part of it, in all directions, into
thine—
—If thou lookest, uncle Toby, in search of this mote
one moment longer—thou art undone.

I protest, Madam, said my uncle Toby, I can see
nothing whatever in your eye.

It is not in the white ; said Mrs. Wadman : my uncle
Toby looked with might and main into the pupil.

Now of all the eyes, whichever were created—from
your own, madam, up to those of Venus herself—there
never was an eye of them all, so fitted to rob my uncle
Toby of his repose, as the very eye at which he was
looking—it was not, madam, a rolling eye—a romping
or a wanton one—nor was it an eye sparkling, petulant
or imperious, of high claims and terrifying exactions,
which would have curdled at once that milk of human
nature, of which my uncle Toby was made up—but
'twas an eye full of gentle salutations, and soft re-
sponses—speaking, not like the trumpet-stop of some
ill-made organ, in which many an eye I talk to, holds
coarse converse, but whispering soft, like the last low
accents of an expiring saint — "How can you live
comfortless, Captain Shandy, and alone, without a
bosom to lean your head on—or trust your cares to ?"

It was an eye—

But I shall be in love with it myself, if I say another
word about it.

It did my uncle Toby's business—

There is nothing shows the characters of my father
and my uncle Toby, in a more entertaining light, than
their different manner of deportment, under the same
accident — for I call not love a misfortune, from a
persuasion, that a man's heart is ever the better for it
—Great God ! what must my uncle Toby's have been,
when 'twas all benignity without it.

My father, as appears from many of his papers, was

very subject to this passion, before he married—but from a little subacid kind of drollish impatience in his nature, whenever it befell him, he would never submit to it like a Christian ; but would pish, and huff, and bounce, and kick, and play the devil, and write the bitterest philippics against the eye that ever man wrote.—In short, during the whole paroxysm, my father was all abuse and foul language, approaching rather towards malediction—yet never concluded his chapter of curses upon it, without cursing himself into the bargain, as one of the most egregious fools and coxcombs, he would say, that ever was let loose in the world.

My uncle Toby, on the contrary, took it like a lamb —sat still and let the poison work in his veins without resistance—in the sharpest exacerbations of his wound (like that on his groin) he never dropped one fretful or discontented word—he blamed neither heaven nor earth, or thought or spoke an injurious thing of anybody, or any part of it ; he sat solitary and pensive with his pipe, looking at his lame leg, then whiffing out a sentimental heigh ho ! which, mixing with the smoke, incommoded no one mortal.

He took it like a lamb, I say.

The world is ashamed of being virtuous, my uncle Toby knew little of the world ; and therefore when he felt he was in love with widow Wadman, he had no conception that the thing was any more to be made a mystery of, than if Mrs. Wadman had given him a cut with a gapped knife across his finger : had it been otherwise — yet as he ever looked upon Trim as a humble friend ; and saw fresh reasons every day of his life, to treat him as such, it would have made no variation in the manner in which he informed him of the affair.

" I am in love, corporal ! " quoth my uncle Toby.

In love !—said the corporal—your honour was very well the day before yesterday, when I was telling your honour the story of the King of Bohemia—Bohemia! said my uncle Toby .... musing a long time. What became of that story, Trim?

We lost it, an' please your honour, somehow betwixt us—but your honour was as free from love then, as I am—'twas, just whilst thou went'st off with the wheel-barrow—with Mrs. Wadman, quoth my uncle Toby —She has left a ball here—added my uncle Toby, pointing to his breast—

She can no more, and please your honour, stand a siege, than she can fly—cried the corporal—

But as we are neighbours, Trim, the best way I think is to let her know it civilly first—quoth my uncle Toby.

Now if I might presume, said the corporal, to differ from your honour—

Why else, do I talk to thee, Trim : said my uncle Toby, mildly—

Then I would begin, an' please your honour, with making a good thundering attack upon her, in return, and telling her civilly afterwards, for if she knows anything of your honour's being in love, beforehand —L—d help her! she knows no more at present of it, Trim, said my uncle Toby—than the child unborn.

Now, quoth the corporal, setting his left hand a kimbo, and giving such a flourish with his right, as just promised success, and no more—if your honour will give me leave to lay down the plan of this attack—

Thou wilt please me by it, Trim, said my uncle Toby, exceedingly—and as I foresee thou must act in it as my aide-de-camp, here's a crown, corporal, to begin with, to steep thy commission.

Then, an' please your honour, said the corporal (making a bow first for his commission)—we will begin with getting your honour's laced clothes out of the great campaign trunk, to be well-aired, and have the blue and gold taken up at the sleeves, and I'll put your white Ramallie wig fresh into pipes, and send for a tailor, to have your honour's thin scarlet breeches turned.

.I had better take the red plush ones, quoth my uncle Toby.

Thou wilt get a brush and a little chalk to my sword.

And your honour's two razors shall be new set—and I will get my Montero cap furbished up, and put on poor Lieutenant Le Fever's regimental coat, which your honour gave me to wear for his sake—and as soon as your honour is clean shaved, and has got your clean shirt on, with your blue and gold, or your fine scarlet—sometimes one and sometimes t'other—and everything is ready for the attack — we'll march up boldly, as if 'twas to the face of a bastion ; and whilst your honour engages Mrs. Wadman in the parlour, to the right, I'll attack Mrs. Bridget in the kitchen, to the left ; and, having seized that pass, I'll answer for it, said the corporal, snapping his fingers over his head —that the day is our own.

I wish I may but manage it right ; said my uncle Toby—but I declare, corporal, I had rather march up to the very edge of a trench.

———

As the ancients agree, brother Toby, said my father, that there are two different and distinct kinds of *love*, according to the different parts which are affected by it,—the brain or liver,—I think when a man is in love it behoves him a little to consider which of the two he is fallen into.

…What signifies it, brother Shandy, replied my uncle Toby, which of the two it is, provided it will but make a man marry, and love his wife, and have a few children ?

…A few children ! cried my father, rising out of his chair, and looking full in my mother's face, as he forced his way betwixt hers and Dr. Slop's—a few children ! cried my father, repeating my uncle Toby's words, as he walked to and fro—

Not, my dear brother Toby, cried my father, recovering himself all at once, and coming close up to the back of my uncle Toby's chair, – not that I should be sorry hadst thou a score:—on the contrary, I should rejoice,—and be as kind, Toby, to every one of them as a father.

My uncle Toby stole his hand, unperceived, behind his chair, to give my father's a squeeze.

There is, at least, said Yorick, a great deal of reason and plain sense in Captain Shandy's opinion of love : and 'tis among the ill-spent hours of my life, which I have to answer for, that I have read so many flourishing poets and rhetoricians in my time, from whom I never could extract so much...

I wish, Yorick, said my father, you had read Plato ; for there you would have learnt that there are two *loves*...I know there were two *religions*, replied Yorick, among the ancients :—one for the vulgar,—and another for the learned ;—but I think *one love* might have served both of them very well...

It could not, replied my father,—and for the same reasons ; for, of these loves, according to Ficinus's comment upon Velacius, the first is ancient,—without mother,—the second begotten of Jupiter and Dione...

Pray brother, quoth my uncle Toby, what has a man who believes in God to do with this ?...My father could not stop to answer, for fear of breaking the thread of his discourse.

This latter, continued he, partakes wholly of the nature of Venus.

The first, which is the golden chain let down from Heaven, excites to love heroic, which comprehends in it, the desire of philosophy and truth ;—the second—

I think the having children as beneficial to the world, said Yorick, as the finding out of the longitude.

To be sure, said my mother, *love* keeps peace in the world...

In the *house*—my dear, I own...

It replenishes the earth, said my mother...

But it keeps Heaven empty,—my dear, replied my father...

'Tis Virginity, cried Slop, triumphantly, which fills paradise...

Well pushed, nun ! quoth my father...

My father had such a skirmishing, cutting kind of a slashing way with him in disputations, thrusting and ripping, and giving every one a stroke to remember him by in his turn,—that if there were twenty people in company,—in less than half an hour he was sure to have every one of 'em against him.

What did not a little contribute to leave him thus without an ally was that if there were any one post more untenable than the rest he would be sure to throw himself into it ; and, to do him justice, when he was once there, he would defend it so gallantly that 'twould have been a concern, either to a brave man, or a good-natured one, to have seen him driven out.

Yorick, for this reason, though he would often attack him,—yet could never bear to do it with all his force.

Doctor Slop's *Virginity* had got him for once on the right side of the rampart, and he was beginning to blow up all the convents in Christendom about Slop's ears, when Corporal Trim came into the parlour to inform my uncle Toby, that his thin scarlet breeches, in which the attack was to be made upon Mrs. Wadman, would not do ; for, that the tailor, in ripping them up, in order to turn them, had found they had been turned before—Then turn them again, brother, said my father rapidly, for there will be many a turning of 'em yet before all's done in the affair—They are as rotten as dirt, said the corporal—Then by all means, said my father, bespeak a new

pair, brother — for though I know, continued my
father, turning himself to the company, that widow
Wadman has been deeply in love with my brother
Toby for many years, and has used every art and cir-
cumvention of woman to outwit him into the same
passion, yet now that she has caught him, her fever
will be passed its height.—

She has gained her point.

.   In this case, continued my father, which Plato, I am
persuaded, never thought of—Love, you see, is not so
much a sentiment as a situation, into which a man
enters, as my brother Toby would do, into a corps, no
matter whether he loves the service or no—being
once in it, he acts as if he did.

The hypothesis, like the rest of my father's, was
plausible enough, and my uncle Toby had but a
single word to object to it, in which Trim stood ready
to second him—but my father had not drawn his conclusion.—

For this reason, continued my father (stating the
case over again), notwithstanding all the world knows,
that Mrs. Wadman affects my brother Toby, and my
brother Toby contrariwise affects Mrs. Wadman, and
no obstacle in nature to forbid the music striking up,
yet will I answer for it that this self-same tune will
not be played this twelvemonth.

We have taken our measures badly, quoth my
uncle Toby, looking up interrogatively in Trim's face.

I would lay my Montero cap, said Trim—Now
Trim's Montero cap, as I once told you, was his
constant wager ; and having furbished it up that very
night, in order to go upon the attack—it made the
odds look more considerable—I would lay, an' please
your honour, my Montero cap to a shilling—was it
proper, continued Trim (making a bow) to offer a
wager before your honours.—

There is nothing improper in it, said my father—
'tis a mode of expression ; for in saying thou would'st

lay thy Montero cap to a shilling, all thou meanest
is this, that thou believest—

—Now, what do'st thou believe?

That widow Wadman, an' please your worship, cannot hold it out ten days.......

After a series of attacks and repulses in a course of
nine months in my uncle Toby's quarter, my uncle
Toby, honest man! found it necessary to draw off his
forces and raise the siege most indignantly. The
shock he received in this affair with the widow Wadman fixed him in a resolution never more to think of
the sex.

Here my heart stops me to pay to thee, my dear
uncle Toby, once for all, the tribute I owe thy goodness. Here let me thrust my chair aside, and kneel
down upon the ground whilst I am pouring forth the
warmest sentiments of love for thee, and veneration
for the excellency of thy character, that ever virtue and
nature kindled in a nephew's bosom. Peace and comfort rest for evermore upon thy head! Thou enviedst
no man's comforts, insulted no man's opinions. Thou
blackened'st no man's character, devoured'st no man's
bread; gently, with faithful Trim behind thee, didst
thou amble round the little circle of thy pleasures,
jostling no creature in thy way; for each one's sorrow
thou hadst a tear, for each man's need thou hadst a
shilling!

The corporal—

Tread lightly on his ashes, ye men of genius, for he
was your kinsman:

Weed his grave clean! ye men of goodness—for he
was your brother. Oh corporal! had I thee, but now
—now, that I am able to give thee a dinner and protection—how would I cherish thee! thou should'st

13

wear thy Montero cap every hour of the day, and every day of the week—and when it was worn out, I would purchase thee a couple like : but alas : alas : alas : now that I can do this, in spite of their reverences, the occasion is lost, for thou art gone ; thy genius fled up to the stars from whence it came ; and that warm heart of thine, with all it's generous and open vessels, compressed into a clod of the valley ?

But what—what is this, to that future and dreaded page, where I look towards the velvet pall, decorated with the military ensigns of thy master—the first— the foremost of created beings ; where, I shall see thee, faithful servant ! laying his sword and scabbard with a trembling hand across his coffin, and then returning pale as ashes to the door, to take his mourning horse by the bridle, to follow his hearse, as he directed thee ;—where—all my father's systems shall be baffled by his sorrows ; and, in spite of his philosophy, I shall behold him, as he inspects the lackered plate, twice taking his spectacles from off his nose to wipe away the dew which nature has shed upon them. When I see him cast in the rosemary with an air of disconsolation, which cries through my ears. Oh Toby ! in what corner of the world shall I seek thy fellow ?

Whilst I am worth a shilling to pay a weeder, thy path from thy door to thy bowling-green shall never be grown up. Whilst there is a rood and a half of land in the Shandy family, thy fortifications, my dear uncle Toby, shall never be demolished !

THE END.

BILLING, PRINTER, GUILDFORD.